BOUND IN LOVE

CAMY TANG

Guideposts
New York, New York

Guideposts.org
(800) 932-2145
Guideposts Books & Inspirational Media

Cover design by Wendy Bass
Cover illustration by Joyce Patti
Interior design by Lorie Pagnozzi
Typeset by Aptara

Printed and bound in the United States of America
10 9 8 7 6 5 4

To the Seekers at Seekerville.net: Thank you for your friendship, support, prayers, scolding, and laughter. I think I managed to get all of you into this book.

BOUND IN LOVE

CHAPTER ONE

C ome on, girls!" Sarah Hart called to her twin grand-daughters as she left the warmth of the spring sun-shine to enter the Maple Hill Library.

The rich smell of books greeted her. There was some-thing in the air in the library that made her feel complete. Maybe it was being surrounded by so much wisdom, so many stories told by so many people. Her granddaughters, Amy and Audrey, seemed oblivious to what was in the air. They immediately headed toward the teen section at the back of the library.

"Wait just a minute," Sarah said. "Didn't you girls say you had to work on your research papers?"

Audrey changed direction without even rolling her eyes, but Amy spoke up. "Grandma, can't we just go see what new graphic novels they have?" She absolutely adored the color-ful novel-length comic books that Spencer, the Maple Hill librarian, had been ordering lately for the teen collection. "It'll only take five minutes, I promise."

"Your five minutes will turn into an hour before you know it. Research paper first, then you can go read the new graphic novels," Sarah said.

Amy turned to follow her sister toward the catalog computers so she could look up the books she needed for her school paper.

Spencer wasn't at the circulation desk. Sarah peered down the length of the library, but saw only the empty oak tables running down the center. She had hoped to ask him if the mystery novel she'd requested had arrived through interlibrary loan. She headed down the stacks, glancing left and right into the nooks made by the bookshelves standing perpendicular to the walls.

As she passed beside the staircase to the second floor, she heard a deep shudder, like something heavy being moved. "Spencer?" she called tentatively.

"Is that you, Sarah?" His voice sounded muffled and faintly out of breath. His head popped into view from around a bookcase. "Hello." A sheen of perspiration covered his reddened face.

"What are you doing? Running a marathon through the stacks?"

He smiled. "No, just trying to get to an old storeroom."

Sarah turned into the space below the staircase. A bookcase had been standing against the wall, but Spencer had removed all the books, laying them in piles on the floor, and he'd angled the empty bookcase outward to reveal a glimpse of a small door in the wall.

"I didn't even realize there was a door there," Sarah said, "but I should have figured there would be a storage space under the stairs."

"Some kids were goofing around last week and accidentally broke a couple of chairs," Spencer said. "It was slow today, and I have some old chairs in the storage area."

"Do you need help moving that bookcase?"

"No, that's fine," he said. "You came about the book you ordered? Sorry, it hasn't arrived yet."

Sarah asked again, "Are you sure you don't need help? Amy and Audrey are here doing research for a school paper, so I have time."

"Well…"

She set down her purse. "Where are we moving this?"

He flashed a grin. "Just far enough so the door can open and we can move the chairs out."

They positioned themselves on either side of the bookcase and heaved. The noise of the wooden bottom scraping the floor echoed through the library, but Sarah found the empty bookcase was much lighter than she had expected. At Spencer's direction, they "walked" the bookcase completely out of the nook so they'd have room to open the door to the storage room, which opened outward.

He dug in his pants pocket and pulled out a key chain filled with a dozen small keys. Each key was labeled with a piece of colored tape and tiny lettering in Spencer's hand. "When I took over the library, I found these keys in the desk and had no clue what each one unlocked. I had to go through the library and figure it out." He found a key with a yellow label and inserted it into the lock on the tiny doorknob.

The door unlocked and swung open, revealing a wall of boxes.

Sarah eyed the boxes. "I don't know how you'll find anything in a room packed so full."

"Have no fear," Spencer said. "I put those boxes there the year I took over the library. Behind them, the room is actually rather empty."

Sarah soon discovered that Spencer's idea of "rather empty" didn't quite match with hers. They removed the boxes blocking the doorway and he flipped on the light switch to illuminate the room. Several smaller bookcases, with a couple more lying on top of them now stood in their way.

"Uh-oh," Spencer said. "I forgot about those. I'll need to move them aside. The chairs are close to the back wall."

They had to crouch to enter the room because of the low, slanted ceiling. The small bookcases stood only two shelves high and Sarah glanced over them toward the back of the room, looking for the chairs. There were a few old student desks, some low metal filing cabinets, and a couple of boxes that weren't stacked, leaving her a clear view of the back wall.

"Spencer," she said, "doesn't the room seem too small to you?"

"I would say so. You couldn't stick another piece of paper in there."

"No, I don't mean too full. I mean, the storage room seems smaller than it ought to be, considering the amount of space under the stairs."

"Really?" Spencer poked his head into the tiny room, then stepped out to look at the stairs. "You're right." The storage room was perhaps twenty feet long, but the area under the stairs seemed much longer, at least forty feet long.

Sarah entered the room and sidled in next to a rusted metal book cart, then climbed gingerly over a solid wooden desk. She picked her way through the student desks and managed to get within a couple of feet of the back wall, with several stacked wooden chairs in her way. "I found the chairs," she called to Spencer.

She leaned forward and knocked on the back wall of the storage room. A dull hollow sound echoed through the small space. She knocked in several places, just to be sure.

"You hear that?" she asked Spencer. "I think there might be another storage area on the other side of the wall. Do you know where the door could be?"

"I think I know." Spencer beckoned to her and, when Sarah rejoined him, led the way along the length of the library, following the wall under the stairs.

"It's got to be behind one of these two bookcases," he said, pointing. "When I took over the library a few years ago, I moved most of the bookcases, but I didn't move these away from the wall because they fit in with how I wanted to reorganize the library furniture. So they've probably been here since the renovation that happened about thirty years ago."

"I remember that. When they expanded the second floor, right? We could check the library blueprints to see if there really is another storage room."

"They're at the courthouse. It'll be faster to move these bookcases aside."

He had a point. "Why don't we each empty a bookcase? Then the two of us can move them aside together."

"Sounds like a plan," Spencer said.

Sarah was careful to keep the books in order as she removed them from the shelves, stacking them neatly out in the pathway down the center of the library, where they were out of the way. Spencer finished before she did, and helped her with her remaining books.

They positioned themselves on either side of the first bookcase.

"Ready? One, two, three!"

Sarah and Spencer scooted the edge of the bookcase away from the wall a few inches. He looked behind it and shook his head. "Nothing."

"Let's try the other one."

They moved the bookcase back into place and shifted around the stacks of books that needed to be put back on the shelves.

Spencer got ready to move the second bookcase and smiled. "Ready to solve a mystery?"

Sarah laughed as she grabbed the edge of the empty bookcase. "There's a chance we moved all those books for nothing."

"Well, here goes nothing!"

This bookcase was a bit heavier than the other two, or perhaps Sarah's muscles were tiring after hefting all those books. They needed two heaves this time to get it away from the wall enough for Spencer to peek behind.

"There's a door!" Spencer said.

"Grandma, what's going on?"

Both girls peered into the nook at the two of them, the askew bookcase, and the books stacked against the sides.

"What are you doing?" Amy asked. The girls each held a small stack of books to check out.

"We found a hidden storage room," Sarah said.

"Did you find any bones?" Amy asked.

"Gross!" Audrey said.

Sarah couldn't help but smile. "I don't know what's inside. We have to clear the way to open the door first."

"We can help." Amy and Audrey set their stacks of research books on a nearby table.

"Good, we'll need all the help we can get," Spencer said. "Amy, you join your grandma on that side of the case, and Audrey, you help me. We're going to 'walk' the bookcase into the center aisle of the library."

It took them longer than Sarah had expected. Because this bookcase was heavier than the other ones they'd moved, all four of them were out of breath when they were done.

"I think that's enough," he said after their last heave-ho. He headed back to the wall and grasped the doorknob, but it didn't budge. "Locked."

He pulled out his key ring and found the same yellow-taped key he'd used for the other door. It inserted into the lock smoothly, but wouldn't turn to open the door.

"Aw," Amy sighed.

"There are still a few unmarked keys." Spencer flipped through the key ring. He tried four other keys before one slid in and turned.

Click. The door unlocked.

It opened to reveal a dark room. Spencer reached for a light switch on the wall and clicked it but nothing happened. "I have a flashlight I left in the other storage room."

"I'll get it," Sarah said. She hurried there and back, her mind swirling with the possibilities of what might be in a room left unopened for at least thirty years. She handed Spencer the flashlight and followed behind him as he stepped into the room.

Unlike the other storage room, they didn't have to crouch because of a low ceiling. Here, the ceiling was high because it was directly under the highest point of the stairs. Sarah immediately spied some tables and old bookcases, smaller than the ones out on the floor and more ornately carved.

"These must have been in the library before the renovation," Spencer said.

"I'm not an expert—Maggie would probably know better—but some of these look like they may be antiques."

"I wouldn't be surprised. The library was dedicated in 1902. Maybe some of this is from back then."

A shriek from one of the twins echoed against the slanted ceiling.

"What's wrong?" Sarah asked.

"I think there are cobwebs in my hair! I'm outta here."

Sarah couldn't see but guessed it was Audrey who beat a hasty retreat.

Sarah, Spencer, and Amy continued to weave their way through a few broken chairs. "I'm surprised there isn't more dust," Sarah said.

"This room seems pretty well sealed," Spencer said. "If it hasn't been opened since the renovation thirty years ago, there probably aren't many cracks in the walls for dust to come through."

Sarah's leg hit the edge of a desk. "Oh." She stumbled, and her toe jammed into something a bit softer than wood, although still heavy and solid. "What's this?"

A cardboard box was hidden under the desk, only an edge peeking out.

Spencer maneuvered the box out with a grunt. "It's heavy." He flipped open one of the flaps. "Books!"

"Let's see if we can get this box out of here," Sarah said.

With more pushing and pulling, they dragged the box out of the storage area. Sarah was happy to leave the dark crowded space for the loftier main area.

"What did you find?" Audrey asked.

"Just books," Amy answered her.

Audrey looked in the box before turning around. "C'mon. Let's go see if there are any new magazines." Amy followed shortly behind.

"Let's sort through these." Spencer dragged the box to one of the oak tables that ran down the center aisle of the library floor.

Sarah and Spencer pawed through the box. It contained hardcover books bound in thick, plain fabrics with the titles stamped in block lettering and also locally printed pamphlets and booklets.

Spencer glanced through the unmarked hardcovers while Sarah laid out the pamphlets and booklets, most of which were literature about local sites. There were collections of essays from the local Rose Growers Society, some Circa-bound genealogies of a few of the oldest families in Maple Hill, and a few pamphlets on locally made ceramics. The publications were all dated 1981.

"I wonder if the historical society will want to look at some of these." Sarah flipped through a Circa-bound book made up of photocopies of the pages of a weather-beaten, handwritten journal, which looked like a personal reminiscence of General Nathaniel Bradford, a Maple Hill hero from the Revolutionary War. The words *Pamela Harders, 1760–1820, book printed 1981* had been stamped on the card-stock cover. If Irene Stuart at the historical society didn't already have a copy of this, she would be salivating to take a look. "Why were all these in the storeroom rather than in the stacks?"

Spencer shook his head. "I have no idea."

"This is odd—all the hardcovers have the same cover design," Sarah said. The hardcovers were green, red, blue, or black, and had the same kind of block lettering stamped on the covers and spines, although the titles were different. Sarah picked one up. The cover seemed newer than the pages. It looked like an old pulp fiction novel, copyrighted 1948. "The hardcover books I read have dust jackets."

"I think these are old books that had been damaged or books that needed more durable covers. The library sends them to a local bookbinder to remove the old cover and replace it with a new one."

"So why weren't they returned to the shelves?"

"Once the books are back from the binder, they have to be processed and the catalog number reattached to the spine before they're reshelved. But none of these were recataloged." He pointed to the clean spine of a book. "No Dewey decimal number."

"You think these books have been in that storage room since the renovation?"

Spencer nodded. "Maybe they were put with the pamphlets and booklets because they all needed to be processed. If the library gets busy, things like that are a low priority. But I don't understand why the books were left in storage rather than cataloged."

Sarah picked up another book, a slim volume with a dark green cover. Strangely, this one didn't have a title stamped on it, although the cover looked like those on the other books. Inside, there was no publisher, no title, and no author.

How odd. Sarah flipped to the first page and read:

I'm telling this story because I can't get the picture of her face out of my mind. When I go to sleep, I can still see her eyes on the day the FBI came to Maple Hill to take her away.

Sarah read the paragraph over again, unable to fully comprehend the words. Was the book talking about *this* Maple Hill?

She kept reading.

I can't keep it bottled up inside anymore. I'm writing this anonymously because my hands are tied and I can't do anything for her. That somehow just seems like a weak excuse.

So, here's the story. It was spring 1960 when Debby Neely moved to Maple Hill. She was about nineteen or twenty years old, a pretty girl. She was quiet, but she was a sweet person.

Sarah drew in a sharp breath. She remembered Debby. Sarah had been about twelve or thirteen years old, with a hazy preadolescent's awareness of anything that didn't involve school. She dredged up a blurred image of a smooth oval face, dark eyes, dark hair, and golden creamy skin. She only remembered meeting Debby a handful of times.

A shiver ran across her skin. This wasn't a book like the others in the box.

Sarah kept reading.

I don't remember when she actually came to town because she kept to herself for much of the first few months. I only know it was spring 1960 because she later told me. I didn't even become friends with her until fall of that year. We started talking and seemed to connect.

When she came to town, she hadn't intended to stay more than a night or two, but Pleiter's shop needed help that year—Al Pleiter had broken his leg, and the only Pleiters able to help out at the store were still in middle school. Debby got a job within a few hours of arriving in Maple Hill, and she stayed for almost two years.

Even though she was in Maple Hill for that long, it was hard for her to form friendships in town. Not because people were unfriendly, she just had her own host of secrets to keep, plus she was a quiet person. She mentioned once how she had always been quiet because her brother was so outgoing and had such a strong personality.

It wasn't like she didn't have any friends, though. She was close to her co-worker and the woman she was staying with, and later with me. I wish I'd pushed harder to get past her reserve, to get to know her sooner than I did. I only knew her for two years, but she changed the way I looked at the world, at myself, at God.

One day, out of the blue, she was arrested by the FBI.

But I know that she went to prison for a crime she didn't commit.

CHAPTER TWO

Audrey's voice startled Sarah out of the book. "Find anything cool?" The girls walked back down the middle of the library.

"Most of these are novels." Spencer plucked a hardcover out of the stack. "Here's an old romance. Look, the girls are in really old dresses." He showed them the page opposite the title page with a black-and-white illustration of two young women. Sarah expected eighteenth-century gowns, but to Spencer the "really old dresses" were from the 1940s or 1950s. The book looked like an old Nancy Drew mystery.

"What's that one you've got, Grandma?" Audrey pointed to the slim volume in Sarah's hand.

"Actually . . . it's a mystery."

"A mystery novel?" she asked.

"No, a real-life mystery."

The girls came to stand on either side of her. "Can we see?"

Sarah opened to the first page and read it out loud for them.

Spencer peered closer. "It isn't a novel?"

"I don't think so. I remember Debby Neely."

"She was real?" Amy asked.

"I was about your age at the time. I remember seeing her around town, or maybe at church. I remember she had beautiful clothes."

"Who wrote it?" Audrey flipped through the blank opening pages, then turned to the last page. "It doesn't say."

"I wonder how the library got the book," Spencer said. "That might help us figure out who wrote it."

"Can you search the computer and find out?" Amy asked.

Spencer chuckled. "I wish it were that easy. When I took over, I only inputted into the computer the books that were in the stacks. For these books, I'll have to look through the paper files."

"Want some help?" Sarah asked.

"Sure."

Amy and Audrey, however, backed away. "We, uh, have research papers."

"Yes, you do." Sarah guided them to a table where their research books sat. "Why don't you two sit here and start taking notes while I help Mr. Hewitt. Spencer, just tell me what you want me to do."

The front door whooshed open and a woman's voice called, "Spencer?"

Sarah recognized Alana Marquez, who worked at the cemetery. When Gerry died, Alana had been very kind and helpful to Sarah.

"Hey, Alana," Spencer said.

"I desperately need your help finding some books on painting," Alana said. "Edward's got it into his head to redo the living room walls, and I didn't know when he started that he doesn't have a clue what he's doing. Oh hello, Sarah." Alana smiled at her.

"Hi."

"Let me get Sarah set up first," Spencer said, "and then we'll look through what the library has."

He led Sarah behind the circulation desk into the office beyond, where there were rows of file cabinets lining one wall.

"There are two places we can search—the donation records or the purchase records." He gestured to one file cabinet. "This cabinet has records of all the books donated to the library—well, before I arrived, at least."

"They're arranged by title?"

"Should be. I'm not sure if the record would be here since the book was never cataloged, but it's worth checking."

He gestured to three other file cabinets. "These are the purchase records for books the library bought, which are also filed by title."

"I'll start with the donation records," Sarah said.

"I'll be back to help you after I help Alana."

Sarah faced the cabinet. The drawers were conveniently labeled A-G, H-L, M-S, and T-Z. How would the previous librarian, Miss Carpenter, have filed an untitled book? Maybe under "Untitled." Sarah knelt to pull open the bottom drawer.

Each donation record page was filled out with Miss Carpenter's spidery scrawl, which was hard for Sarah to read. She squinted to make out the words.

Unfortunately, there were no records under "Untitled." Same for "Unknown," "No Title," and "No Name." Maybe the librarian had filed it under "*Anonymous*" for the anonymous author? She found one record, but the donated book had actually been titled *Anonymous*. She pursed her lips. But then she remembered that it was unlikely the library received untitled books very often.

Maybe Spencer was right and the book wasn't in the files because it hadn't been cataloged. Was there a way to find out? All the donation records she saw had the books' catalog numbers on the form. What about the other books in the box? They hadn't had catalog numbers, either, so she could check to see if those titles were here in the drawer.

Sarah went to the box, still on the oak table where they'd left it, and selected a few booklets. She grabbed a few hardcover books too. There was no sign of Alana and Spencer, but she heard a murmur of voices from behind a few bookcases to her left.

The first booklet she had grabbed was the photocopied pages of the reminiscence about Nathaniel

Bradford, handwritten by Pamela Harders. The cover of the booklet had only the words *Pamela Harders, 1760–1820, book printed 1981*. Sarah looked through the file cabinet.

There! A piece of paper with the title, *Pamela Harders, 1760–1820, book printed 1981*. The author was also listed as "Harders, Pamela." According to the donation record, the booklet had been donated by a woman named Cara Harders, with a notation that it was one of twenty booklets printed by Cara because the original journal had been too fragile. At the bottom of the record, the field for the catalog number was blank.

Good. That proved that if the mystery book had been donated, the record would be in the file cabinet even though it had never been cataloged.

Maybe the untitled book had been purchased, like the hardcover books. Sarah repeated the search for the untitled book in the filing cabinets for purchased books. Nothing. But this time, when she cross-checked a couple of hardcover books, they didn't show up either.

Maybe the hardcover books had all been donated? She might as well check. But her search turned up nothing in the donation records cabinet either.

"How are you doing, Sarah?" Spencer asked as he walked into the office.

"There's something here that doesn't make sense. If a book is bought by the library, the record would be filed here, right? Even if the book had been damaged and sent to the binder?"

"Yes, that's right," He said.

"Well, none of these hardcover books are here in the purchase records."

"You're right, that doesn't make sense."

Spencer picked up one of the books from where Sarah had laid it on his desk, and fingered the cover as he thought. Then he snapped his fingers. "The librarian kept detailed records of every order sent to the binder. They're all filed...here." He pulled out a bottom drawer from a different file cabinet and scanned through the hanging file folder tabs. "Here they are. They're filed by date."

"Try 1981," Sarah said. "The booklets and pamphlets in the box were all dated 1981."

He searched through the files until he pulled out a thin manila file folder. "Here's one marked 1981."

He opened the folder, and the first page was the order sheet for the book binder. "It looks like all the books in the box were part of this order." He flipped the page. "Yup, here are all the books' missing purchase records. It looks like the librarian put them in this folder so all the records would be in one place."

"I wonder why the books weren't cataloged and reshelved after they came back from the binder."

"Maybe the box was put in storage temporarily during the renovation, but then forgotten about."

Sarah looked down at the folder in Spencer's hand, with the date "1981" printed on the folder tab.

She headed back to the donation records cabinet. "You know, I couldn't find the book earlier under 'Untitled,' but what if the book had been filed under the donation date instead?" She pulled open the top drawer and started from the very beginning.

There was no record dated "1981," but she did notice a record titled, "1963," three years after Debby Neely came to Maple Hill. Could this be it? Sarah pulled the record out of the file drawer and deciphered the librarian's handwriting.

Title: None—1963.

Author: Unknown.

Donation date: November 1963.

Notes: Dark green hardcover book, no title, no author, no other markings or indications. Appears to be a story about Maple Hill.

The field for the catalog number was blank.

Then at the very bottom, next to *Donated by*: was the name *Ruth Drayton*.

Sarah's mother.

CHAPTER THREE

After dropping the twins off at their house, Sarah headed to The Spotted Dog Bookstore and Café to treat herself to some chai. Liam's corgi Murphy greeted her at the door, his furry backside wiggling his pleasure at seeing her.

Sarah scratched behind his ears. "You're looking quite chipper today, Murphy."

"What else would you expect when my dog is silly in love with you?" Liam asked from behind the café counter, giving her a broad wink.

"That's flattering, Murphy, but you really should get to know a girl better before you fall in love with her." Murphy, however, continued frantically licking at her fingers.

There was a pause. Liam looked for a moment as if he was about to say something, but then he continued leisurely wiping the counter with a dishcloth. "When you're ready to pull yourself away from my fawning dog, Sarah Hart, you can tell me what you'd like today."

"Women like a little fawning once in a while," Sarah said with a grin. "I don't want anything to eat, but I'd like a chai latte with—"

"Let me guess, no whipped cream."

"No—"

"Yes ma'am, your usual without whipped cream."

"Liam—"

"Coming right up." His green eyes sparkled as he reached for the whipped cream from the refrigerator.

While Liam was making her chai, Sarah sat at a table and took the "mystery book" out of her bag to read a little more. After the shock of finding Ruth Drayton's name on the donation record, she had begged Spencer to let her borrow the book. He had good-naturedly processed it quickly and checked it out to her.

When Liam set her steaming chai in front of her—topped with the biggest mound of whipped cream he'd ever given her—he caught sight of the book. "Library book? It doesn't look like any of the books at the bookstore."

Sarah told him about finding the box of books in the library, about how the book claimed to be a true account of something that happened in Maple Hill, and also how her mother, Ruth Drayton, had donated the book to the library almost fifty years ago.

"May I?"

Sarah let Liam riffle through it. His silver eyebrows rose as he read the first page. "A woman imprisoned for a crime she didn't commit?"

"I remember Debby Neely, although I didn't know about the FBI. I was only in middle school at the time."

"Do you think it's true?"

"I think I can figure that out if I can find out who wrote the book." Sarah said.

"Another mystery?"

"It'll be interesting reading, that's for sure."

Another customer came into the café and Liam turned to help him just as Sarah heard Martha's voice behind her. "Hi there, Sarah." She turned just as her best friend slid into the chair next to her.

"You're the perfect excuse," Martha said.

"Excuse for what?"

"For getting a mocha double-chocolate almond latte." Martha plopped her crochet bag on the table.

"Since when do you drink a mocha...chocolate...what was that again?"

"Mocha double-chocolate almond latte with a dusting of cinnamon on top. Karen made it for me the last time I came in with my granddaughters." Martha had already pulled out her current crochet project, which looked like a granny square for an afghan. Her stainless steel hook flashed in and out as she worked. "She made it for all of us. It was *wonderful*."

Karen Bancroft, Liam's part-time waitress, was passing behind them with two plates of sandwiches. She overheard Martha raving and flashed a smile. "Does that mean you'd like another one today?"

"Yes, please!" Martha said. Then to Sarah, "It's the perfect cure after spending so much time at the bank this afternoon. All I wanted to do was deposit some money in my grandchildren's savings accounts."

"Well, you do have ten grandchildren."

"And that tenth one is cute as a button." Martha paused her needlework to pull out of her workbag several squares in different patterns of light pink, cream, and chocolate brown. "What do you think? It's for my new granddaughter."

"Yummy color combination. Reminds me of Neapolitan ice cream."

"Me too." Martha noticed the book on the counter for the first time. "What's that?"

"Spencer and I found this book hidden away in a storage room at the library."

Martha opened it and read the first paragraph. "Maple Hill? *Our* Maple Hill?"

"I'm almost positive. Do you remember Debby Neely?"

Martha's crochet hook paused and she stared unseeing at her granny square. "The name sounds familiar...."

"We would have been about twelve years old."

"Yes, I remember her but only vaguely. She was a lot older than us, wasn't she?" Martha asked.

"She was only nineteen, but I guess to a pair of twelve-year-olds, she would seem a lot older."

"Didn't she have a beautiful green dress...?"

"Yes, I remember that too," Sarah said. "She caught me staring once and smiled at me, and I got up the courage to ask her about it. She let me touch it. I was fascinated.

Thinking back now, I want to say that it might have been quilted. Do you remember?"

Martha shook her head. "You're the quilter, not me. I just remember it seemed to almost shimmer."

Sarah sighed. "I wish I'd paid more attention, so I could remember it better now. I didn't really get into quilting until after Gerry and I got married. I think it was quilted. I remember the feel of tracing a line of stitches with my finger, and the puffiness of the fabric."

"What happened to Debby?" Martha asked.

"The book says she was arrested by the FBI."

"What? Who wrote the book?"

"That's what I intend to find out. But the record at the library says it was donated almost fifty years ago by my mother."

Martha stopped crocheting. "Do you think she wrote it?"

"I'm not sure," Sarah said. "The fact that she donated the book doesn't necessarily mean she wrote it."

"Does it say why the person was writing about Debby in the first place?"

"I haven't read very far, but the author became friends with Debby a few months after she arrived in Maple Hill in the spring of 1960." Sarah sipped her tea. "I wonder if the book's author is one of the people mentioned in the book. The writer might do that to throw the reader off the scent of who he or she really is."

Martha tilted her head to one side. "I can see the logic in that. So you need to find the people mentioned in the book. Who's mentioned?"

"I haven't read very far, but I know Debby worked at a shop called Pleiter's Handmade Gifts, though I don't think it exists anymore."

"The only gift shops in town now are that New Age gift shop and The Galleria, right next to Maggie's shop."

At that moment, Karen delivered Martha's drink with a flourish. "The Bancroft Special. A latte with dark and milk chocolate, a shot of almond syrup, topped with whipped cream and a dusting of cinnamon."

"Karen, this drink will make you famous," Martha said.

"I certainly hope so." Karen winked and left them, responding to a customer calling her.

Sarah eyed the confection. "I have to admit, it looks decadent."

"Try some." Martha slid the glass closer to her.

The hot drink was incredibly creamy, probably from the two types of chocolate and the whipped cream. She could taste just a thread of almond flavor and a hint of cinnamon. "Very chocolaty," she said. "But I'll stick to my chai."

"I knew you'd say that."

"After knowing me for so many years, I'm not surprised."

Sarah's words made Martha pause thoughtfully midsip. "You said your mother donated the book to the library. She may not be the author, but at the very least, she probably knew the author. Do you remember if she was friends with Debby?"

"No, I don't remember them spending much time together."

"So maybe the author was one of your mother's friends back then. Someone who was close to Debby too."

Sarah thought back to the various women her mother had been close to, but the faces and names were hazy. "Mom's things are in the attic, and I remember she had an address book she used every year when she sent out Christmas cards. One of the friends in the address book might be the author."

"I hate sorting through boxes in the attic," Martha said.

Sarah sighed. "I'm not fond of it myself, but my mother's things are organized fairly well. I don't think it will take me long to find the address book."

The next morning, Sarah sat down at her breakfast table with a cup of coffee. After she and Martha had left the café yesterday, Sarah had peeked into the attic and noticed that the afternoon light barely penetrated the enclosed space, so she had put off searching for her mother's address book. She had intended to read more of the book last night, but after dinner, the previous day's exertions—moving the bookcases and searching through the library records—had left her too tired to do more than collapse into bed.

But this morning, the attic light bulbs didn't turn on when she flipped on the switch. She had taken a flashlight with her, but she'd need to buy new light bulbs to have enough light to search through the boxes.

She absently flipped through the book as she sipped her coffee. As she read it, she thought she ought to make a list of the people mentioned. There was a chance that one of them might be the author, like Debby's co-worker at Pleiter's gift shop.

The New Age gift shop was relatively new, but The Galleria had been around for many years. She had assumed Pleiter's had closed years ago, but maybe it had just changed names under new ownership. The new owner might still have old records. It had been a long time, but it was worth a shot. She was going to go to the hardware store to get light bulbs, so she might as well stop by The Galleria and even the New Age shop just to be safe.

"Good morning, Sarah," said Chloe in her rolling Virginia accent. Sarah's new boarder breezed into the kitchen. Her smooth brown hair was still damp, and her fresh, youthful face had a pink glow from her shower. She wore a button-down shirt with faded jeans tucked into calf-high work boots, tightly laced.

"Good morning. What sheep farm are you off to today?"

Chloe pulled a carton of milk from her shelf in the refrigerator. "I talked to an owner yesterday. Her sheep farm is about thirty miles from here, and she said she has a Merino-Rambouillet-Polworth cross that she's willing to sell." She poured some milk into a glass.

Chloe's uncle, a sheep farmer, was letting her bring fleece sheep—as opposed to mutton sheep—into his flock to try their hand at wool production. As an avid spinner, Chloe was selecting her sheep with a critical eye from farms all over Massachusetts, and had pitched camp in Maple Hill since it was centrally located from the farms she wanted to visit. Upon buying a sheep, she arranged to have it transported to her uncle's farm.

"How many sheep have you bought for your uncle's farm?"

"Six," Chloe said. "He's letting me buy an even dozen to start breeding."

"Is this your last farm in this area?" Sarah asked.

Chloe nodded. "I'll be out of your hair by next week."

"You've been a wonderful boarder. You can stay as long as you like and come back anytime."

"Thanks a bunch." Chloe swallowed the last of her milk, and nabbed a breakfast energy bar from a box she kept on the counter. "I have to get ready to go. I'll see you later."

"Bye. Have a good day."

Chloe headed upstairs back to her room.

Sarah looked up The Galleria's number in the phone book and dialed.

A young, perky voice answered the phone. "Hello, this is The Galleria. How can I help you?"

"Hello, my name is Sarah Hart. I would like to speak to the owner."

"Is there anything wrong with your purchase, Ms. Hart?"

"Oh no, nothing like that," Sarah said. "I just want to ask a few questions about the history of The Galleria."

"Oh. Well, you'd need to speak to my Uncle C.J."

"Will he be at the shop today?"

"Yes, he'll be here at about one o'clock."

"Could you please leave him a message to let him know I'll be coming by?"

"Oh sure, Ms. Hart." The girl also took down Sarah's cell phone number.

Sarah couldn't remember the name of the New Age shop—something Unicorn, she thought. She'd have to go downtown and walk in, hoping the owner would have time to talk to her.

One this afternoon. That left Sarah plenty of time to go to the hardware store, and then visit with her daughter-in-law Maggie at her antique store right next to The Galleria. In fact, she could call Maggie and ask if she wanted Sarah to pick up a couple of sandwiches for lunch for both of them. That would be fun.

She was washing her cup at the sink when she heard a horrible bumping sound coming down the stairs. There was a moment of dead silence, then a low groan.

Sarah rushed from the kitchen and found Chloe crumpled in a heap at the bottom of the stairs. "Chloe!" She knelt beside the young woman.

Chloe grimaced in pain. "My leg."

Sarah didn't want to touch her leg in case it was broken. "Don't move. I'll call an ambulance." She got her cell phone and made the brief phone call from Chloe's side. "They'll be here in a few minutes."

The woman's face was pasty, her eyes closed tight with pain.

"Is there anything I can get you? Are you cold?"

Chloe shook her head. "I'm sorry, Sarah."

"Don't be sorry! It wasn't your fault you fell down the stairs."

"I was rushing. I wasn't paying attention." Chloe glanced up and tried to smile. "I guess I won't be moving out next week after all."

CHAPTER FOUR

Upon coming home after a trip to the hospital, Sarah helped Chloe hobble up the stairs to her bedroom. Her leg had been broken, but it had only been her fibula, the smaller bone in her lower leg, so the cast only came up to her knee. Chloe had had knee surgery a few years before, so she used the crutches on the stairs with ease.

"I'm so sorry to be causing you all this trouble," Chloe said as she maneuvered onto her bed.

"You're not any trouble. I'm sorry you're in so much pain."

"It feels better now that the cast is on." Chloe gave a huge yawn. "Sorry."

"You've had an eventful morning. Is there anything I can get you?"

"I'll be fine. That pain medication helps a lot, but it sure makes me sleepy." She yawned again. "I'll rest a bit."

"Are you sure?"

"Positive," Chloe said.

Sarah tucked a quilt around Chloe, making sure not to jostle her cast.

After eating a bowl of soup for a quick lunch, Sarah got in her car and headed into downtown Maple Hill. After picking up a package of light bulbs at the hardware store, she checked her watch. Still thirty minutes before one o'clock, so it was too early to head to The Galleria. She drove to the New Age gift store, passing Liam's café and bookstore on the way.

As she parked in front, she glanced up at the store's name—The Crystal Unicorn. She had only visited the shop twice before, both times to speak to the owner, Annie Harper, but none of the items the store carried interested her. Many of the gifts were based on horoscopes or mysticism, and they made Sarah feel a bit sad that people would depend on these sorts of lifeless things for healing and happiness. When she prayed, God always answered and helped her through whatever difficulties she was experiencing.

As she entered the store, a thick cloud of something spicy wafted to her. Annie stood beside the register, just lighting a new stick of incense.

She glanced up. "Hello. I remember you, we spoke about Genie Collins. But I'm afraid I don't remember your name."

"Sarah Hart." She extended her hand, and Annie shook it.

"Did you come to find out more about Genie?"

"Actually, I'm looking up information about a very old gift shop that used to be in town and I wanted to know if you'd be willing to tell me about when you first opened your shop in Maple Hill."

"I've owned The Crystal Unicorn for only five years," Annie said.

"Did you start it yourself or buy it from someone else?"

"I started about fifteen years ago as my own mail-order company for herbs and plants used in alternative therapy. I was one of the earliest online stores and soon made enough to be able to open this shop."

Sarah was impressed—it was difficult being a business owner these days, especially as a single woman. "That's fantastic. It must have been a lot of hard work."

"It was, but it's been worth it."

"Do you know what store this used to be?"

"I'm pretty sure it was a pet shop," Annie said. "The Realtor didn't tell me, but when I was cleaning up before moving in, I found things like birdseed, rabbit food pellets, an empty box that was printed with a fish food brand on the outside."

"That's right, now I remember. This used to be Sirpless Pet Supplies. Buster Sirpless ran this store for years." How sad that she hadn't remembered that until this moment. "His grandchildren do a lot for the community."

"Can I help you with anything else? Or could I interest you in some chamomile tea?" Annie held up a small brown paper sack with a label stuck to the side. There were several on the counter. "I picked the flowers last week from my garden and they finished drying today. All organic."

"I love chamomile." Sarah found Annie's price reasonable for whole leaf chamomile tea. She loved the soothing applelike scent in the evenings before bed.

"The Roman chamomile from my garden is very good. I think you'll enjoy it." As Annie handed Sarah the receipt, she smiled. Sarah realized she hadn't seen Annie's smile before, and it lit up her face. Annie had enjoyed talking about her business, and she obviously loved her garden, but her life seemed a little lonely. They might not agree on spiritual philosophy, but that didn't mean Sarah couldn't be friendly. She was glad she'd supported a local business owner.

Sarah decided to walk the block to The Galleria. The fresh spring air after so many months of winter always gave her extra energy.

At The Galleria, a young woman behind the counter was helping a customer when Sarah entered the shop, so she wandered around, looking at the items for sale. A local glassblower artist had several large wall hangings and light fixtures along one wall, right next to several local artists' paintings and a table with some scupltures, also from local talent. In the corner stood a quilt rack with two handmade quilts, and Sarah gently fingered the delicate stitches and studied the vibrant color combinations. Several people had urged her to sell her own quilts at The Galleria, which sold the items on commission, but she always seemed to have a particular person or use in mind when she made a quilt, and so she never had an "extra" to sell.

A rack held some touristy items like mugs, keychains, and magnets. Sarah chuckled at the contrast with the rack next to it, which held hand-spun yarn and hand-knitted items made from local sheep's wool. A small bookcase held books by local groups or about local history, books about General Nathaniel Bradford, and a couple of copies of a book of recipes compiled by the Maple Hill Women's Soccer League.

She was standing in front of another wall filled with delicate porcelain dishes and figurines when the young woman from behind the counter approached.

"May I help you?" she asked.

"My name is Sarah Hart. I called earlier about speaking to the store's owner."

"Oh yes, I spoke to you on the phone, Ms. Hart." The girl smiled. "I'm Allie."

Close up, Sarah could see that Allie was probably no more than sixteen or seventeen. "It's nice to meet you, Allie."

The girl glanced at the handmade copper clock mounted on the wall behind the counter. "I'm afraid Uncle C.J. isn't here yet. Is there anything I can help you with?"

There was a chance her Uncle C.J. hadn't even been born when Debby Neely worked in town, but Sarah figured there was no harm in asking. "How long has your uncle owned The Galleria?"

"I'm not sure. As long as I can remember."

"Do you know who owned it before?" Sarah asked.

She shook her head. "My mom told me once, but I don't remember."

Sarah smiled. "I'm sorry, but I don't even know your uncle's last name."

"Oh, it's Wyatt. Same as mine."

Sarah had been half-hoping the Pleiters still owned the shop. Well, it was hard for any small business to be successful over the long term anywhere, much less in a small town like Maple Hill.

The phone rang and Allie excused herself to go to the counter to answer it. "Hello? ... Oh hi. ... Ms. Hart is here. ... Okay. Bye!" Allie hung up the phone. "Ms. Hart? He said he's sorry he's running late, and he'll be here in about thirty minutes."

"That'll give me some time to visit my daughter-in-law," Sarah said. "Thank you, Allie. I'll be back in half an hour."

She nipped next door to Magpie's Antiques, a fitting name for the store since Jason's nickname for his wife, "magpie," was due to Maggie's penchant for collecting antiques. Her hobby had turned into her dream, an antique store in the heart of historical downtown Maple Hill. The store had been difficult for Maggie at first, but recently she had achieved a balance between working at home and at the store.

The bell over the door jangled cheerfully as Sarah entered the shop. Maggie looked up from where she had been staring intently at some papers on the counter. "Sarah! This is a nice surprise."

"I hope I'm not dropping in at a bad time."

"Not at all. I just finished with a customer and I'm eating a late lunch." She gestured to a half-eaten chicken salad sandwich next to her papers. "Do you want some?"

"No thank you, I already ate."

Maggie fished inside a paper bag on the counter and held out a golden brown roll. "I made these last night."

Just the sight made Sarah's mouth water, not because she was especially hungry but because Maggie's rolls—her mother's recipe—were absolutely wonderful. Crisp on the outside, soft and fluffy inside, with a faint honey flavor. "Are you sure? I don't want to eat your lunch."

"You won't." Maggie held open the bag so Sarah could see five more rolls inside. "I brought them to snack on this afternoon. Here's a napkin."

Sarah took the roll and pulled off a small piece. A few flakes from the crusty round top broke off and settled on the napkin. She popped the morsel in her mouth, where it melted like a sweet snowflake. "Mmm. These are so good."

"So what brings you downtown today?"

Sarah told Maggie about the book and everything she had discovered so far about Debby Neely. "I want to talk to the owner of The Galleria about the previous owner. I might be able to find out if The Galleria used to be Pleiter's gift shop, or if the owner knows about Pleiter's back in the sixties."

"I've chatted with C.J. a few times," Maggie said. "He's really nice."

"Has he ever mentioned how he acquired the shop?"

"Actually, I do remember him saying he bought it from a developer who lives in New York."

"Really?"

Maggie nodded. "It seemed strange that someone all the way in New York would have invested in a tiny gift shop here in Maple Hill. C.J. said the previous owner had been a tourist who happened to stop in Maple Hill, saw The Galleria for sale, and bought it on impulse."

Sarah finished her roll.

"Do you want another one?" Maggie reached for the paper bag.

"Oh no, thank you. You're trying to fatten me up," she teased.

"It's because I'm living with two adolescent girls who seem to eat everything in sight."

They chatted about the twins for a while, and then Sarah caught a flash of chrome outside the store windows. A dusty Jeep Cherokee slid into a parking spot in front of The Galleria, and a man about the same age as Sarah's son Jason climbed out of the vehicle.

Maggie leaned over the counter so she could peer out the storefront window. "That's C.J."

"Oh good. I'll see you Sunday?"

"The girls are already excited about the picnic."

With a smile, Sarah exited the store and hailed C.J. just before he entered The Galleria. "Hello. I'm Sarah Hart."

"Nice to meet you, Ms. Hart." He held out a large, square hand and gave a smile that made his blue eyes crinkle.

"Call me Sarah."

He opened the shop door for her. Inside, a couple were looking at some leather shoulder bags and an elderly woman held up a hand-knitted wool lace shawl for inspection in another corner of the store. Allie was talking with the couple. "Let's go to my office in the back," C.J. said.

He led the way through a narrow doorway in the back corner of the store, almost hidden by a bookcase stuffed with figurines of General Nathaniel Bradford and mugs and plates with his likeness stamped on them.

The small office had a massive desk taking up most of the space, with an old leather chair behind it and a newer, smaller chair in front. He waved Sarah to the smaller chair, and as she sat down, she noticed a closet door taking up most of the wall behind the desk. The rest of the wall held old pictures and photographs of various people.

"Allie mentioned you wanted to know the history of The Galleria?" C.J. settled in the leather chair. It creaked loudly under his slim frame, but he didn't seem to notice.

"I'm looking into a woman who worked at a store named Pleiter's Handmade Gifts in the 1960s. I realize The Galleria may not have even been around then, but I thought I'd ask just in case—"

C.J. held up a hand. "Your complicated story has a very easy but complicated answer. My full name is Charles James

Pleiter Wyatt. The Galleria used to be called Pleiter's Hand-made Gifts."

Sarah could hardly believe her luck. "Why did it change names?"

"That's the complicated part." C.J. pointed to one of the old-fashioned pictures on the wall, a man with a brilliant expression in his eyes despite his somber pose. "My Great-Grandpa Jake started Pleiter's gift shop in the 1940s. It passed to his son, my Grandpa Al." He pointed to another picture of a thinner man with bags under his eyes. "Grandpa Al died in 1972. The shop fell to his brother, my Great-Uncle Joseph."

C.J. sighed, "Uncle Joseph hated the shop. One day, a rich tourist from New York came through Maple Hill and stopped by. He chatted with Uncle Joseph about how he loved the shop, and my uncle offered to sell it to him on the spot."

"If he hated it so much, why didn't your Uncle Joseph sell the shop to one of his relatives instead?" Sarah asked.

He shrugged. "He never said, according to my mother. Personally, I think it was because he had inherited the shop from his brother, and he resented the fact that he was expected to take over to keep it in the family. I think he deliberately sold the shop out of the family."

"How sad." Sarah studied the pictures.

"The new owner changed the name to something more 'modern,' at the time, The Galleria."

"So your family owned Pleiter's Handmade Gifts in 1960?"

"Yes, ma'am. You wanted to know about a woman who worked here back then?"

"In 1960, your Grandpa Al broke his leg and hired a woman named Debby Neely. I have a very hazy adolescent memory of noticing Debby's dress, which I think was quilted—I'm a quilter myself. I'm looking for more information on Debby Neely. So I'm tracking down any friends and co-workers of hers."

"I should be able to tell you about her co-workers." C.J. twisted in his chair to reach into a file cabinet behind him. He pulled out an old, overstuffed ledger and flipped through the pages. "This is an old payroll register that starts in the forties. My Grandpa Al never threw anything away. All his paid employees should be recorded here. When did Debby Neely arrive in Maple Hill?"

"Spring of 1960."

C.J. turned a few pages, then frowned. "It's not here."

"Debby's name?"

"No employee payments at all. These pages only have consignment payments." He flipped ahead. "There are employee payments in the seventies and beyond, but not before that."

"Could the payroll records be somewhere else?"

"They must be." C.J. turned to look through the file cabinet drawer. "However, I'm not sure where they are."

"Would you be willing to look for me?"

"It might take me awhile." She wasn't in any hurry, but... "Is there any other way to find out who worked at Pleiter's with Debby?"

"My mother would have been too young to work in the store at the time, but she had to go there after school every day. She might remember who was working there."

"Who is your mother?"

"Cheryl Pleiter Wyatt."

The name sparked Sarah's memory. Of course. She remembered Cheryl Pleiter from school, although they had been a year apart in grades, so they hadn't been in any of the same classes or hung out with the same friends. "Do you think she'd mind if I gave her a call?" Sarah asked.

"I'm sure she wouldn't mind a visit if you have time to drive over to see Mom right now. I can call her and tell her to expect you. She has a doctor's appointment later this afternoon."

"Now is fine." Sarah smiled.

C.J. made the call to his mother, then gave Sarah the address and directions.

Sarah drove to Cheryl Wyatt's house on the outskirts of Maple Hill. She enjoyed the beautiful rolling hills and lush trees, several still sporting their bright green spring foliage.

The tiny farmhouse had cherry red trim, newly painted. On the wraparound porch were a couple of rocking chairs next to a low white wicker table, where a cat drowsed in the sunlight. Sarah climbed up the short flight of steps and paused to scratch the cat's ears before knocking on the screen door.

The inner door flew open to reveal an energetic, petite woman, around Sarah's age, with snow white hair and blue eyes that matched her son's. Her eyes crinkled as she smiled at Sarah. "Hi there! I remember you. We went to school together, didn't we?" Cheryl's hand flapped like a hummingbird's wing, sparkling with three or four ruby rings. "Come on in!"

"Nice to see you again." Sarah stepped into the cozy living room. Cheryl obviously loved the color red, because it was splashed as an accent color over the floral overstuffed chairs and ran in slender stripes down the curtains at the large picture windows. She also had china plates with scarlet trim around the edges displayed on the distressed wood mantle. "Thank you so much for agreeing to see me today."

"It's no trouble at all. I just put a kettle of water on to boil. I'll be right back."

Sarah was immediately drawn to the pictures in frames on a worn oak bookcase. She had picked up a picture of a tall, gangly young man when Cheryl zipped back into the living room with a tray holding a fat red teapot and matching mugs, which she set on the low cherrywood coffee table. "I hope you don't mind decaf tea—goodness knows, if I added caffeine to the mix, my body would probably explode.

"That was my husband Joel," Cheryl said, looking at the picture Sarah held.

"He looks like a teenager in this picture."

"He was. Seventeen. We married the year after that was taken."

"You married young."

"Our wedding anniversary is next week." Cheryl sighed, and her energy level seemed to wane. "I'm grateful for every year I had with him."

Sarah stared at the photo. "I can relate. It was hard to think that way when I first lost my husband. The days afterward were so...dark."

Literally. After Gerry had passed away, she had gone home and the walls had seemed paper thin. The house seemed to have deflated. And everywhere she turned, every room was dim. The sunlight hadn't been able to penetrate the windows somehow, and every lamp feebly glowed like a fifteen-watt bulb. She had wandered the house, expecting Gerry to turn a corner and enter a room. And when he didn't, she had stood silent and cold, unable to cry because she hadn't been able to breathe.

One day, a few days before he'd died, he had said to her, "Sarah, don't center your life around death." It had been Gerry's words that brought her out of those terrible days.

"What do you mean?" she had asked. The hospital bustled around them, nurses hurrying here and there, doctors flipping through charts, IV stands rolling along with patients. They all were the sounds of sickness and death to her.

"Take advantage of every moment," he said, his breath coming in shallow gasps. "Keep nagging Jason to move the family home to Maple Hill. Make that wall hanging quilt of Mount Greylock you've been talking about doing for so long." He touched her hand. "Move on. Enjoy the life God has given to you. Don't center your life around death." His.

After he had gone and she'd been wandering the echoing house, those words had penetrated the fog of her mind. And so one day, she dressed, put on her shoes, and went to the Wild Goose Chase fabric store to look for fabrics for that Mount Greylock quilt.

Sarah shook herself, realizing she and Cheryl had dipped into a long moment of silence. Then Cheryl's natural zing returned full force, and she plopped into a cream-colored armchair with fluffy red pillows. "Have a seat."

Sarah replaced the picture on the bookshelf and seated herself on the sofa, which was all rounded corners and patterned in a strawberry patch design.

"I remember your husband Gerry." Cheryl poured the tea with so much gusto that a little splashed over the rim. "He was so friendly, and he was the most highly recommended accountant when we asked around. He helped us with our finances the year Joel got sick."

Sarah hadn't known that, but then again, Gerry hadn't often spoken about his clients to her. "I'm glad he was able to help you. I enjoyed meeting your son C.J. today."

"He's such a dear boy. I don't know how he turned out so well. He's so calm, and look at me! But here I am, going on. Get me started and I won't stop talking about my family. C.J. said you had some questions for me?"

"I'm interested in a woman who worked at Pleiter's Handmade Gifts when we were in school."

"I didn't work there at the time, but I went to my father's shop every day after school. My mother had recently passed away, so my sisters and I went to the store to do our homework until Pleiter's closed for the day. I practically grew up there."

"Do you remember a woman who worked at the shop named Debby Neely?" Sarah asked.

"Debby! Yes, I remember her. She only worked there for a few years, I think. I never knew what happened to her. Why do you ask?"

"I'm a quilter, and I have a vague memory of a dress she wore that I think was quilted. I thought I might be able to talk to one of Debby's friends or co-workers. Do you remember who worked with her at the shop?"

"Why, of course. It was Olive Cavanaugh."

"Olive? She was my son's Sunday school teacher."

"Mother had been working at Pleiter's, but after she passed away, none of us kids were old enough to work there. My father hired Olive to help out. A few years later, when he broke his leg, he hired Debby."

"How long did Olive work at Pleiter's?"

"Several years. When I turned fifteen, I started working at the shop with Olive. She quit a few years later, when my brother started working there," Cheryl said. "I may have been young at the time, but I do remember she and Debby were very close, despite the difference in their ages."

The author of the book also had been good friends with Debby. Before Sarah forgot, she had to at least ask Cheryl. "Do you remember anyone else who was close to Debby besides Olive? There's a possibility my mom was friends with her."

"What was your mom's name?"

"Ruth Drayton."

Cheryl shook her head. "Doesn't ring any bells."

Sarah thanked Cheryl and rose to leave, her mind absorbed with more questions. She hadn't found any clues as to why her mother had donated the book to the library, but she had at least discovered who Debby's co-worker was.

Olive had helped her with a mystery once before. Maybe she'd help her again.

 CHAPTER FIVE

S arah arrived home to find Chloe trying to navigate
her way from the breakfast table to the sink with her
crutches while holding an empty plastic bowl. She
had the bowl clamped between her teeth when Sarah walked
in.

"Oh Chloe. Let me help you."

"I don't want you to have to wait on me."

"It's no trouble at all." Sarah set the bowl on the counter
and noted the box of cereal already there, while the carton of milk still sat on the breakfast table. Chloe must have
just eaten. "How in the world did you get the milk to the
table?"

Chloe grinned. "Very carefully."

"Want me to put it away for you?"

"If you don't mind. I don't want to risk dropping it."
Chloe swung easily but slowly on her crutches. "When I had
knee surgery before, I had a messenger bag to help me carry
things. I'll have to find something similar to use."

Sarah put the milk in the fridge. "I have a fanny pack you can use, and I also have a cloth tote bag and an old backpack. Would any of those work?"

"Thanks. The tote would be great."

Chloe balanced gingerly on her crutches as she washed her bowl and a spoon, her movements slow and measured.

"Do you hurt very much?" Sarah asked as she put a kettle of water on the stove to boil.

"I do have a few bruises. I play soccer at a recreational women's league back home, so I'm used to aches and pains. But it hurt a lot when he did the cast, and I'm exhausted."

"I'm not surprised. Did you want me to make you anything more substantial than cereal for dinner?"

"No, I'm not very hungry, but I thought I should eat something small before bed. Which is strange, since I've slept most of the afternoon. So did you find Debby's co-worker?"

Sarah made her tea while telling Chloe about her conversations with C.J. and Cheryl. "She remembered Debby working at Pleiter's."

"Did she remember Debby's co-worker too?"

"It was Olive Cavanaugh. She was my son's Sunday school teacher and now she lives at the same assisted living home as my father."

"Wow. What are the odds of that? So are you going to visit her?" Chloe's words were enveloped in a huge yawn. "I'm sorry."

"You should get to bed."

"I think I will." She had been leaning against the kitchen counter, but now she turned around on her crutches and headed toward the door. "Good night."

"Good night."

"Oh I almost forgot." She turned at the kitchen doorway. "I thought about this while you were out. Did you search for Debby Neely online?"

"In fact, I was going to do that tonight."

"I hope you find something." Chloe turned and made her way up the stairs.

Sarah sat back down at the table and sipped her tea. She had a lot to do, so she decided to make a list. She got a pad of paper and a pen from her sewing room.

1. Search attic for Mom's address book
2. Look for Debby Neely online
3. Talk to Olive Cavanaugh
4. Finish reading the book

She felt a bit guilty that she had been so busy running around town that she hadn't had more time to read the book. She'd do that tonight, after doing a quick search online for Debby.

Sarah made a simple dinner for herself—a pork chop with rice and steamed broccoli—and then headed into her quilting room to fire up her computer.

She searched for *Debby Neely* but got no useful results. There were no articles about a Debby Neely arrested by the FBI. There were a few blogs by women named Debby

Neely, some social networking pages, and two newspaper journalists, but they were all too young to be the Debby in the book. She also found a newspaper article about a woman named Debby Neely who had a baby with an enlarged heart.

She searched for *Deborah Neely* and found even more false hits. Then she saw a newspaper article on a woman named Deborah Neely who was incarcerated in a prison in North Carolina.

Her hopes rose as she read the article, which mentioned the woman had been convicted of murder but had recently been able to find her missing daughter from the confines of prison and reach out to her. But then the article went into more detail about her crime, which hadn't occurred until the eighties.

Sarah sat back in her chair and glanced at the clock. She had about an hour before bedtime.

She drew the book out of her purse and set it on her desk. She also flipped to a new page in her notebook so she could take notes as she read. After turning on the bright gooseneck lamp, she opened to where she had left off earlier.

Debby didn't make friends easily, but I guess a lot of people are like that too. There aren't many people who can readily strike up conversations with strangers.

Gerry had been like that, and when they were at gatherings with people she didn't know, Sarah had been content to stay in the background while he talked and made friends. Every year, they would be invited to Christmas parties or

Fourth of July picnics, usually with family friends or some of Gerry's clients. Even when Sarah knew everyone at the party, something about the sheer number of people, gathered in clusters, made her a little shy. She'd stand beside Gerry while he chatted with people, and he always made sure to include her in the conversation. He would always be sure to say hello to people, ask them about their families or their hobbies, or maybe a trip he knew they had been on. He'd been so good at that—asking questions to get people to open up to him, to make them feel comfortable, to show them that he genuinely cared about them.

Sarah was happy to simply stand beside him and smile and listen. Gerry had been entertaining to the people he talked to, and also considerate to her—he didn't press her to talk more than she felt comfortable doing. Sarah could relate to Debby's shyness. Not everyone could be an extrovert.

There were times, though, when Debby seemed to draw inside herself. She almost became smaller, even though she was only a little bitty thing already.

I think that's why I didn't get close to her very quickly, even though I saw her so often. I always talked to her, of course, and she seemed friendly enough, but she was definitely tense with people, in that quiet way of hers. She rarely smiled. It was only when I got to know her later that I ever saw anything in her face besides a guarded mask.

The only time she really was carefree was when she was with children. Debby loved children, loved making them laugh and playing games with them. She almost became a different person with kids, someone ten years younger. The parents at church liked Debby because their children liked her, although Debby would always revert to that polite, friendly but reserved way of talking to adults. I think it kept even the parents from getting close to her, despite the fact that she got along so well with their kids. I didn't really understand why she liked kids so much until years later.

I remember one time, after church. She'd been singing the hymns, same as always, with quietness, but it always looked like the songs moved her in a sort of painful way. She didn't sing timidly, and she didn't sing neutrally or just mouth the words. It was as if she loved the hymns but they pricked her too. You could see it in her face, especially when she sang songs like "The Solid Rock" and "I Know That My Redeemer Lives." I myself never sang very strongly, but the words of the hymns didn't hurt me like they seemed to hurt her.

After church one day, a group of us were gathered outside the front doors, same as always. C. had picked up a bunch of sandwiches and we were going to go to the park to have a picnic lunch, but I noticed Debby wasn't there, in the circle of friends. I went inside to find her, thinking maybe she had stopped to speak to someone or perhaps play with one of the kids from Sunday school.

I saw her in a corner talking to the pastor, and she seemed a little more serious than normal. Then again, her face was always sort of sad. I wasn't sure if it wasn't just my imagination.

I only remember her talking to the pastor that one time. Later, when we were closer, we talked a lot about God. I think her faith had been very strong, before she came to Maple Hill, but with everything that had happened to her, when I knew her, her faith was a bit shaky.

When I asked her once about what she had talked about with the pastor, she didn't answer me. By then I knew her better, so I didn't pry. But it made me wonder. I still wonder about it. If I had been a stronger person and pushed her for an answer, would it have enabled me to help her any better? I don't know. I guess it's useless to think about the what-ifs.

I think she was happiest when she was talking about her dresses. She loved making them. She said they were each inspired by something she had seen or heard or felt. To her, they were artwork.

She loved beauty, I think. She liked giving beautiful things to people, even to animals. She liked taking things that seemed like nothing just by themselves, and combining them to make them special. Like in her dresses.

Not many people knew that about her—her love of beautiful things. Not that she bought a lot or had a lot. She had very little. She seemed used to having very little.

But she saw beauty in things that other people didn't see. And it seemed like she wanted things and people around her to be beautiful. She made little hats for the mailbox flag where she lived, cheerful things like a red stocking cap in winter and a pink flower hat in spring. And she made bright scarves from cloth scraps and gave them to the little girls at church.

She didn't get very close to anyone until the last few months she was in Maple Hill. I wish she had. People liked her. She was part of our community.

But I guess since she was on the run, she wouldn't naturally want to get close to people. It just doesn't seem fair, since she didn't do anything. But without proof, what could she do?

Sarah had jotted down notes as she read, clues that might lead her to the identity of the author, and she scanned the list.

No kids.

The author was apparently someone without children yet. So perhaps someone Debby's age, maybe in her twenties? Or younger? Would Debby be close friends with someone younger than nineteen? Things the author had said, like calling Debby a "little bitty thing," made Sarah think the author might be a little older than Debby rather than younger.

Didn't sing very strongly.

Further down had been the phrase, "if I had been a stronger person and pushed her." Maybe the author wasn't a very bold personality? Sarah could relate to that—she didn't feel she was a very strong personality, while Martha was a determined, "git 'er done" type of person. It was one of the things she admired about her best friend.

Church.

Apparently Debby had gone to one of the Maple Hill churches. But which one, Bridge Street Church or the Congregational Church?

Circle of friends. C.

From what the author wrote about that day after church, it seemed there was a group of people who might have hung out with Debby, including the person referred to as C.

Sarah couldn't help wondering if maybe C. was the author, mentioning himself that way in the book to hide his (or her) identity.

So far, the only people she knew were connected to Debby—or possibly friends with her—were Olive Cavanaugh and Sarah's mother. She'd known her mom's church friends very well. They were mostly women Mom's age, and Sarah distinctly recalled the four or five women her mother spent the most time with. She didn't remember her mom spending time with Debby Neely at church. Her memories of Debby were at places around Maple Hill.

Still, even though she couldn't remember her mom talking to Debby Neely at church, it didn't mean Debby didn't attend services. She would talk to Pastor John Peabody on Sunday. He hadn't been in Maple Hill in 1960—goodness, he had probably been only a toddler—but he might know which church members might know anything about Debby, and if she had gone to Bridge Street Church in the early sixties.

Debby made dresses.

Sarah recalled Debby's magnificent dress, which was now more vivid in her memory than even Debby's face. Had Debby made the dress Sarah had touched? Apparently she'd made several, and liked combining things to make them special. Like quilting—taking different fabrics and combining them to make a design that painted emotions greater than the individual fabric pieces would have evoked. Perhaps her fuzzy memories were correct and the dress had been quilted. Once again, she wished she had paid more attention, to both the dress and the woman.

Sarah closed the book with a sigh. Time to head to bed. She had her notes to look over before chatting with Olive tomorrow. Maybe Olive had even been one of that circle of friends, or might know who C. was.

She couldn't wait to talk to Olive Cavanaugh.

CHAPTER SIX

The lawns around Bradford Manor were like lengths of spring green silk rippling under the sunlight as Sarah drove up the private gravel driveway. She parked in the parking lot and enjoyed a deep breath of air scented with the freshly mowed grass before heading into the colonial-style building.

As she walked in the front door, Tiffany Henderson, one of the nurses, was pushing a man in a wheelchair toward the piano. She caught sight of Sarah. "Hello, Mrs. Hart. I think I saw your father out on the back patio."

Sarah went to the patio to say hello to her father first. William Drayton sat in his wheelchair next to another man in a chair, both of them facing the view of the mountains. The blue sky faded to white haze as it touched the snowy tops of the peaks in the distance.

Her father was chatting with the other man, who looked positively ancient. His brown face was a mass of lines like Maggie's antique crackle-glazed bowls, and heavy lids covered his dark eyes. His mouth moved constantly in a slow, rotating motion, and Sarah guessed he had lost all his teeth and wasn't wearing dentures.

"And so when Ted Williams hit that home run, we jumped to our feet like there were hot potatoes under them," her dad said.

The other man's smile didn't change, although his eyes were focused on William's face. Sarah wondered if he had the hearing to listen.

"Hi, Dad. It's Sarah."

He turned in his chair and smiled at her. Then he nudged his neighbor. "See, I told you she'd come today."

The other man turned to look at Sarah, and gave her a friendly nod but didn't say anything.

"How are you doing today?" Sarah pulled a chair close to her father's wheelchair and sat down.

"I was telling him about last week's game," he said, pointing to the other man.

Sarah held her hand out to him. "I'm Sarah." She pitched her voice a bit louder than normal.

He shook her hand and silently nodded.

"What's your name?"

He simply nodded and smiled.

"Dad, did he tell you his name?"

"What?"

"Do you know his name?"

He hesitated, then said, "I don't remember." He turned to his neighbor. "What's your name again?"

The man again nodded and smiled.

Sarah simply patted her father's hand. "He seems very nice." No need to know someone's name to enjoy a good conversation with them. Especially if it was one-sided. "What have you done today?"

"We had eggs for breakfast. They made them just the way I like." He winked.

Sarah laughed, glad to see him in such fine humor. The joke was that her father loved eggs any way they were prepared. He had often told her mother, "Surprise me," when she asked him how he wanted his eggs.

"Is there a game this week?" he asked. "That Ted Williams sure is on a winning streak."

"Ted Williams hasn't played in years, Dad."

"Is that so?" He leaned closer to her and lowered his voice, gesturing with his thumb at his silent neighbor. "He doesn't follow baseball."

Sarah wondered if she could get old baseball games on DVDs and give them to her father to watch. She'd have to look into that and find out when Ted Williams played for the Red Sox.

"I was telling him about my batting average," William said. "Your mom brought you to our games. You were only a little tyke, but you always cheered the loudest."

Sarah did remember going to a few of her father's recreational baseball games with her mom and her brother, although as a child, she hadn't been very interested. "I remember playing with the extra balls on the sidelines."

Her father yawned. "It's nice out here."

"Did you want me to take you back to your room so you can nap?"

"No, I think I'll snooze a little right here." His eyes drifted shut.

Sarah kissed him on the cheek. "See you later, Dad."

She headed inside toward the nurse's station so she could ask if they knew where Olive was. But as she entered the front sitting room, she glanced around to see if Olive was among the residents there.

A soft hymn rolled out of the console piano standing against one wall, played by the man she'd seen earlier in the wheelchair with Tiffany. Several people had drawn chairs close by to listen.

Directly across from the piano was a cage filled with small, colorful birds, and nearby were chairs and low tables for people to sit, chat, or nap. Sarah scanned the chairs and was pleased to see Olive Cavanaugh's white head bent over some work in her lap.

"Hello, Olive." Sarah sat down next to her.

She looked up, and her blue eyes were bright. "Sarah Hart! Trying to sneak up on me? Well, you're getting better at it. Have you come to visit your father?"

"I left him dozing on the patio." She noticed that Olive had several scraps of colorful fabric in her lap, and she was cutting them into narrow strips with a pair of scissors. "What are you doing?"

"Why, I'm designing my new dress for the Academy Awards." Olive delivered the line with a completely straight face and a twinkle in her eye.

"How glamorous!"

Olive fingered the colorful pieces. "Once every few weeks, I cut pieces of cloth into strips and give them to the birds."

"I've seen the cloth pieces in the birdcage every so often." The cage was cleaned regularly, so she had never paid much attention to it before. "I didn't realize you were the one giving the scraps to them."

"I've been doing this for...my goodness, I don't know how long. Since I was married. I'd give the scraps to the birds in my backyard, and sometimes I'd see some mighty snazzy nests in our oak tree." Olive snipped a long strip from a piece of blue calico. "So what can I do for you, Sarah?"

"Am I that obvious?" she asked.

"No, not really. You know I always enjoy chatting with you. But today you have a certain gleam in your eye. It reminds me of the last time you hunted me down to help figure out one of your mysteries."

"I'm always grateful for your help. And I heard that you used to work at Pleiter's Handmade Gifts."

"Pleiter's! I haven't heard that name in a long time. Al Pleiter was the sweetest man. We grew up together, did you know that? I think at one point he was sweet on me, but I cured him of that pretty quick." Olive chuckled. "He was a huge boxing fan—he was one of those people who were fans of Muhammad Ali when he was still Cassius Clay. When he won the gold medal in boxing in the 1960 Summer Olympics, Al wouldn't stop crowing about it," Olive said.

"Do you remember working with a woman named Debby Neely? Nineteen sixty is right about when she would have started."

At the mention of the name, Olive fumbled with a piece of purple taffeta. "Wh-who did you say?"

"Debby Neely. Cheryl Wyatt mentioned you were working at Pleiter's when Al Pleiter hired Debby."

"Oh yes," Olive said. "Little Debby. Sweet girl."

The way she said it reminded Sarah of the words the author had used in the book. "Can you tell me about her?"

The snipping slowed slightly. "She was a good worker. Very quiet. I liked her."

How strange. Olive seemed reluctant to speak of her, but Sarah couldn't figure out why. "What else do you remember about her?"

"Not much," Olive said. "Why are you interested in her anyway?"

"I was only twelve or thirteen, but I remember meeting Debby and being fascinated by her dress. Looking back, I think it was quilted, and I wanted to know for sure. You know me and quilts," she said with a smile.

Olive's busy fingers stopped, and she caressed a strip of scarlet grosgrain. "Well, your memory's pretty sharp. Debby made the most beautiful dresses and blouses."

Sarah leaned forward. "And were they quilted?"

"Yes, she hand-quilted them herself. I loved her clothes." Olive sighed, with a half smile on her lips. "Her dresses and blouses were in high demand."

"She sold them?"

"Through Pleiter's. As I recall, Myra Johnson was the one who got her to start doing that, and once she started, she couldn't keep those dresses on the shelves. As soon as she finished one, someone always bought it within a few days. She took special orders too."

The amount of money Debby made working at Pleiter's was probably barely enough to support a young woman alone in 1960, so the dresses would have brought in extra income. If Debby sold her garments to local women, perhaps Sarah would be able to find out who bought them. She would love to see them, even if they didn't help her find out who wrote the book.

Sarah leaned back in her chair and watched as Olive finished snipping her last length of fabric. "Were you close to Debby?" she asked.

"We chatted some." Olive took the handful of strips in her lap and fed them, one by one, into the bird cage. "She wasn't one to talk about herself. She would sit there, doing her sewing and listening to whomever felt like talking. She was a good listener."

Sarah wasn't sure how to bring up the subject of her mom or C. without telling Olive about the book. But she wanted to keep secret the fact that she was searching for the book's author. The problem was, it seemed Olive was reluctant to talk about the only other topic she could mention, which was Debby herself.

"Did you know any of her other friends?" Sarah asked.

"She kept mostly to herself."

"Not for long, I'm guessing. You and Mom are a lot alike, introducing people, making sure people don't feel quite so alone."

There was a long pause before Olive continued the conversation. "Your mother was a dear, so gentle and caring. I do remember Debby chatting with her every so often. Your mother seemed to make an effort to try to make her feel welcome when she first came to town."

Maybe Sarah hadn't been with her at those times or simply didn't remember. It didn't rule out her plans to search through the attic for her mother's address book. But if her mom only chatted with Debby "every so often," it was unlikely she was the close friend of Debby's who had written the book.

"I'm sorry to cut our conversation short, but I'm feeling a little tired and I'd like to take a nap." Olive didn't look very sorry—in fact, she looked relieved for the excuse. She twisted in her wheelchair to wave in the direction of the nurses' station in the far corner.

"I'll take you to your room," Sarah offered.

"No, that's fine."

Tiffany walked over. "Where would you like to go, Mrs. Cavanaugh?"

"My room, please."

The young woman seemed surprised at Olive's somber tone. "Sure thing." She undid the wheelchair brake.

"Goodbye, Olive," Sarah said as Tiffany began to wheel her away. "Thanks for your help."

Olive didn't answer right away. She was already halfway across the sitting room when she responded. Sarah could barely hear the soft voice across the room.

"In this instance, I think you should let the past go, Sarah." Her voice sounded tired. "Some mysteries aren't meant to be solved."

Her words were the last thing Sarah expected to hear. Before she could answer her, Olive was down the hallway and out of sight.

CHAPTER SEVEN

Sarah's cell phone rang just as she exited Bradford Manor. She saw "Martha" in her caller ID. "Hello," she greeted her best friend.

"I'm having lunch at Liam's today. Want to join me?"

"That sounds good. I'll be there in a few minutes."

When Sarah arrived at The Spotted Dog Café, Martha was sitting on a bright red stool at the counter, chatting with Liam. She smiled at Sarah and patted the empty seat next to her, but Sarah was waylaid by a wriggling roadblock that sat panting on top of her shoes.

"Goodness me, what was I thinking? To enter the café and sit down before greeting you, Murphy. Where are my manners?" She scratched his chin, which he stretched out and leaned into her hand.

"Now Sarah, I know Murphy's the only reason you come here, but you've got to at least pretend you enjoy my dazzling personality as well." Liam winked at her.

"I'll do my best to appear entertained, Liam, but no promises," she said.

Liam sighed in mock despair. "Now I know I'm getting old when a pretty lady chooses my dog's company over mine."

Liam often offered compliments, but Sarah felt warmly gratified when he called her pretty. She reminded herself he was just a friendly person. In fact, in some ways, his outgoing personality made her think of Gerry, making her always feel comfortable and welcome.

"What can I get you?" he asked.

"Chai with extra whipped cream," she said, then glanced at the daily special. "And that spinach bacon quiche."

"Any luck finding that mysterious author?" Martha asked.

"Maybe." She told her about The Galleria/Pleiter's gift shop and about her talk with Olive.

"How strange for Olive to act that way," Martha said.

"She seemed so sad talking about Debby, but there was something else too. Almost like remorse," Sarah said.

"What would she have to be sorry for? Did the book say anything more about Debby's co-worker?"

Sarah shook her head. "But I haven't finished reading it yet. I've been following a few leads, and they seem to keep me busy. Where does the time go?"

"Story of my life," Martha said with a chuckle.

Liam set Sarah's chai and quiche in front of her and slid a plate with a turkey sandwich over to Martha. They both bowed their heads for a quick prayer of blessing before digging in.

"What else did Olive say?" Martha asked.

"Olive did confirm Debby's dress was quilted. And in fact, Debby made garments to sell at Pleiter's."

"I should have known you'd be right about anything to do with quilting."

"I remember now how beautiful it was. It couldn't have been made out of cotton like my day dresses. Maybe more expensive fabric? Like the kind of dress you'd save for a special occasion. People probably didn't wear them very often," Sarah said.

"That's kind of sad, if you think about it. Maybe I shouldn't wait to wear my 'special' dresses and just gussy myself up every chance I get."

Sarah laughed. "Wear one of them to church and dazzle the congregation. Life's too short to waste on regrets, after all."

At her words, Liam's eyes fell and he blinked rapidly as he suddenly started wiping down the counter with a cloth. Sarah wondered what he was thinking.

"Speaking of church," Sarah said, "the book mentioned Debby talking to a pastor, but it doesn't say which pastor or which church."

"I wonder if it was our church." Martha tapped on the counter with a finger as she thought. "Fifty years ago ... that was probably Reverend Radcliffe. Do you think Bridge

Street Church has records of members dating back to the sixties?"

"I'm not sure. I'll ask Pastor John after the service tomorrow."

"Pastor John's home with a cold today," Sarah told Martha as they sat down in the church pew. They'd both arrived several minutes before the service started. Martha helped her husband Ernie scoot into the pew. He smiled and waved at Sarah but didn't say anything, simply looking around at other people filing into the sanctuary for the church service.

"Ask him what?" From the pew in front of them, Mavis Hoyt turned as she spoke.

Sarah realized that Mavis, as head of women's circle events, might be able to help her. "I'm trying to find out if a young woman attended this church from 1960 to 1962. Her name was Debby Neely."

"Neely? I don't recall the name, although in the early sixties, I was only a little girl."

"Do you know if the church has records that go back that far?"

"Hmm. Pastor John could probably tell you for sure, but I think we had a set of books that recorded the church membership—addresses, telephone numbers, names and birth dates of children, that sort of thing. But a bunch of them were in the storage room in the church basement when there was that flooding that happened about fifteen years ago, do you remember that?"

Sarah did remember.

"I still can't believe it," Martha said. "The rain that year! Pouring buckets. And all those rivers that overflowed—no one had ever seen the like, not even Hattie Hepperson, and she's the oldest person in town. I know you and Gerry were lucky, but we piled sandbags around the house and had a tense few hours while waiting to see if the water would rise any further," Martha added. "We ended up with only minimal damage to the basement, but I remember the east part of town was nearly six feet deep in water!"

"Unfortunately, the church had gallons of water in the basement," Mavis said. "I helped with clean up, and I remember throwing away boxes and boxes of old papers and water-damaged furniture after the water had gone down. But what am I saying? I saw you there too, Sarah."

Sarah nodded. "We were so grateful we had such little damage so we could spend more time helping at the church. Those floods were just terrible. It's too bad the records were destroyed. Is there any other way to check church membership or attendance?"

"Actually, there might be, but it depends on how firmly your ear is attached."

"Why is that?"

"Because Julie Lessman and Sandra Pohlman will talk it off if you let them." Mavis had a rather disdainful expression.

Sarah tried not to smile. That was the pot calling the kettle black, indeed. But Mavis's idea was a good one. Julie and Sandra were among the oldest members of Bridge Street Church, and the best of friends. They also could both talk a mile a minute without taking a breath, and they hadn't slowed down at all with the passing years.

Mavis said, "Just the other day, I had to ask Julie for help because she has a recipe for whitening antique lace with buttermilk, and she kept me there for two hours. I couldn't get a word in edgewise, although I have to admit the woman can multitask. While she was whitening my lace, she talked about every goal her great-grandsons made this season in soccer, and then her granddaughter expecting twins around Christmas time—now that's something I love, Christmas babies, don't you?—and she even started talking about old Christmas parties they used to hold at Bridge Street Church in the fifties. And she didn't stop working on my lace the entire time."

If Julie remembered Christmas parties from the fifties, there was a good chance she might remember a young woman who attended services in the early sixties. "So you think Julie and Sandra will remember if Debby attended the church back then?"

"If they don't know, they'll definitely know who will."

Mavis turned back around in her seat as the music started and the service began. One of the deacons quoted from Hebrews 10:22: "let us draw near to God with a sincere heart in full assurance of faith, having our hearts sprinkled to cleanse us from a guilty conscience and having our bodies washed with pure water."

Sarah thought about Debby Neely and wondered whether she had had a "guilty conscience." Debby had gone to church when she could have stayed away. Today, the culture seemed to revel in the fact that you could choose any religion that fits you—and Sarah fleetingly thought about Annie Harper and her New Age gift shop—but even in the sixties, church attendance wasn't mandatory. It was all about freedom of choice. And yet Debby had chosen to go to church.

But the book mentioned the pain she had seemed to feel when singing the hymns. Had she been pained by a guilty conscience, or had she been pained because, despite her innocence, she was on the run from the FBI? The author had described her personality in minute detail, as if trying to find proof of her innocence in all the things remembered about Debby. Who had Debby Neely really been?

After the last prayer was said and the congregation dismissed, Martha turned to Sarah. "So what are you going to do now?"

"Now? Jason said the twins want to make lunch for me...."

"I meant in your search for the book's author," Martha said.

"Oh. Well, I'll go talk to Julie and Sandra, and then I'll probably have to brave the attic to find Mom's address book."

"I can help you tomorrow if you'd like."

"Are you sure?"

"Definitely," Martha said. "Besides, some of the grand-daughters are taking Ernie out for a 'Grandpa Day' today. I predict he'll be completely tuckered out all day tomorrow."

Sarah leaned forward to speak to Ernie, sitting on the other side of Martha. "A 'Grandpa Day,' huh? Sounds like a lot of fun!"

He lifted his eyes to the ceiling and gave a long-suffering sigh, although a smile twitched at the edges of his neatly trimmed moustache.

Martha said, "So, I'll be over at nine tomorrow morning. Sound good?"

"The attic is pretty dusty," Sarah warned her.

"I'll leave my ball gown at home, then," she replied.

Sarah laughed, then excused herself from Martha and Ernie to seek out Julie and Sandra.

The two friends were sitting on a bench outside, sheltered from the sunshine by a budding tree waving in the slight breeze. They were watching an impromptu soccer game on the lawn, and Sarah recognized their great-grandchildren among the players. Sarah's granddaughters Amy and Audrey were also there playing with three of Martha's grandchildren.

"Hello Julie, Sandra," she said as she approached.

"Oh hello Sarah," Julie said, sliding over on the bench. "Have a seat."

"Come to watch your grandkids?" Sandra asked.

"Actually—"

"They're springing up," Julie said. "Look how big they've grown. It seems like only yesterday they had just come to town and were such little things."

"You just said that about your own great-grandchildren," Sandra chided her.

"Did not. They didn't come to town, I saw them being born."

"You said 'It seems like only yesterday they were such little things, and now they're monsters.'"

"Did not! I said that it seemed like only yesterday they were such little things *being carried around by their mothers*, and now they're playing soccer. Sandra Pohlman, you need a hearing aid."

"I have a hearing aid. You need a new memory."

"I remember just fine. In fact, I remember Sarah coming over looking like a woman with a mission." Julie turned toward Sarah with bright eyes and a wide smile.

Sarah had actually been vastly entertained by their banter. "I hope I wasn't too obvious. I do need to ask you something."

"It's bound to be more exciting than us two rehashing the same arguments," Sandra said. "Shoot, girl."

"Do either of you know if a woman named Debby Neely ever attended our church?"

"Who?" Sandra asked.

"Debby Neely. She might have attended Bridge Street Church in the early sixties, but I'm not sure."

"Nineteen sixty? Land sakes, girl, that's fifty years ago," Sandra said.

"I was barely a toddler fifty years ago." Julie ran a hand over her silver hair, but her brown eyes twinkled.

Sandra nudged her with a bony elbow. "You had already pushed out three babies, you big liar."

"I wasn't *that* old, and if I was, it means you were too!"

"I need a calculator. In nineteen sixty, I was how old?" Sandra asked.

"We were—ahem. In our early thirties," Julie said.

"I *loved* the sixties."

Julie smiled. "The sixties were all about the Beatles."

"You really do need a new memory. It was Elvis all the way!"

"Oh how could I forget?" Julie shook her head, then leaned close to Sarah. "She dragged me to every single one of his movies, each one worse than the last."

Sandra swatted her friend. "How dare you say such a thing about Elvis? Plus, I seem to remember someone going gaga over a British boy band."

Julie grinned. "I confess John Lennon was a little young for me, but you have to admit he was cute."

Sarah couldn't help smiling. "I was in high school when the Beatles had begun to hit it big in America."

"Oh that's right. Elvis was in the army while my little boy band was playing overseas." Julie sighed. "You know, it's funny how I can't remember where I put my hearing aid this morning, but I can remember Elvis and Beatles trivia."

"What were we talking about, again?" Sandra asked.

"Sarah mentioned a girl named Debby Neely," Julie said. "How old was she?"

"Maybe nineteen or twenty," Sarah said.

"Hmm, a little young for us to have hung out with. Debby Neely, Debby Neely...," Sandra muttered as she thought. "The name's familiar, but my gut feeling is she didn't attend this church."

Julie nodded. "Me too. And you know my gut is completely reliable—"

"Your gut has indigestion. *My* gut, on the other hand, is totally accurate."

Julie threw her hands up. "Well, I bow to the gut. Especially because in this instance, I agree. Sorry, Sarah, we don't *think* Debby Neely attended this church. Then again, we weren't exactly in her age group at the time."

"Do you know of anyone who might have been closer to Debby's age?" Sarah asked.

"Olive Cavanaugh?" Julie suggested.

"Lenore Lawton." Sandra gave a superior smile.

"Oh." Julie was momentarily nonplussed, but then a smile broke out on her face. "That's a good idea. Lenore knows everybody, young and old, and that woman's mind is a steel trap. Where is she?"

"I saw her walking back to the church without her son only a few minutes ago," Sandra said.

"Thanks to both of you." Sarah headed to the church.

Sarah scanned the people standing outside the front doors of the church but didn't see Lenore. She headed inside and immediately spied her collecting a fuzzy light blue scarf from where it lay over a pew.

"Lenore?"

Lenore didn't seem to hear her, but when she turned toward the door, she saw Sarah heading down the aisle. "Oh hello Sarah."

"Do you have a minute?"

"What?" she asked.

Sarah raised her voice. "Can I ask you a few questions?"

Lenore draped the scarf dramatically around her throat and over her shoulder. "Sure, but I've only got a minute. Neil's waiting in the parking lot, and he gets more impatient than a starving man ripping open a bag o' chips."

Sarah laughed. "Do you remember Debby Neely? She was in Maple Hill from 1960 to 1962."

"Gracious, that's a long time ago." Lenore's leather handbag dropped down from her shoulder to her forearm, but she didn't seem to notice. "Was Debby young or old?"

"About nineteen."

"I believe I remember her. Beautiful clothes. Quiet. I didn't know her well. But she didn't go to this church, she went to the Congregational Church. She might have come to Bridge Street Church once or twice, but she knew more people over at the other church."

That was the confirmation Sarah had been hoping for. "Thank you so much."

"You're welcome. Now I've gotta run or my son'll come looking for me." She headed back up the aisle toward the door, her gait slow and measured despite her words about needing to hurry.

So Debby went to the Congregational Church. Well, it looked like Sarah would be attending services there next week. She should talk to Liam—he was a Congregational Church member, and he could introduce her to people. She hoped the members would be willing to talk to her.

She had a flash of Olive's closed expression. So far, the one person who had known Debby beyond a passing acquaintance had been strangely close-lipped about her. Would Debby's fellow church members be the same?

CHAPTER EIGHT

"We made everything ourselves, Grandma," Audrey said as she unpacked the gigantic picnic basket.

"We didn't get any help from Mom," Amy added. She placed a bucket of ice and sodas on the ground next to the picnic table.

"Well, we did get a little help from Dad," Audrey said, "because the stove burners weren't working at first."

"But your old man worked his magic and saved the day." Jason grinned as he helped carry a second picnic basket to the table from the car.

Maggie leaned in close to whisper to Sarah, "His 'magic' consisted of lighting the pilot light."

Sarah had to stifle a giggle.

The afternoon was unusually sunny, making it seem like summer was closer than the calendar said it was. But it wasn't too hot, because a light, cool breeze rushed down the thickly forested hills next to Patriot Park and wrapped around the picnic area before blowing off and tangling in the maple trees over the playground.

"Do you need help?" she asked as the twins unpacked plastic forks and knives and large plastic containers of food.

"No," Audrey said. "We have everything covered."

Amy scooped some ice from an ice chest into a cup and asked Sarah, "What do you want to drink, Grandma?"

"What are my choices?"

"Fresh orange juice, which we squeezed by hand," she said with a touch of pride. "And Mom also made us bring soda and water in case you didn't want orange juice."

"Who would want soda when there's hand-squeezed orange juice? I'd love a glass."

Amy passed her a full cup, which Sarah sipped gingerly to prevent it from spilling over.

The tart juice had a few pieces of bitter white pith floating in it but otherwise tasted very bright and fresh. "Excellent," she said.

Sarah looked up, enjoying the view, and saw a figure in the distance—no, two figures. One tall, the other short and squat. Very short and squat, rather like a waddling basketball.

"Oh that's Liam walking Murphy. Do you mind if I speak to him for a moment?"

"Invite him to join us," Jason said. "The twins made enough for General Bradford's entire army." He nodded at the bronze statue of Bradford in the center of the park, seated on his horse with his right arm perpetually extended in front of him.

Sarah hurried to intercept Liam's loping figure. Murphy saw her first, darting away from his master to beeline toward her. Liam saw her then, and he looked pleased to see her. Something in her chest seemed to light up, but she forgot about it when Murphy launched himself at her legs, propelled by his running momentum.

"*Oof*! Murphy, are you trying out for the football team? Nice tackle." She scratched behind his ears and on top of his soft head.

"There's a man who knows how to greet his lady properly," Liam said, striding up to her. He gave her a smile that made her tingle from her head to her toes.

"I'm so glad you're here today, Liam. I was going to see you tomorrow at the café, but this is even better because I won't feel guilty for taking you from your customers."

"I would always find time for you, Sarah," he said.

Warmth crept up her neck. "Well, I have a favor to ask of you."

"Would this happen to have something to do with that mysterious book you've been reading?" A half smile pulled at his mouth as he spoke.

"Guilty," she said. "I think Debby Neely went to your Congregational Church."

"Do you, now?"

"Would you be willing to introduce me to people at church next Sunday? I'm hoping someone remembers her, or might even have been close to her."

"Such an onerous chore, introducing you to my church family." His green eyes twinkled. "I'll do it if you'll do something for me."

"Oh?" She couldn't think of what she could do for Liam.

"On Friday night, I need you be my dinner partner for about two or three hours."

It took a second for the words to connect. "Liam! Are you asking me out on a date?"

He scratched the back of his head. "I might be, if the answer's yes. If the answer's no, then no, I wasn't."

"Liam!"

"Sarah." He smiled, but Sarah noticed a trace of anxiety around the corners of his eyes. Then he blinked and it was gone, and he was the same teasing Liam.

A date. How strange. This didn't feel like when she was younger and Gerry had first mustered the courage to ask her out.

"You like to go dancing, don't you?" Gerry had asked her.

"Well…" Sarah had been searching for a way to confess she had two left feet, deathly afraid he'd completely write her off for not being as graceful as Ginger Rogers, but he barreled ahead.

"Great! I'll pick you up at five."

Later, Gerry had confessed he'd been so nervous that after talking to her, he had gone to the bathroom where he promptly lost his lunch.

This, however, with Liam, felt...odd. Gerry had been gone for only six years. Was it wrong for her to even think about someone else?

But then she remembered Gerry's words, recalled only a few days ago in Cheryl Wyatt's house: "Sarah, don't center your life around death."

Lord, Gerry was such a kind, generous man. So is Liam, in a different way. I'm not sure what to think, but I know you'll help me. She couldn't think of a better place to leave it than in the hands of her Father in Heaven. He would guide her.

"I promise I don't burp at the table or eat with my fingers," Liam said.

"Liam..."

"Is that, 'Liam, no, I wouldn't be caught dead with you,' or 'Liam, I'd love to eat dinner with you'?"

She couldn't help a short burst of laughter. She felt silly. But she replied, "I'd love to have dinner with you."

For a moment, his smile seemed brighter than the sunlight. "Friday night, then. I'll make reservations at the Old Mill."

"Great." There was a brief, awkward silence, then she remembered what Jason had said. "Would you like to join us for lunch?"

"I don't want to interrupt you and your family—"

"We'd love to have you. We even have enough for Murphy's bottomless stomach." Murphy's ears perked up as he realized she was talking about him.

He glanced over at the picnic table, and Sarah turned in time to see Jason and the twins waving at the two of them.

"Come on," he said. "Let's eat!"

Martha arrived at Sarah's house bright and early, wearing a pair of work coveralls and a smile.

"You look chipper today," Sarah said as she opened the door to her. "Coffee?"

"That would hit the spot. I left home after only eating a bagel."

"Let's have a cup now before we brave the attic," Sarah said.

Sarah poured her a mug of coffee from the pot on the counter while Martha sat down at the circular table in the breakfast nook. "I have a confession, Martha."

Martha calmly got out her crochet bag. "Unless Liam asked you out on a date, you can't surprise me."

Sarah turned from the kitchen counter to stare at her friend. "How did you know?"

Martha turned wide eyes to her. "I was only kidding! He did?"

Sarah sat down at the table and related how he'd asked her.

Martha laughed. "That sounds just like Liam. What cheek."

"Do you think it's okay for me to be even considering this?" Sarah asked.

"Oh, Sarah." Martha reached over and clasped Sarah hands. "I would think that it's natural to doubt yourself, but Gerry's been gone several years. He would want you to be happy and move on. He was that kind of person."

"You're right."

"It's only a date. Just enjoy yourself." Martha squeezed her hands and then released them.

Sarah grinned. "I'm sure I will."

"So did you read more of the book yesterday?"

"I didn't have time to read much of it—I picnicked with Jason and the family for most of the afternoon. I was a bit tired by the evening, so I read only a few pages." She sipped her own coffee and sat down across from her friend.

"Did you learn anything interesting?"

"I read about Debby making her dresses and selling them at the shop, which I already knew, thanks to Olive. She apparently sold them to tourists as well as local women. The author described some of the women but doesn't give any names."

"We might know some of them. Did you recognize anyone?"

"Not really, although there was one woman who sounded a little like my neighbor Imogene Dowling. But I couldn't be entirely sure."

"What made you think it was Imogene?"

"Well, the woman was described as being a bit competitive with her cousin, and I've talked with Imogene about her friendly competition with her cousin Rosemary. Also, the woman was apparently an avid fan of the TV show *Guiding Light*."

"*Guiding Light* was on TV in the sixties?"

"I checked online, and apparently it started airing in the fifties."

"My goodness. I had no idea it was on for so long."

"I know Imogene loves soap operas, so that made me think of her too," Sarah said. "The book also describes how Debby sang in the church choir. I'm hoping that means that several people in the choir got to know her well, and maybe one of them is the author."

"I think Olive is the author. Why else would she be so secretive when you talked to her?" Martha asked.

"I'm not ruling her out, but I also want to keep my eyes open. If Olive didn't write the book, I don't want to miss the real author."

"What else did you find out?"

"I didn't get much further than that. I fell asleep while I was reading."

"Well, I'm eager to get to it." Martha rose to her feet.

"Today might be downright dirty. I have dust masks for us, but there's nothing to protect our hair or clothes." She led the way upstairs.

They entered the attic, which seemed even dustier than the last time Sarah had been up. The morning sunlight tried to fight its way in through a tiny window set high in the attic wall, close to the eaves, but grime covered the glass, which had always been difficult to clean because it was out of easy reach.

Sarah was glad for Martha's longer reach to replace the old bulbs in their naked sockets on the low ceiling while she held a flashlight for her. When she was done, she flipped on the switch. The light cast a warm glow over the trunks and boxes filling the stifling space. The air felt thick and full of fine grit that coated her eyelashes.

"Ernie said that today'll get hot, according to the weather report," Martha said.

"We'll have to remember to stop and drink water." She grimaced at the dust in the air. "I don't think I'll want to stay up here for hours at a stretch, anyway."

"Where do you want to start?"

"You can start anywhere, but I think the best bet is in the far corner."

"Do you remember what the adress book looks like?"

"No, sorry. But it will probably be with other things from my mother's desk."

Martha nodded and began searching along the wall.

Sarah moved deeper into the corner. When her father had moved into Bradford Manor and she had cleared out his old house, she had instructed the movers to set those boxes in the far corner of the attic because she didn't expect to need anything from them anytime soon. She hoped she'd be able to find them now.

She noted with dismay two very tall stacks of boxes. On a couple of boxes, the contents were clearly labeled— "Dad's mementos," "Mom's old dresses"—but for many of the boxes, the side where she'd written the contents in black marker was not facing her.

She started with the first stack of boxes, rotating the top box to see what the writing on the far side was. "Dad's trumpet music." Her father had several music books with him at Bradford Manor, but he had said he hadn't wanted to take all the music he had, so she'd stored the rest here. She took the box from the stack as well as the next one, which had "Dad's postal worker uniforms" plainly visible, and laid them both on the side.

She swiveled the next box and the one below that, and still had no luck. She repeated it with the next stack of boxes, and again didn't find the box with the contents of her mother's desk.

There was a trunk next to the boxes, unlocked, so she popped open the clasps and lifted the lid, which squeaked as it opened. The strong scent of mothballs hit her, even through the thick dust mask.

The first thing she saw were several pictures in silver frames. There was an old picture of her mom and dad on their honeymoon, a picture of Sarah and her brother when they were toddlers, a shot of Jason, Maggie, and the twins at the hospital when the twins were born, and a last picture of Jenna and David at their wedding. Mom had passed away before Jenna's kids were born.

Sarah remembered these pictures sitting on her mother's desk. She might be on the right track here.

She peeled back a layer of brittle yellow tissue paper to reveal a delicately embroidered baby gown in faded pink satin.

Sarah didn't remember wearing the dress, and it was so tiny, she had probably outgrown it by the time she turned two. She traced the intricate flowers and leaves stitched into the bodice and at the base of the skirt. It billowed out slightly, crinkly with the stiff tulle sewn underneath to make the skirt blossom out like an upside-down tulip.

She carefully set it on a nearby box and peeled back the next layer of tissue paper. She found an old tuxedo with water-stained lapels, complete with a yellowed white dress shirt.

Under the tuxedo lay a peach-colored formal dress with a fitted bodice and yards of peach gauze flowing over a peach satin underskirt. Sarah had a sudden vague memory of her mother wearing the dress, perhaps at a wedding? She remembered the scent of orange blossoms, and her mother's hands encased in white lace gloves and holding a small bouquet of rosebuds. Her mother could have been a bridesmaid.

The next layer of clothes looked dark through the thin tissue paper. Sarah laid the peach dress carefully where she'd laid the tuxedo, on another nearby box, and peeled back the last piece of tissue paper.

Dark blue fabrics in different shades seemed to shimmer in the bottom of the trunk. Sarah gently unfolded the stiff fabric, revealing a beautiful quilted dress.

"Oh my goodness," she breathed. It was ten times more magnificent than her feeble memories of Debby's green dress, especially now that she could appreciate it with a quilter's eye. The different fabrics had been artfully chosen and placed next to each other to create a stunning visual effect that would make the surface seem to ripple with the wearer's movements.

Unlike the boxy quilted dresses Sarah often saw, this dress had a fitted shape, designed by an experienced dressmaker. Most quilted dresses also had only a patchwork top layer, but this dress not only had a pieced top layer, but the top layer was quilted to a lining fabric with both running stitches and embroidery stitches. It looked like there wasn't a middle batting layer, just the top and inside layers.

The bodice was made of dozens of small pieces of cloth cut and sewn together to hug the curves of the woman underneath without being overly formfitting, while the quilting stitches created lovely, figure-flattering lines instead of bulkiness across the torso. The modest neckline was edged in dark blue lace, as were the edges of the gently puffed sleeves. Over the entire bodice, there wasn't a single strip of fabric longer than six inches or wider than two inches—all of it had been painstakingly sewn together. The pieced strips that made up the sleeves had been positioned vertically, producing a striped effect, while the pieced fabrics on the bodice looked like gently rolling water.

The skirt was also a patchwork of fabrics, but with larger pieces in a vertical geometric pattern. The various blues produced the illusion of running water flowing from the bottom edge of the bodice. Dark blue lace edged the bottom of the hem as well.

"Martha?" Her voice came out in a high pitch. "I think I've found one of Debby's dresses."

Martha walked over to stand next to her and gently caressed the fabric. "It's gorgeous."

"I'm going to take this to my sewing room. I'll look it over later with better light." She made sure to put the other things back in the trunk, then she went downstairs.

In her sewing room, she gently laid out the dress on her quilting frame, smoothing the creases and brushing dust from the surface. The fabric was a bit stiff with age, so she was careful as she twitched the skirt to lie out flat.

This work of art must have taken hours, plus it seemed to be custom-designed for her mother's frame. But it was fancier than any dress Sarah had seen her mother wear, which might be why it had been stored away with the keepsake baby gown and the bridesmaid's dress. Sarah wondered if her mother had bought it for a special occasion.

She cast a last glance at it before heading back upstairs to rejoin Martha, who wiped her brow with the back of her hand as Sarah entered the attic.

"Tired?" she asked.

"Dusty." Martha turned back to the box she was looking through and Sarah headed back to her corner of the attic.

But only a minute later, Martha called, "Sarah, I think I've found something."

Sarah hurried over to the other side of the attic. Because of the low ceiling, Martha was stooped over as she looked through several boxes filled with papers. She handed something to her.

It was a small brown leather book with "Addresses" stamped in faded gold lettering on the cover, its edges curled and worn. "You found it." But as she fingered the pebbled cover, she had to admit to herself that she had expected her mother's address book to be larger, more flowery. This book looked very masculine. She opened it up.

Her father's slanted handwriting stared up at her. "Oh it's Dad's."

"Would your mom's friends be in there too?" Martha asked.

The book was filled with mostly men's names—her father's friends, some business contacts, a few cousins, both male and female. "None of Mom's friends are in here, but I wouldn't expect them to be."

"I guess I'll just keep looking, then."

"You got it out of this box?" Sarah peered into the box and pulled out a few of the papers. "These are Dad's, probably from his desk." She held what looked like an inventory of his fishing tackle box. Another sheet was a to-do list of things needing repair around their house, with notes and additions in her mother's handwriting. It made her smile. "If I had the time and inclination, I'd go through these and toss what he doesn't need anymore."

"I can set these boxes aside for you."

"No, put them back where you found them. I don't think I'll get to them anytime soon."

Sarah returned to the far corner. She turned her attention to more boxes but was dismayed to note that several had dark water stains on the sides. She glanced up at the walls and saw more water stains coloring the wood, coming down from a point in the roof. The spot in the attic was right above her bedroom, and she hadn't noticed leaking water this past autumn and winter. She hoped that meant the leak was small.

But the boxes were simple cardboard, and the attic rarely dried out in wintertime. She carefully took the top box and laid it on a clear space on the floor, feeling the bottom sagging with the weakened cardboard. She gingerly opened the lid and peered inside.

The distinct odor of mildew reached her nose even before she could see the contents. Inside the box were stacks of papers, the edges curling from water damage, with large ash gray splotches marring the text. She took several pages out and noted the mold damage that made many sheets almost unreadable.

She didn't look through the entire box but instead opened the box that had been underneath it. The damage was not as great in this one, which was filled with paperback books—it looked like the water had mostly saturated the top box. The box under the books was filled with letters and had very little water damage.

Sarah returned to the box that had sat on top and pressed her lips together at the icky mess inside. She was tempted to simply throw the entire box away, but she knew she should roll up her sleeves and go through it, no matter how unpleasant the task. She started lifting papers from the top.

Pages stuck together, and for some, the water had caused the ink on the pages to run, obliterating most of what had been on them. On other pages, the mildew made it hard to read what was there, but Sarah could make out some of the text. It looked like some of the papers were in her mother's handwriting—possibly a few recipes jotted down, what looked like a list of Christmas presents, and a page that appeared to be Bible verses copied by hand. Sarah began to wonder if this came from her mother's small desk in her bedroom, and while her excitement mounted, so did her dread. All of these papers were horribly damaged.

At the bottom of the box were several pens, a ruler, a pair of rusted scissors, a silver envelope opener so tarnished it looked nearly black. Sarah sorted carefully through the items so she wouldn't cut herself, and found a stapler, a staple remover, and several cracked erasers.

And then at the bottom, a small book with a warped cardboard cover. Sarah lifted it out of the box.

Almost the entire cover was dark gray with mildew and felt rough under Sarah's fingers. Rust from the metal items lying on top of it had left reddish brown scars on the cardboard. When she opened it, she saw with a sinking heart that the pages were tabbed with the letters of the alphabet in white capital letters on faded black tabs. She flipped to the As and saw her mother's handwriting almost entirely melted away by a gigantic water stain.

She turned to more pages, but they were all the same. Some pages had readable names, but the addresses had been erased by the damage. Other pages had addresses or telephone numbers, but Sarah couldn't make out the names.

It was her mother's address book, but it was completely useless.

CHAPTER NINE

S arah, I'm sorry."

Sarah looked up. Martha had left an hour before, so Sarah had sat down to peruse her mother's address book in her sewing room. Chloe now stood in the doorway, leaning on her crutches. "Sorry for what?" Sarah asked.

"I accidentally broke that antique lamp in my bedroom," Chloe said. "I'm so sorry. I'll pay to replace it."

"No, don't be silly. I bought the lamp because it was pretty and cozy, not because it was an antique or there was any sentimental value to it." Sarah set aside the damaged address book. It had been only wishful thinking that she would be able to make out some of the names and addresses in the brighter light of her sewing room. "Besides, my daughter-in-law owns that antique store downtown. I'm sure I can replace it very easily."

"I still feel bad. I'm just too clumsy with these crutches. I'll be more careful, I promise."

"Chloe, you didn't do anything wrong." Sarah rose and placed a hand on the girl's arm. "Can I make you a cup of tea?"

They decided to sit out on the wraparound porch with a view of the garden. The early evening light made the white-painted railing glow, and a few butterflies flitted above Sarah's baby sweet pea plants.

Sarah set out the kitchen chairs for them since Chloe couldn't quite sit down in or get up from the low Adirondack chairs, and they slowly sipped tea made with the chamomile she'd bought from Annie Harper. It really was quite good—a slightly floral flavor compared to the plain chamomile bags of tea Sarah usually got.

"How is your leg feeling?" Sarah asked.

"I feel better every day," Chloe said. "I can't believe I broke it only a few days ago."

"I'm so sorry you had to cut short your sheep-buying trip. What are you going to do now?"

"I had only a couple more farms I wanted to visit. I could go home and make do with the sheep I've already bought. Or I could go to the farms later, after I've healed, to look over what they have."

"I guess it's still early in the year. Is that going to be okay?"

"To be honest, I'm not entirely sure what I'm doing," she said. "My uncle and I are treading new ground with these fleece sheep. He knows sheep, and I know fleece, so we're just muddling through."

"You're close to your uncle?"

"He practically raised me. My dad ran out on us when I was six."

"I'm so sorry. How tough on you and your mom." Sarah's heart ached for the young woman. "Your uncle must be a wonderful man."

Chloe's smile was fond but a little sad. "He's pure gold. He's a bit gruff, but he's very caring." She stifled a yawn.

"He sounds like my friend Martha's husband Ernie. He's always been a bit quiet, sometimes a little dour, while Martha is bright and chatty. But Ernie's really so caring and considerate of her and his grandkids. He always shows it in little ways." Sarah laughed at a sudden memory from a few years ago. "I remember once, Ernie went to the auto parts store—actually, he was there getting a part for my car, because it had a strange rattling sound. Anyway, Martha's favorite yarn store is right next to the auto parts store, and he noticed they were having a huge sale. The day before Martha had mentioned in passing that she needed more pink yarn for a project she was crocheting. So Ernie walked into that yarn store and bought three giant bags of different kinds of pink yarn and brought it all home to her."

"Aw. Now that's love. I can't quite see my uncle walking into a yarn store, much less buying pink anything." She ended her sentence on another huge yawn. "Well, I think I'll go to bed early. I seem to be doing nothing but sleeping since I broke my leg."

"I'm sure it's exactly what your body needs. Leave your cup right there. I'll take it in. Good night, Chloe."

"Good night." Chloe hobbled back inside the house.

It was still quite light outside, and the air felt balmy. Occasional puffs of breeze carried the pearlike scent of early spring flowers. Sarah went inside, gathered the book, her notebook, and a pen from her sewing room, and took them out to the porch so she could read in the early evening light.

Debby had a pretty voice, and she loved singing in the choir. It took her awhile before she joined, though, and I think she only sang for a year or a few months before she was arrested.

She made a lot of friends in the choir, although she kept everybody at a slight distance. Like she was surrounded by an invisible wall. She was always friendly, never rude, but there was still that sense of a part of herself she wasn't letting anyone see. I think the choir members thought she was open with them, but by then I knew her well enough that I could see that while she spent time with people and enjoyed their company, there was always something about her that was aloof. Maybe that's what intrigued me about her. The way she kept apart from her friends was different from just quietness. I'm quiet, but it's shyness rather than wanting to keep people from getting too close. It was my shyness that kept me from reaching out to her and becoming friends sooner than I did.

The first time I talked to her was a few months after she'd come to Maple Hill. She'd been going to our church for a while, and we'd say hi to each other, chat but nothing more than that. I remember the day because C. and I were outside even though it was lightly snowing, but we hadn't wanted to be overheard by any of the older people because we were talking about how Kennedy had recently won the presidential election over Nixon. C. is pretty liberal, but she keeps it secret from her family. I'm not staunchly conservative, but I don't like to rock the boat. C., on the other hand, would rock it enough to make it flip over.

I'm not sure why Debby was outside that day. It was about half an hour after the church service had ended, and there weren't many people still around by then. C. said something emphatically about Kennedy, and Debby was standing a few feet away. I think she'd been there for only a minute or two, having just come out of the church. She said, "It's people who change the world, not a single man."

We got into a discussion, and it was amazing how C. seemed to calm down when Debby was there with us. Not that Debby was conservative, but she had a kind of soothing way about her. I couldn't quite keep up with her and C., but Debby never made me feel ashamed of it. Instead, she challenged me to think—really think—about what I believed and why.

I'm glad she did, although this time my shift in thinking has come too late.

After that day, Debby and I became closer friends, but it took more than a year before she confided in me that she was running from the law. I understand why it took so long, and a part of me wishes she hadn't told me. Then all this misfortune might never have come to her.

We especially became closer a few weeks later when I heard about a small fire that had broken out in her boardinghouse. Everyone knew Clapham was a fire trap, an accident waiting to happen. She'd had an offer to rent a room in a house, but she'd *been hesitant to accept. It was that invisible wall again, except this time I think it was a fear of what could happen if she lived in someone's home. In the boardinghouse she didn't really talk to anyone because they all had their own rooms, although she said she got along fine with a few of the other girls there. In a house, there was a chance she'd get close to the woman she lived with.*

But I spent some time talking to her one day. It was strange, because our personalities were almost reversed—I was the strong one, and she was the one in fear. But I convinced her to move out of Clapham, that it would be safer if she did. I know I kind of bullied her, but it was for the best. She got close to her new landlady because of it.

At last, a tangible clue. Sarah wrote *Clapham boardinghouse* at the end of her list of notes. She knew that there had been a street on the west side of town that had been lined with old boardinghouses for women who worked at the mill when it had been operational. The houses had fallen into disrepair and been torn down, but because they had been a part of Maple Hill history, there was a chance the old rooming house records were at the Maple Hill Historical Society. If Sarah could see a list of boarders in 1960, she might find the name of someone who knew Debby Neely, and that person might still be here in town.

Sarah might even be able to talk to Debby's landlady.

She glanced at some of the other notes she had taken tonight.

Choir.

She had hoped that as she read it would become more obvious whether the author had been in the choir with Debby, but she still couldn't tell. Maybe the author had done that deliberately.

C. appears to be separate from author, and is female.

That had been both an exciting clue and a disappointing one. While it had been nice to see from the passage that C. was a separate person, it also eliminated someone who might have been the author. On the other hand, if she could discover who this C. person was, she might find out more quickly who the author was. *Conservative, doesn't like to rock the boat.*

The more she read, the more the author seemed like a very timid person. Even the writing style was soft, a little hesitant.

There were more and more phrases that seemed sad and regretful. Like, "It was my shyness that kept me from reaching out to her and becoming friends sooner than I did," "my shift in thinking has come too late," and especially, "a part of me wishes she hadn't told me. Then all this misfortune might never have come to her." That last statement implied that the author was the cause of bad things that had happened to Debby. Was the author talking about Debby's arrest?

She had so hoped her mother's address book would list someone close enough to her mother that he or she would have felt comfortable about asking Ruth to donate the book that was written to the library. At the same time, Sarah realized that her own mother could have been the author. Her mother had been a bit shy, just like the author.

Yet the phrases Sarah had picked out seemed emotional, maybe even a touch melodramatic. They didn't quite match what she remembered of her mother's calm personality. She couldn't imagine her mom saying something like "a part of me wishes she hadn't told me. Then all this misfortune might never have come to her." Her mom had always said not to waste energy on regrets but to move forward and try to walk in obedience to the Lord. Rather than spending so many pages on sadness and worry about what had happened, Sarah thought her mom would be more likely to confess exactly what she had done, apologize for it, and then rest in the fact that whatever the consequences, God would be with her through it all.

She looked at the passages again. What had her mother's political stance been in those days of the early sixties? In 1962, President Kennedy hadn't yet been assassinated, and Dr. Martin Luther King hadn't yet made his famous "I Have a Dream" speech at the Lincoln Memorial. What had her parents thought about the rising civil rights movement, the early days of the Vietnam War?

Maybe she could ask her father about it the next time she visited him. If he remembered old baseball players, there was a slim chance he remembered some of Mom's friends.

Sarah blinked and realized the garden was now shrouded in darkness, her only light from the porch bulb. Had she really been out here for so long? She rose to her feet, stifling a yawn.

Sarah couldn't shake the conviction that the author must have been someone her mother knew well. She also had a feeling the author's identity would surprise her.

CHAPTER TEN

When the Maple Hill Historical Society opened its doors the next morning, Sarah was there waiting to be let in.

"Hi, Sarah," Irene Stuart said as she unlocked the door. "You look like you're raring to go."

Sarah followed Irene inside the building, the wide pine planks squeaking under her feet while the smell of cedar—stronger today than the usual smell of parchment—wrapped around her. "I guess I am a bit impatient. I'm hoping you can help me. Do you happen to have records from a boardinghouse called Clapham?"

As she thought, Irene idly played with her charm bracelet. "You're talking about the old boardinghouses on the west side?"

"Yes."

"I think we do have some old records. I've never looked through them, but they'd be in the filing cabinets. You can check the computer catalog to help you find them. I'll give you a hand when I finish opening up."

Sarah sat down at the computer workstation in the corner while Irene went about her opening procedure, setting out the bell on the counter that edged through the arched doorway and around the corner and turning the lights on for the display cabinets.

She inputted the name *Clapham* in the search box and hit Enter.

No results.

Had she spelled it wrong? She tried other spellings, but they all came back the same—no results. She tried *boardinghouses* but came up with too many listings, and she didn't know which houses had been the ones in that particular row.

"How are you doing?" Irene asked, approaching to stand behind her.

"For some reason, it's not showing up. I know Clapham was a boardinghouse here in Maple Hill, but it's not in the database."

"Hmm. Let's double-check that the boardinghouses' records really are here. Try *Postway*—that's another one."

Sarah typed *Postway* into the search box, and immediately came up with a listing. Irene checked the reference number and moved unerringly to the right file cabinet and pulled out a manila folder. "Here you go," she said as she handed it to Sarah, and peered over her shoulder as she opened it.

"So what are you looking for?" Irene asked.

Sarah said, "I found a beautiful quilted dress in a trunk of my mother's. I remember there was a woman named Debby Neely who made quilted garments and I learned she lived in the Clapham boardinghouse. I was hoping to find out who her fellow boarders were, maybe her landlady, or a forwarding address."

"I'm not sure about the forwarding address, but I'd guess the other things would be there."

The folder first held the deed for the house, but it also showed that Postway had apparently been one of ten boardinghouses owned by the same man, Rodney Gilman. The folder also held photocopies of the guest book pages for the house.

"It proves we have the records from those boardinghouses," Irene said. "But that doesn't explain why there isn't a listing for Clapham."

"Gilman owned ten houses, but this folder doesn't list all their names. But maybe there are records under his name that would tell us." Sarah inputted *Rodney Gilman*, but came up with no results. She shortened it to *Gilman*, which yielded a listing for *Gilman properties*.

Irene retrieved another file folder. As Sarah opened it and the two of them peered at the first page, Irene said, "Bingo! It looks like Rodney came through for us."

Rodney Gilman had died in 1945, but his son Richard managed the Gilman properties until the houses had been demolished in 1983. Women had originally lived in the houses when the mill was operational, but after it closed down, the houses opened up to anyone who needed a place to stay. While the buildings had been historical properties, all the boardinghouses on the row had been abandoned sometime in the midseventies and were so unstable in 1983 that they'd been destroyed rather than restored.

There were real estate records that listed all of the Gilman properties by name and also street addresses. There was also a rough map of their locations. They had been situated five in a row, on each side of the street.

"There! Clapham." Irene pointed to the name on the record.

"But if Gilman owned Clapham, where's the record? What could it be filed under?"

They continued to look through page after page of property documents, but after the copies of the deeds for the houses, there was a fire marshal report in the back of the file.

"Oh no." The report stated that due to faulty electrical wiring in 1974, three of the Gilman houses had been burned in a fire. No one had died, but the damage had been complete.

"So the guest book records were probably burned," Sarah said.

"I wonder if that's why the boardinghouses were abandoned," Irene said. "Even if your house didn't burn down, watching three houses destroyed on the same street might induce you to move."

A typed note at the end of the file said that Richard Gilman had died in 1997, and his son had donated all the

Gilman property records to the historical society because of the significance of the original boardinghouses.

That was it. She'd hit a dead end.

That afternoon, Sarah opened the windows wide to let the bright sunlight into her sewing room, and her eye fell on the glorious blue dress.

She had intended to spend more time reading the book, but the dress called to her irresistibly. She hadn't worked on her latest quilting project in a week—it had been set aside while she investigated the book's author. Especially after the disappointment of this morning, she wanted to feel the fine fabric under her fingers, study the combinations of different shades of blue, trace Debby's quilting stitches and embroidery patterns.

Setting aside her plans to read more of the book, she bent over her quilting frame to examine the dress. Just for a few minutes.

She was surprised to hear a knock at the backdoor, but as she looked up from her work, her neck ached. She had been bent over the dress for longer than she intended.

"Sarah?" Martha's voice called into the house.

"Come on in. I'm in my sewing room."

"Figured you would be," her friend said. "Oh you're looking at your mom's dress? It's even more beautiful in the sunlight, isn't it?" She peered closer at a puffed sleeve. "I still can't believe your mom had this and never wore it."

"Mom liked simple clothing. I'm a bit curious why she bought it in the first place."

"Maybe she wanted to support Debby. Did you read more of the book? Did it mention your mother?"

Sarah told Martha about what she'd read the night before, and also about the search for the boardinghouse.

"Well, that's too bad. Where can you look now?"

"The only other clue I can think of is to try to find C."

"C., hmm? How in the world are you going to find out who she is?"

"I'm not sure. That's also partly why I got sidetracked and decided to look at the dress this afternoon." She frowned down at the underside of the skirt, which she had been going over when Martha arrived. "The dress is puzzling."

"How?"

"It's a work of art—the fabrics she chose and the way she positioned them, the shapes she cut them in to form the curves of the bodice, the patterns of the quilting stitches. I was in awe until I turned the dress inside out.

"What's wrong?"

"I just don't understand it. The stitches visible on the top are neat and beautiful. But the stitches visible on the inside are ... skewed."

"Let me see."

Sarah flipped the dress over. "You can't tell from the top, but on the inside the stitches aren't lined up neatly, and sometimes it looks as if the needle went into the fabric at a strange angle. I just can't understand it."

It was as if Debby had cared only about making the outside neat, whereas the inside betrayed her insecurity. At first Sarah had thought she was a lazy quilter, but if that were so, the stitches visible on the outside would be only marginally acceptable. But the outside stitches were clearly painstakingly done.

"That is strange," Martha said. "Especially when the dress looks like it took so long to put together. She might have been rushing to finish it."

"No, when a quilter rushes, the stitches usually get larger as well as uneven." Sarah could picture the stitches in her mind, like an odd bird track across the fabric. "I'm wondering if she couldn't see the underside as well for some reason."

"But how could you find out something like that?"

"I'm not sure. Maybe the book will mention something about it."

"Speaking of books, I was at the bookstore this morning just as Liam was opening a box of new books." She brandished a glossy hardcover by Sarah's favorite author with a flourish.

"Ooh," Sarah took the book from Martha's hands. "I was wondering when the next one would come out." She cracked it open, loving the crispness of the spine and the scent of clean paper. She turned the first few pages, then turned them again, feeling the paper flip back and forth on her fingers.

"What is it?" Martha asked.

"I guess I've been reading that book about Debby for too long. Feel this." She had Martha touch the white page.

Sarah picked up the anonymous book from her desk and opened it. After touching the pages of the new mystery novel Martha had bought, these pages now felt brittle, thin, odd. She gave the book to Martha. "Now feel this."

"Huh. It's almost like onionskin paper, but not quite."

"Exactly. I've been reading only this book for the past week and I haven't touched a modern book, so I didn't even notice the difference in the pages until I touched that novel."

"It doesn't even feel like the pages of those old hardcover books we had to read for school. Do you remember those?"

She nodded. "These pages are completely different, but the cover looks the same as those rebound books Spencer found."

"I wonder if the pages feel this way because the book's so old."

"I'm not sure, but I'm hoping that's not the case."

"Why?" Martha asked.

"If the book was printed in a unique way, then maybe I can track down the printer and see if they have records of who paid to have the book made."

"How are you even going to find out who printed it? The Chamber of Commerce?"

"I have a better idea—Spencer."

The library was much noisier this time when Sarah entered it. Several families were there with their children to pick up new books. There was also a smattering of teenagers in both the teen section and the reference stacks.

Spencer was busy checking some books out for a patron. Sarah waited until he was done.

He smiled at her and indicated the book in her hand. "What did you find out about Debby Neely?"

Sarah gave him a quick summary of what she'd discovered so far.

"Did you figure out the connection to your mother?" Spencer asked.

"Not yet. She hasn't been mentioned in the book so far."

"Did she write the book, do you think?"

"I'm not sure. The author seems terribly regretful about what happened to Debby, but Mom was very gentle and very practical. She didn't waste time on regrets—she always believed in full disclosure, getting things off her chest. I don't think it's her, but...," she let her voice trail off. "I discovered something about the book itself that you might be able to help me with. The pages feel strange to me."

She handed the book to him. He rubbed a page, then thumbed through the book, letting the pages fan.

"You're right. Granted, books published in the sixties had different paper than books published now, but these pages don't even feel like the other books in the library collection from that time frame."

"So what does that mean?"

"Now that I think about it, this book was probably self-published."

"How does that make it different from other books?"

"Most of the library's books were produced by publishing companies. If you look on the first few pages, usually you'll see the publishing company's name on the bottom of the title page. Even the older books have that. That means the publishing company bought the manuscript from the writer and then produced the book.

"Self-publishing means the writer didn't sell his manuscript to a publishing company, but instead arranged to have the book printed and bound, all by himself. These days, that's pretty easy—there are lots of companies where you give them your manuscript and they'll produce your book, for a fee. The self-publishing company's name will be on the title page, just like any other book. The writer gets a certain number of copies of his book—whatever he's paid for—and he has to go about selling it, as opposed to the publishing house selling it for him."

"Oh okay. I think I see the difference."

"But back in the sixties, there weren't those types of self-publishing companies. Or, at least, they weren't very common. If someone wanted to self-publish a book, he or she had to be a little more creative." Spencer said.

"So what do you mean by 'being creative'? Do you know where this book could have been printed?"

"I think these pages were printed on a magazine press. But the cover was probably done by a traditional book-binder."

"You mean like the other hardcover books we found in that box?"

He nodded. "In fact, it's probably the same bindery the library uses, Suffolk Bindery. I can give you their information. They're the only one within a hundred fifty miles of Maple Hill, and we've been using them since the forties, according to the library's records."

That took care of one question. "Did Maple Hill have a magazine press fifty years ago? I don't think there's one now."

"That you'd have to check with the Chamber of Commerce."

"Thanks, Spencer."

After getting the bookbinder's information from him, she hurried to the Chamber of Commerce offices, which were only a few blocks away. The spring sunshine had held for several days and cheered up her mood immensely. She had found the binder, and now she could find out which magazine press was in business back in the sixties with one quick trip.

Though "quick" might not be the word for it. The surly redheaded young man at the counter handed her a stack of papers to fill out when she stated what she needed.

"I need to fill all these out?"

"For each business you want to look up."

"But I don't know what the business was called. I was hoping to get a list of magazine presses that were in business back in the sixties..." She glanced at his name tag. "...Paul." She looked again—Paul Barclay. "Are you related to Tim Barclay, the clerk for the Register of Deeds at the courthouse?"

"He's my cousin," Paul said.

"So is it possible to get that list?"

"Sorry, lady. I don't know how to do that."

"Well, who does?"

He shrugged. "Dunno."

"Well, how about your supervisor?"

His eyes slid away from her. "Don't got one. Sorry." He turned away from her and went back to the comic book he was reading behind the counter.

Sarah was miffed, but aside from pounding on closed office doors, she didn't know what else she could do. She also was in such an agitated state, she knew that if she did find someone to speak to, she would probably not be very controlled or polite, so it was just as well. She turned around and marched out.

Paul Barclay might have barred her way today, but she was determined to get the information she wanted.

CHAPTER ELEVEN

Sarah couldn't help the flutter in her stomach as she smoothed down her cream slacks and straightened her blue silk blouse. She glanced at the mirror to check that her makeup was fine, then looked at her watch. She had finished getting ready for her date with Liam a full ten minutes early.

This was just Liam. But tonight, she seemed to think a different Liam was coming to her door.

The doorbell rang. Five minutes early.

Sarah had to grasp the front doorknob firmly to open it. "Hello, Liam."

He held out to her a slender bouquet of yellow bearded irises that glowed in the light from the house. "For you, my dear."

"Oh how lovely." The flowers were a little unusual. Wasn't that just like Liam? But they also brought the cheerfulness of spring into her home, which she had a feeling was what he had intended to do for her.

"They're almost as pretty as you." He winked.

"You need to watch that silver tongue of yours, Liam Connolly," she said, though she smiled as she said it.

"And what's the fun in that?" He held out his arm in an old-fashioned gesture. "Shall we?"

She took his arm, and suddenly her nervousness disappeared and she was simply enjoying an evening out with a good friend.

Liam drove them to the Old Mill, a restaurant frequented by both locals and tourists. It had originally been a working grist mill perched on the edge of the Clear Springs River, but the owner had been enterprising enough to renovate the historic building and hire an excellent chef.

The hostess led them through the restaurant, busy on this Friday night. Sarah's pumps thudded softly on the solid oak floorboards as they wove between the half walls that separated different areas of the restaurant and created a more intimate setting.

The hostess gestured to a small square table right near a window overlooking the Clear Springs River. The evening dusk made the rushing waters seem softer, slower.

Sarah's nervousness returned when she took in the red rosebud in a porcelain bud vase on the table, flanked by a tea light candle in a squat glass holder. But her jitters disappeared when Liam leaned his elbows on the table and asked, "So what were you thinking, to bring Amy and Audrey to the café twice after school this week?"

"They begged..." Sarah gave a helpless gesture. "I really am a doting grandma sometimes."

He said, "Karen is going to put me out of business. The week before, your son brought your two granddaughters in, and Karen gave them both a chocolate chip cookie from the pastry case. Waited to tell me until after the damage had been done."

"So that's why they wanted to go to the café!"

"Were Jason and Maggie busy this week?"

"Maggie was invited to an exclusive estate auction in Richmond."

"She drove?" Liam asked.

"She thought about flying, but since it was only five hours by car, she decided to drive so she could bring back a few items with her rather than shipping everything she bought. She left early Wednesday morning to get to the auction by one o'clock, and Jason had meetings on Wednesday and Thursday afternoons, so the girls couldn't go to his office after school. So I volunteered." She couldn't help smiling as she recalled the two afternoons this week. "They had to work on a special school project with Zoe, one of their friends. I feel like I ought to get some credit for this project too. I took them to the library last week so they could do research, and then this week, they wiped me out of all my toothpicks."

"Toothpicks?"

"They're learning about physics and architecture. They have to build a bridge using only toothpicks and school glue, and then they'll have a competition in class about which group's bridge can hold the most weight."

"That sounds rather interesting."

"It was a fun two afternoons, let's put it that way. Full of girly stuff."

"No boys allowed?"

"I admit I enjoyed playing dress-up with Jenna much more than I enjoyed playing trucks with Jason," she said. "Didn't you do girly things with Caitlin?"

At the mention of his daughter's name, Liam stared at the candle's flame for a moment. Then he replied cheerfully, "Caitlin was every father's dream, a right proper tomboy."

Sarah hesitated. A part of her wanted to ask him if everything was all right, to get him to open up to her about Caitlin. But she didn't want to pry, either. And maybe eventually he'd feel comfortable enough to talk to her. *Lord, help Liam with whatever he's going through right now.*

The waitress interrupted them at that point with a basket of fresh-baked rolls. "Good evening. May I start you off with something to drink?" she asked.

Sarah stuck with decaf coffee, and Liam followed suit, but with regular coffee. When the waitress bustled away, Liam said, "We should figure out what we're eating."

When the waitress returned with their drinks, they were ready. Sarah had been tempted to order the crab cakes, which she loved, but the special sounded scrumptious—grilled salmon. Liam asked for the pork chops and spring peas.

There was an awkward pause when the waitress left. Sarah realized that even though she and Liam had been friends for several years, she didn't really know that much about him. He always had an easy smile for her, and his conversation was always lighthearted, but he didn't talk about himself much. Instead, he was unfailingly willing to listen to people. It was his gift.

"So how're things going with the mystery of that book?" Liam asked.

"Oh, I have so much to tell you," she said as she buttered a roll. "I was excited on Monday night because the author mentioned the name of Debby's boardinghouse before she moved, but I found out that the boardinghouse burned in a fire along with all the records. The author also mentioned a woman by her first initial, C., who knew Debby."

"How will you find her?"

"I'm hoping some members of your church will help. Apparently, C. attended services there as well. Oh, and Martha helped me discover an interesting clue that I hadn't even considered." She told him about the book being printed on a magazine press and then bound by the local bindery. "I got the information from Spencer, and I called the bookbinder numerous times this week, but no one ever picked up the phone, so I left several messages. So far, no one has returned my calls." She sighed. "I'm starting to wonder if I ought to drive out to see them even though it's two or three hours away." She also told Liam about her frustration at the Chamber of Commerce when she tried to find the magazine press.

"Young people these days," he lamented. "Let me see if I can do anything for you."

"That's so kind of you. You're already helping by taking me to church with you on Sunday."

At that moment, the waitress appeared with their dinner salads. Liam said grace for them.

Sarah speared a cherry tomato on her fork. "I was busy with the twins for a couple of days this week, but I managed to read more of the book. I found out why Debby was arrested."

He glanced up at her, all ears.

"Debby's brother had been actively involved in an extremist civil rights group. With both her parents dead, she got involved with her brother's violent crowd and started dating one of the guys from that extremist group, a man named Josiah. He made a bomb and planted it in a federal courthouse."

"That's pretty serious. Was anyone hurt?"

"Apparently one person was killed—a judge—and several others were wounded, some severely. Debby tried to stop Josiah from setting off the bomb but had to run for her life. Witnesses saw her running from the courthouse."

"That's pretty incriminating, being at the scene like that," Liam said.

"Debby admitted that she should have gone to the police when she suspected Josiah of making the bomb, but she had been involved in that group herself and was afraid she'd be arrested. Then the FBI caught Josiah, and he insisted

Debby was the one who had made and set off the bomb and that he had been trying to stop her. He even passed a lie detector test. So she ran. She came to Maple Hill eventually and ended up staying despite her intention to move on quickly."

Liam set down his fork on his empty plate. "So here's the million dollar question. Is it true?"

Sarah shrugged. "The author believed it all."

"So far, you've only heard about Debby's character from three people—the author, and the little that Olive and Cheryl Wyatt gave you. You don't know that much about her besides the fact she was quiet." The edges of his mouth suddenly quirked upward. "And you don't really know if she was a 'timid' quiet or a 'psychopath' quiet."

Sarah couldn't help smiling at his choice of words. "True."

The waitress glided into view, holding their two entrees. "Here you go," she said, and set their plates in front of them, then removed their salad plates.

A lemony scent from the salmon made her nose tingle. "Mmm."

"You took the words right out of my mouth," he said, gazing at his brown-crusted pork chops.

"Enjoy," the waitress chirped, and left them.

Sarah took a bite of her fish, and it melted in her mouth. The dill brought out an earthy tang, while the lemon gave it a spark of freshness. Liam seemed to be enjoying his meal as well.

They ate in companionable silence for a few minutes, then Sarah spoke. "How are things going at the shop?"

"I had a mystery of my own the other day."

"Oh?"

"There is a group of about ten women, maybe ten or fifteen years older than us, who meet in the shop every Thursday at nine. They chat for about half an hour in the bookstore, then they go to the coffee shop for some refreshments. They're always knitting and crocheting together—and one woman even spins wool into yarn with a drop spindle sometimes—so I figured they were some sort of club."

"I remember Vanessa telling me once about a knitting group that meets at her store every so often, but unless they all sit around the fabric cutting table, the store is a bit crowded for a group as large as ten people. I wonder if that's them?"

Liam's eyes twinkled as he continued, "I admit I usually don't pay much attention to them. They sit around the large table near the back of the bookstore—the one the high school students use to study after school—and since the register is up front, I can't hear what they're talking about if I'm working in the bookstore as opposed to the café. But the other day, I happened to be shelving some new reference books near the back and I caught some of their conversation.

"One woman said, 'Well, if it drops any further, I'm pulling out faster than a fox from a henhouse at the sound of a shotgun.'

"Another one who was crocheting a blanket answered, 'I don't know, I think I'll stick it out and see.'

"'Well, aren't you a daredevil!' the first woman said.

"'Just call me Evie Knievel,' she replied."

Sarah blinked at this odd conversation. "What in the world?"

Liam continued, "I happened to need to move closer to shelve some other books..."

"Naturally," Sarah said with a grin.

"Another woman nodded her white head and said, 'Well, Jane's batting average so far has been pretty good, so maybe she knows what she's talking about.'"

Batting average? Maybe this was about baseball? Sarah was completely confused.

"The first woman said, 'You can always tell when Katie's been watching the Red Sox with her husband. She starts talking like a sports announcer.'

"Katie said, 'I don't see how that's bad. Sports, the Market—they both deal with numbers.'

"Then the woman named Jane said, 'I'm sure my recommendations have been better than that fool financial magazine Angie keeps quoting.'"

Sarah blinked in dawning realization. "Are you telling me they're an investment group?" It seemed incongruous with the picture of a bunch of white-haired women knitting and crocheting together, but it also proved there was no age limit on what a woman could do these days.

"Katie said, 'I think I'll stick with it even if it falls a bit further. I'm game for an adventure.' Then they decided to head to the coffee shop." Liam took a bite of mashed pota-toes. "I'm almost jealous of all the excitement in their lives."

"We'll have our own adventure on Sunday when you take me to your church."

"I don't know how much use I'll be."

She winked at him. "You can use that Irish charm on the ladies and find out if they knew Debby Neely."

CHAPTER TWELVE

unday dawned cloudy and chilly, a sharp contrast to the warm weather of the weeks before. Liam picked Sarah up at her house and they drove to the Congregational Church.

She'd felt a lift in her spirits when he came to the door. She tried not to read into his expression or body language any more than what he was saying, but she had been curious about how their relationship might have shifted since their date.

On the drive to church, she asked him, "How's Caitlin?"

Liam responded with his typical good cheer, "Likely to turn my whole head white before long. In other words, a typical twenty-something."

Sarah wondered if she'd imagined the emotion she'd seen cross his face on Friday night, but she didn't push.

The church steeple rose above the trees at one end of the village green in downtown Maple Hill. On this Sunday morning, the street parking spaces in front of the various shops and restaurants on either side of the green were filled with churchgoers' vehicles, so they had to park a little distance away in front of a clothing boutique.

They walked through the green toward the church, enjoying the rustling of the wind through the trees and occasionally greeting other people also on their way to the service. As they neared the building, the brick sanctuary came into view with double doors opened wide, and a small crowd gathered just outside, chatting and greeting one another.

Sarah felt a bit like an outsider as they neared the doors, but Liam took firm hold of her arm and made a way through the crowd into the quieter foyer of the church, nodding to several people but not stopping to speak to anyone. "I'll introduce you after the service," he said.

A young woman with a stack of programs and a sweet smile stepped up to them. "Hi, Mr. Connolly."

"Carol, this is Sarah Hart."

"Welcome. Is this your first time here?"

Sarah nodded.

The girl smiled wider. "That's wonderful. Here are your programs." She then turned to gesture behind her to the wooden swinging doors. Through the small windows built into them, Sarah could see the sanctuary beyond, brightly lighted, and a large wooden cross hanging over the front of the room.

"Let's go into the sanctuary and find a seat." Liam opened one of the doors for Sarah and she immediately heard the muted roar of conversation echoing off a high ceiling. They entered the sanctuary together.

The ceiling was indeed high but plain white with simple crown molding around the edges. The walls, however, had Bible verses etched on light-colored wooden panels that ranged artfully around the perimeter of the room. At the front was a low dais with a pulpit at the center, and behind the pulpit was a low railing that separated the choir seats from the front of the stage. The choir members were seated on benches and dressed in simple blue robes. Some choir members chatted with each other, while others flipped through their music.

Wooden pews were ranged on either side of a center aisle and a deep blue carpet runner. Sarah and Liam sat in a pew midway down the aisle. She looked through her program, which was a simple sheet of paper folded in half. On the front was a color photograph of yellow daffodils and a Bible verse printed underneath, and beneath the verse, "Congregational Church, Maple Hill, Massachusetts." Inside on the left side was a listing of the pastors of the church, the worship leader, the choir members, and the ushers and greeters. On the right side were a few announcements. On the back was a listing of church events such as weekly Bible studies and the youth group meeting, and also the main telephone numbers of the church.

Sarah scanned the list of pastors again. There were three of them: a youth pastor, an associate pastor, and the senior pastor, Reverend Charles Yauger. Sarah was acquainted with

Reverend Yauger. He had been pastor of the Congregational Church for many years, but she doubted he had been here fifty years ago. However, he would certainly know who in his congregation she could talk to who might have known Debby.

The music of a piano filled the hall, signaling the congregation to take their seats quickly. The worship leader stepped up onto the low stage and signaled for them all to rise, and then the choir erupted in a rendition of "The Sweet By and By."

Reverend Yauger gave the sermon, which was on Jesus's trial. Sarah couldn't help wondering if Debby had had an unfair trial too, or if she had truly been a murderess.

After the last prayer and the worship leader's dismissal of the congregation, Liam and Sarah made their way up to the front of the sanctuary.

"Hello, Liam," Reverend Yauger greeted him. "Who's your friend?"

"This is Sarah Hart," Liam said.

She smiled and held out her hand. "Hello. We met once before, years ago."

"Yes, yes, I remember. Hello, Sarah. Welcome to our congregation today." He had a faintly disorganized air about him, but his handclasp was warm and friendly. "So nice to see you. So what brings you to the Congregational Church today? Ready to jump ship from Bridge Street Church? I can rib Pastor John about that the next time we have coffee."

"Not quite yet," Sarah said. "I'm hoping you can help me. I'm interested in finding out about a woman who attended this church in the early sixties."

"Early sixties? I'm afraid I wasn't pastor then. Barely into my teens, in fact."

"Do you know if there are any church members who could have been here then? Who might remember a young woman who attended church for a year or two?"

His full, steel-colored beard twitched as he thought. "Yes, yes, perhaps. You might ask some of the older ladies in the choir. Several of them have been at this church for over fifty years." He took them to a small door to the left of the front stage and led the way inside. Sarah could hear chattering voices.

They entered a small room cramped with choir members who were hanging up their robes in the tall oak wardrobes that stood against the far wall. All of the other walls were covered with photographs, some of which looked rather old, but others which were obviously more modern. The photos were all of the choir in their robes, with a year at the bottom of each frame.

Several of the choir members turned to greet Reverend Yauger, but stared curiously at Sarah and Liam.

The reverend introduced them to three older women who were sitting on two low benches in front of one of the wardrobes. "Virgie, Linda, Janet, this is Sarah Hart, and you might recognize Liam Connolly as a regular church member. Mrs. Hart has some questions you might be able to answer." He then nodded to Sarah. "I hope you find what you're looking for. Good-bye, good-bye." He smiled and left the room.

"Hello," Sarah said.

Linda, a thin, regal woman with a beak of a nose, gave a supercilious nod. "What is it you wish to know?"

"I'm hoping you might have known a woman named Debby Neely who sang in the choir in the early sixties. Perhaps between 1960 and 1963."

Linda gave a decisive shake of her head. "I never knew anyone by that name."

The woman sitting next to her, a plump woman with fluffy silver curls, gave Linda a hesitant look. "Are you—" she began to say, but was cut off by Virgie, who sat on the second bench.

"We've been singing with the choir since we started attending this church," Virgie said. "If she did sing in the choir, it wasn't at this church."

"Or if she was at this church, she didn't sing in the choir," said Linda.

Janet tried to speak again. "There was—"

"Are you sure this Debby person attended this church?" Linda asked.

"Relatively sure," Sarah said.

"What makes you think she sang in the choir?" Virgie asked. She had deep grooves along the sides of her mouth that made her look like she was always scowling.

Sarah hesitated. She didn't want to tell them about the book, but she couldn't lie either. "Someone mentioned how she loved singing in the choir."

"She didn't sing in this choir," Linda said. "We should know."

"Well—" Janet began.

"We're some of the oldest church members, been part of the choir for decades," Virgie added.

Sarah was hard-pressed to remain polite in the face of such rudeness. Not only the two women's rudeness to her, but also the fact that they wouldn't let Janet finish a sentence. Sarah had been taught that to interrupt someone was rude, and these women thought nothing of running roughshod over someone else.

Liam's face also looked a bit clouded, but he took his cue from Sarah and didn't say anything.

Linda stood. "If you'll excuse us, we're quite busy this afternoon," she said. She began to march out of the small room, followed by Virgie and, reluctantly, Janet.

The women seemed to have taken a dislike to Sarah, so the situation needed some finesse. She gave Liam a pleading look.

With a charming smile, Liam stepped forward to detain the women. "Now, ladies, we mean no disrespect. If we're mistaken, we sorely apologize for taking up your time."

But Linda wasn't charmed. "You're most certainly taking up our time. Out of my way." She poked at him with the dirt brown purse hanging over her wrist.

Sarah touched Janet's sleeve. "Janet, were you trying to say something?"

"I had thought ... perhaps ... "

"Janet, are you coming?" Virgie had an impatient edge to her voice.

Janet bit her lip and gave Sarah a nervous glance. She whispered quickly, "Talk to Dale Wexler."

"Do you remember Debby?"

"Janet!"

Janet nodded to Sarah and Liam and scurried after Linda and Virgie.

Sarah sighed as she walked to where Liam stood near the door. "I wish I'd been able to talk to her more. Do you know her telephone number? Maybe I can call her and meet her for coffee. Without Linda and Virgie."

"I could probably get it for you," Liam said. "Sometimes I give the church secretary the extra cookies that are left at the end of the day, for her little ones. Her husband's been out of work for several months, so her kids don't get many treats."

"Liam, that's so kind of you."

"'Give, and ye shall receive,'" he said with a twinkle in his eye. "I'm only doing it so someone will bring *me* cookies someday."

As Sarah started to exit the choir room, the black-and-white photograph just to the left of the door caught her eye. The date under the choir photo said 1970.

"What is it?" Liam asked.

Sarah pointed to the picture. "That isn't too far off from 1963." She and Liam searched around the photo, but all the photos were more recent.

"Looks like 1970 is the oldest," he said.

"But the wall is pretty packed." Sarah turned in a circle in the middle of the room. "There's a photo for last year, but not for this year, yet. And from what I can see, there's no space for it, either. I wonder if they remove the older pictures to make room for newer ones? Maybe the older ones are stored away in a box somewhere?"

"You know who would know?"

"Who?" Sarah asked.

"Janet."

He was right. "Well, let's find the church secretary. It looks like she is my next lead."

CHAPTER THIRTEEN

T he rest of Sunday was filled with warmth as Jason and the family came over for dinner. Sarah didn't think about Debby Neely or the mysterious author until she settled into bed with the book again that night. She had managed to get in touch with Janet just after church and they had arranged for Sarah to go to Janet's house Monday morning for breakfast.

As Sarah drove into the rising sun to Janet Dean's house the following morning, she carefully read the directions Janet had given to her over the phone. She pulled up in front of a beautiful Southern-plantation-style home, although on a much smaller scale than Tara in *Gone with the Wind*. It had four simple white columns in front, which flanked the steps leading up to the front porch and continued through the second story wraparound balcony. Both the front porch and the balcony had wooden railings, painted white. Gabled dormers peeked from the sloping roof.

Sarah rang the doorbell and waited, noticing the pots of tulips scattered over the porch. The door opened, and she was surprised to see Tiffany Henderson, one of the nurses from Bradford Manor.

"Hi, Mrs. Hart," Tiffany said cheerfully. "Come on in. Aunt Janet's in the kitchen."

"I didn't realize you were her niece."

"Great-niece, actually," Tiffany said. "I come by and check up on her Monday, Wednesday, and Friday mornings before I head in for my shift."

Janet was waiting for them in the kitchen, sitting at a lovely walnut nook corner dining table, with an L-shaped bench nestled into the corner of the kitchen in lieu of chairs. "Sarah, thank you so much for meeting me here," Janet said. "Tiffany gets so upset if I miss a checkup."

"I certainly don't mind if you're okay with it." Sarah laid a paper bag on the table. "I bought fresh bagels."

"Thanks, Mrs. Hart," Tiffany said.

Janet reached for the bag. "Oh I'd love a chocolate chip—"

"No, you don't." Tiffany snatched the bag away and looked inside. She pulled out a whole wheat, multiseed bagel and put it on a plate in front of her aunt.

"You take the fun out of everything," Janet said. "Sarah, there's coffee in the pot and I made some eggs and Canadian bacon, which are on the counter. Help yourself."

Sarah took a poached egg and a piece of Canadian bacon. Tiffany got a plate of food for her aunt, and after they were settled at the table, Tiffany picked up her purse from the kitchen counter. "I'm off. Behave, Aunt Janet." She gave them both a smile and left through the front door.

"Will you say grace?" Janet asked Sarah.

After a short prayer, Sarah cut into her breakfast. Tiffany had helpfully left low-fat cream cheese and jam on the table for the bagels.

"How do you know Tiffany?" Janet asked.

"My father is at Bradford Manor, and she has always been so kind to him. She's his favorite nurse."

"Mine too," Janet laughed. "Although I detest this diet she has me on. Low fat, low salt, low everything."

Sarah asked, "Do you mind if I ask you some questions about Debby Neely?"

"Go ahead. I'm sorry about Linda and Virgie yesterday. Years and years ago they saw Debby arrested after Sunday service, and ever since they've believed Debby is a cold-blooded killer."

"She was arrested after church?"

"I didn't actually see it happen, but they did. Virgie said that Dale was helping Mrs. Griggs to her car when the FBI drove up, got out of their car, and marched straight up to Debby as she was walking out the front door of the church. They knew exactly what she looked like."

"What did Debby say?" Sarah asked.

Janet sighed. "Linda said it looked like Debby just gave up. She hung her head and didn't say a word."

"Did you know why they arrested her?"

"Not at the time. Of course, afterward the rumors flew. There were a dozen different stories. No one knew for sure what the truth was."

"It must have been very shocking."

"I think it was worse because Dale and I were in the choir with her. We'd gotten to know her pretty well over the past year."

"Who else was in the choir at the time?"

"My memory is so terrible these days." Janet said. "I can't remember, not with any certainty. I might be remembering later years in the choir."

"Virgie and Linda weren't in the choir?"

"I do know they joined a few years later. They didn't in fact sing that well, but this really cute boy happened to be in Maple Hill one summer with his grandparents, and he sang in the choir, so ..." She shrugged. "They stayed even after he left, and their singing improved too."

Sarah realized that her next question might help. "I noticed that the pictures on the wall of the choir room are only from 1970 until the present. Are there older pictures in storage somewhere?"

"Of course! Why didn't I think of that? Ivan Hillman."

"Was he the photographer?"

"Yes. Up until about five years ago, Ivan Hillman took the choir Christmas picture every year. We've been giving the older photos back to Ivan to make room for the newer ones, so they're in his house somewhere." Janet made a face.

"Good luck with that. Ivan couldn't organize himself if he only had two pencils and a cup."

"And the photos go back to 1960?"

"They go back even further, but you'll probably want nineteen sixty or 1961. I can't quite remember when Debby joined the choir, but it was a year or so before her arrest." Janet sighed. "It would be fun to see that photo again. And it might jog my memory about who else was in the choir with us."

"Do you have Ivan's telephone number?"

Janet got the telephone number for Sarah, and said, "Have you talked to Dale Wexler yet?"

"Do you think he'll mind if I give him a call?"

"No, he won't mind at all. He and I have been good friends for many years. In fact, he married my best friend. The four of us, Dale and I and our spouses, used to get together all the time for cards. Anyway, he might remember more about Debby than I do."

"Was he close to her?"

"About as close as I was to her, but he has a better memory." Janet dimpled at Sarah. "There's nothing like getting older."

"But hopefully we're getting wiser too." Sarah rose to take her leave but then stopped and said, "I almost forgot to ask. I was wondering if maybe my mom knew Debby. Do you remember a Ruth Drayton who was close to her?"

Janet shook her head. "Sorry, the name doesn't sound familiar to me at all."

Olive had said her mom chatted only occasionally with Debby, and now Janet said she didn't even recognize Mom's name. What was her mom's connection to the book? "Thank you so much."

"You're very welcome. I hope you find out more about Debby," Janet said. "Everything that happened just seems so … unfinished."

After running errands to the bank and the grocery store, Sarah arrived home famished. She entered the kitchen to the smell of butter and the slight hiss of the frying pan.

Chloe stood in front of the stove, propped up with her crutches while making grilled cheese sandwiches. She turned as Sarah approached. "Oh good, you're home. I made a sandwich for you too."

"That's so nice, Chloe. You don't have to do that. You're the injured one, after all."

"I was already making one, so why not two?" Chloe handed Sarah a plate with a crispy sandwich.

"Thank you. Let me carry your plate for you." Sarah took both sandwiches to the table while Chloe hobbled over.

"I just started the coffee, so it'll be a minute," she said. "Um … would you say grace for us?"

Warmth filled Sarah's chest at the request. "Of course." She said a short, sincere prayer for them.

As soon as she had said "Amen," Chloe said, "It just seemed kind of weird, me always just sitting here while you said grace by yourself. So I figured I'd join you."

"You're welcome to join me anytime." *Lord, I pray that you can touch Chloe's heart through me.*

They spent a pleasant half hour while Chloe talked excitedly about genetics charts, and waxed poetic about a sheep breed called California Variegated Mutant, of all things.

When they were done eating, Sarah started to collect her plate, but Chloe stopped her. "No, I'll clean up."

"No—"

"No, I insist."

Sarah supposed that the traits that enabled so young a woman to venture into entrepreneurship—her ambitious sheep breeding project—would also make her strong willed. Still, it upset her to see Chloe slowly and painstakingly hobble back and forth from the table to the counter with each plate and cup.

"Thanks for lunch," Sarah said, and headed back to her quilting room.

She dialed Dale Wexler but got his voice mail and left a message. Then she called Ivan Hillman.

A woman's voice answered. "Hello?"

"Hello, my name is Sarah Hart. I'm looking for Ivan Hillman."

"Oh hi, Sarah. This is Alana Marquez."

"Did I dial the wrong number?" Sarah asked.

"No, Ivan is my dad."

"Is he around? Could I speak to him?"

"He's napping right now."

"No, I'm not!" came an irate voice in the background.

"I'm trying to get him to nap," amended the woman in a long-suffering voice.

"I don't need a nap," groused the old man in a gravelly voice. "It's only noon."

Alana's voice was muted as she spoke to her father. "You wouldn't need a nap if you hadn't gotten up at four this morning."

"It wasn't four, it was four-thirty," he said.

Sarah couldn't help grinning. "Should I call back later?"

"Is there anything I can help you with?"

"I wanted to ask him if he had a photo he took of the Congregational Church choir at Christmas in 1960."

"Oh good heavens, yes, please call back later." Alana's voice dropped. "If you ask him now, he'll spend all afternoon searching for it rather than taking a nap, and at ninety, he really does need one."

"What time should I call back?"

"The way things are going…" She sighed, and Sarah could hear Ivan muttering to himself in the background, with a few choice words about "dictator daughters."

"How about calling back around four? He'll be up from his nap by then."

"No problem."

"Are you still on the phone?" Ivan asked. "If you're on the phone, then I don't have to take a nap…."

"I'd better go," Alana said.

"Thanks. Goodbye." Sarah hung up the phone. Ivan sounded like quite a character—and quite a handful for his daughter too.

Dale Wexler called Sarah back that afternoon. He invited her to meet him at Patriot Park, where he was watching his grandchildren.

She didn't see any children playing on the playground or seated at the picnic tables, but she did see several boys playing basketball on the brand new basketball court that had been laid out next to the playground. She headed toward them and recognized Tim Wexler's athletic form as he went for a layup. She could see why he was already getting calls from college scouts.

An older man tried to guard him, while two younger boys, perhaps a year or two younger than Amy and Audrey, waited to see how the play went. Tim spun around to avoid the man and sank a basket. One of the two boys cheered.

"No fair," the other boy said. "I think it should be all three of us against Tim."

"I second that," the man said, his hands on his knees as he caught his breath. "Especially considering all three of your ages added up is still younger than me."

Tim caught sight of Sarah and waved. "Hi there, Mrs. Hart."

The man looked up and smiled. "Hello, you must be Sarah. I'm Dale Wexler." He held out his hand. "You know Tim?"

"He's always a big help when I'm looking for something at the historical society." Sarah shook Dale's hand. "When you said you were watching your grandchildren, I didn't know Tim was one of them."

"These two are Oscar and Andrew, Tim's younger brothers," Dale said.

"Hi," they each mumbled in that embarrassed way of pre-teen boys.

"Okay, you two play with Tim," Dale said. "I need to talk to Sarah for a few minutes."

"You can only use one hand," Oscar stipulated for his older brother, but the two younger boys seemed to relish the game despite their disadvantages in height.

"If they're anything like Tim, they'll sprout up before their freshman year," Dale said as he led the way to a nearby picnic table. "I wasn't even half as tall as that kid when I was in school."

Despite his words, Sarah noted Dale was also rather tall. He was probably around seventy, but he still carried himself with an athletic grace similar to his grandson's. He picked up a towel that lay on the table and mopped his face. "You wanted to know about someone from church?"

Sarah sat next to him. "Do you remember Debby Neely?"

"I do. Wow, that was a long time ago. Why do you ask?"

She recited her quilting angle as motivation for her questions.

Dale gave a rueful smile. "You're asking the wrong guy. What I know about quilting would fit in a thimble."

"I was hoping you could tell me more about Debby and any of her friends. One of them might be able to tell me more."

"Well..." He scratched at his hair, still brown gray. "I don't know as I knew her that well. But I think I was one of the first people to talk to her when she came to Maple Hill."

"Oh?"

"When I was a rookie cop, I got all the worst shifts. Back then, the civil rights movement had already started rumbling. Maple Hill had a few sit-ins during the day, but at night, I'd often come across a bunch of stupid teenagers—of mixed races—using the political atmosphere as an excuse to misbehave. That's how I met Debby. One night, I saw a few hoodlums making some noise on a street corner in a residential area on the north side. I dropped my lights and brought my squad car to a crawl and pretty much snuck up on them. When I got closer, I realized they were harrassing a woman."

Sarah had been so young at the time, and only partially aware of the social changes just starting to take place. This perspective from a former policeman was interesting.

"The first thing I noticed was they weren't drunk, like I had originally thought. The next thing I noticed was that there were four of them, and only one of me. So I flipped on my brights and hit my siren once to let them know I meant business. The poor woman looked like a rabbit about to have a heart attack. Those big brown eyes couldn't have been any more scared.

"I got out of the car right quick and said, 'Boys, I think it's about time you moved along.' Bogart would have been proud."

Sarah smiled. Dale certainly knew how to tell a story.

"They looked me up and down, and I knew exactly what they were thinking. They were sizing me up, figuring they could take me. For good measure, I said, 'I already called for backup. So I'd rethink what you're thinking right now.' Now, I hadn't called anybody, but they didn't know that.

"And then, I kid you not, in the distance we heard a siren. I recognized it as an ambulance siren, but those four goons didn't know the difference. They went whiter than my grandma's buttermilk, and next thing you know, it's just me and Debby.

"I said, 'Ma'am, may I escort you to your destination?' As if I were a fancy chauffeur. And I drove her to one of the old boardinghouses on the west side."

"Grandpa," Andrew called from the basketball court, "last time you told that story there were only three guys."

Sarah laughed, but Dale said, "That really is how I met Debby. I told her about my church and she started coming a few weeks later, I think."

"Did she have many friends at church?"

"She was a bit reserved, but she was a pretty nice girl once you got to know her. She seemed to get along with everybody."

"Was there anyone she was closer to?"

"It's hard to remember. It was a long time ago."

But he had remembered meeting Debby very clearly. "Someone mentioned that my mom might have been close to Debby," she said. "Do you remember a woman named Ruth Drayton?"

"The name sounds familiar, but I don't know that she and Debby were friends."

How in the world did her mom come to donate that book to the library?

"Have you talked to anyone else besides me?" Dale asked.

"Debby's co-worker, Olive—"

Dale snapped his fingers. "Olive Cavanaugh. I had forgotten they worked together. What did Olive say?"

"Not much."

"I wonder why. Did she seem nervous? Agitated? Did she respond to anything in particu—" He cut himself off with a laugh. "Sorry, didn't mean to interrogate you. It's the cop in me."

"Did you know Chief Webber, then?"

"I trained Nate. He was my replacement."

"Your replacement? You were Chief of Police?"

"Yup."

"So that's where you get your investigative nature."

"It's hard to stop being police chief and remember I'm a *retired* police chief."

That explained his questions to Sarah, but a part of her was a bit suspicious at his curiosity. One could argue he was simply interested in a woman he hadn't thought of for fifty years.

On the other hand, perhaps he had a different reason for being so inquisitive about Debby. Maybe he was trying to figure out how much she already knew, so he could gauge how much information to give her.

"Grandpa." Tim jogged up to them, the basketball under his arm. "Time to go. Mom'll be home soon."

Dale stood. "I hope you find what you're looking for."

"Thanks," Sarah said. As she drove away, something about Dale nagged at her, but she couldn't figure out what it was.

His language was extremely different from the timid voice of the author. But he'd also been aggressively curious about what she'd learned so far.

She realized that she had been hoping the author of the book would reveal him- or herself in more obvious ways, such as reacting to Debby's name in remorse, since the writer had been full of remorse when writing the book. But then again, maybe fifty years had changed the way the author felt.

And as she drew up into her driveway, she realized: Dale had spent so much time talking about how he met Debby, he'd managed to avoid mentioning singing in the choir with Debby or seeing her arrest.

CHAPTER FOURTEEN

couring the Internet for the bombing Debby had been involved in was as frustrating as herding cats. After her previous failed search for Debby Neely, Sarah had decided to focus on the event. She tried *bomb* and *Josiah* and *federal courthouse*. She tried synonyms and more general terms, and dropped Josiah's name in case he hadn't been mentioned since he ended up being a witness.

She tried changing the year, since the bombing would have happened earlier than the year Debby arrived in Maple Hill, but that didn't give her any promising results. She got a lot of Web pages talking about present-day bombings and very few articles about bombings that occurred in the year she had plugged in.

She also had the sinking feeling that Debby Neely hadn't been a real name. It would make sense, since the woman had been on the run. And if it wasn't her real name, Sarah didn't think she'd be able to find the bombing at all, much less any news articles from fifty years ago.

Searching for Debby's crime also didn't answer the question the book and her interviews still hadn't addressed—was Debby innocent, as she claimed, or guilty? The author seemed to believe in Debby, but Sarah would guess that there had been at least a few more people like Linda and Virgie who didn't.

After three hours in front of her computer, she leaned back in her chair and rubbed her gritty eyes. Her stomach rumbled.

Before she could dig up a snack, Sarah got a call from Martha.

"I baked cookies this morning for my granddaughters and had a few extras I thought you might want," Martha said.

"I'll be happy to help you get rid of them," Sarah replied. "Are you busy with something else right now? I'd love to come by."

"Come on over."

As Sarah pulled up in front of Martha's white Cape-Cod-style home, the blue shutters seemed gray-blue in the overcast morning light. Her car startled a flock of pigeons that had gathered on the edge of the front porch roof, and they burst into flight, finally settling on one of the two chimneys that flanked the ends of the home.

She had just reached the low steps up to the front porch when Martha opened the door and gestured her in. "Come in to the kitchen. Tea?"

"I'd love some."

Martha put a kettle on the stove to boil, and set out two mugs and two tea bags on the oak Mission-style kitchen table. She then set a plate of cookies between them.

Sarah reached for a snickerdoodle, still a bit warm from the oven. The cinnamon scent tickled her nose as she bit into the cookie, crispy on the outside but a little chewy on the inside. Martha's recipe was award winning.

"So how did your date go?" Martha asked, leaning in with a gleam in her eye.

Sarah laughed. "I knew you had an ulterior motive for inviting me over for snickerdoodles. You just 'happened' to make extra cookies, huh?"

"Yes, yes, guilty as charged. So how did it go?"

"It was really nice. At first I was a bit nervous, but then I remembered, this is Liam, my friend, and I relaxed."

"I'll bet he doesn't want to be only a friend anymore," Martha said.

"He called me yesterday, just to chat and see how I was doing. Then he said in that audacious way of his that we'd set a precedent and that it was our civic duty to plan to go out again in a couple of weeks."

Martha laughed. "What a scoundrel."

Sarah smiled. "I feel a bit like a silly teenager again."

Martha shuddered. "If I were you, I'd be heartily glad *not* to be a silly teenager again."

"Our teen years weren't that bad," Sarah said.

"And what would you call *my* first date with Ernie?"

Sarah burst into laughter. "How could I have forgotten about that?"

Ernie had taken Martha to a movie. Being a perfect gentleman, he'd bought her popcorn and a soda, but he was so nervous that he forgot to buy anything for himself, and he didn't realize it until they had sat down and the movie was about to start. Martha naturally offered to share with him, but as she passed him the cup of soda, he'd fumbled it—Ernie always said later that it was a good thing he had never been interested in playing football. The soda went all over Martha's brand-new dress and Ernie's pants. What was worse was that Martha had been so shocked by the sudden cold liquid splashing on her that she dropped the bag of popcorn she had been holding, and the popcorn stuck all over them too. They'd cut out of the movie early, still shaking popcorn off themselves, and he'd had to take her home barely an hour after picking her up.

"I guess it was memorable," Martha said.

"If you hadn't felt so sorry for him, you might not have given him a second date."

"Are you going to give Liam a second date?"

Sarah tilted her head to the side. "If he asks me."

"And why wouldn't he ask you?" Martha gave her friend a hard stare. "You didn't talk about nothing but quilts, did you?"

Sarah's face grew warm. "That was only that one time with Gerry, and we were already married. I felt comfortable enough with him to talk about my new hobby."

"For an entire anniversary dinner," Martha said dryly.

"We talked about his shop, and about our kids, and I also told him what I've discovered about Debby Neely."

"What have you discovered?" Martha asked.

Sarah realized she hadn't talked to Martha since last week when she went to the library, so she started off explaining about the self-published book, the magazine press, and her aborted mission to the Chamber of Commerce. "At first I was too busy to go back," Sarah admitted, "and then I forgot about it."

Martha, however, had worked herself up into a fine temper. "Those Barclay boys. Come on." She popped up to her feet. "We're going right now."

"Now?"

"We're going to get that information if I have to shake it out of Paul Barclay with my bare hands."

This time when Sarah entered the Chamber of Commerce, Paul didn't even look up from his comic book as they walked in. Martha had to bark, "Paul!" before he jumped and looked at them.

"Oh, uh…can I help you?" Paul's eyes shifted to Sarah. "Didn't you just come by? I told you that you can't get those records unless you give me a specific business name—"

"Now Paul." Martha was definitely using her "mom voice" inside the echoing room. "I don't want to hear any of your nonsense. I know you can look this information up on that computer right there." She stabbed a finger at the dusty monitor on the counter next to him. "So you're going to find us the information right now."

A cherry red color had started to glow from Paul's neck and ears, but his mouth remained set. "Or what?"

Martha leaned in slowly. "I have five gorgeous grand-daughters," she said, "and they are all boy crazy. I could accidentally let them know you think they're cute. And give them your phone number."

Paul's face paled to the color of strawberry cream. He slapped his comic book down on the counter and started typing at the computer keyboard.

"See? That's not so tough." Martha smiled.

Sarah was speechless for a moment. Then she leaned in to whisper to Martha, "But Sylvie's only two."

"Well, she does love her father very much. That counts as being boy crazy, right?" Martha whispered back.

"What did you need?" Paul asked.

"The names of any magazine presses in Maple Hill between 1960 and 1963, although they may have opened long before then and closed long afterward."

Paul tapped on the keyboard with very hard strikes, but he did what Martha asked. Finally, he turned the computer monitor to face them, leaned back in his chair, and crossed his arms.

Sarah read the record on the screen. Only one item found: "*The Berkshire Heart* magazine," she said. "It looks like the only magazine press that was ever in Maple Hill. It went out of business in 1966."

"Owned by Jerry Hobbs," Martha read.

"Oh," Sarah said. "I know him."

"You do?"

"He used to be friends with my father—they went to ball games together. He was a teacher at the high school. I never realized he owned another business on the side."

"That's great," Martha said. "You can talk to him and ask about his magazine press."

Sarah shook her head. "He died several years ago, and his wife died only a few months after he did."

"Oh no."

"Thank you," Sarah said politely to Paul. He gave a snort of acknowledgement and picked up his comic book again, but she noticed he avoided looking at Martha.

As they got back to Sarah's car, Martha asked, "Now what?"

"Well, I've been leaving messages at that book bindery, asking about the order record for this book. I want to know who ordered the book to be bound—it might be a clue."

"It might be the author," Martha said. "Would the book-binder still have its order forms from the sixties?"

"If anyone had returned my phone calls, I would know. Since no one has, I've been thinking I should drive out to pay them a visit, but they're two or three hours away."

"I'm game. Tomorrow? Ernie's nurse is scheduled to come."

"Are you sure?"

"You. Me. Road trip!"

The next day, as they drove to Suffolk Bindery, Sarah and Martha chatted about family and friends, then talked over what Sarah had discovered so far.

"I don't understand why Olive didn't want to talk to you." Martha shook her head.

"It was almost as if she felt guilty about something," Sarah said.

"Guilty about what? She didn't turn Debby in to the FBI, did she? I can't believe that of Olive."

"I can't, either. She's such a gentle soul. I could see her trying to convince Debby to turn herself in but calling the FBI? No."

"Do you think maybe she wrote the book?"

"I'm not sure. It's crossed my mind a few times, and I think it's possible, but there's no proof. All I know for certain is that she refuses to speak about Debby, but the book mentions that she and Debby were close."

"Who else is in the book?"

"Debby's landlady, and a woman named C."

"And out of all the people you've talked to who knew Debby, none of them was her landlady and no one's name starts with the letter C."

"If this trip doesn't turn up anything," Sarah said, "the only clue we'll have will be Ivan's photo."

"Did you talk to him?"

"I chatted with him yesterday. He was very excited to start looking for the photo for me."

They arrived at Suffolk Bindery, which had a small parking lot in front of a low office building, with a larger warehouse behind it. As Sarah got out of Martha's minivan, she marveled at the silence—the only thing she could hear were the birds tweeting in the trees that flanked the office building, and the occasional rush of a car that drove past on the two-lane road.

They entered the office and paused just inside the door. Behind several desks piled with papers and manila folders was a man who looked like he'd just been zapped by a few thousand watts. His eyes were wide and round, and his longish salt-and-pepper hair stood out around his head in a stiff, wide halo. He darted back and forth in sharp, short movements, picking up papers here and laying them down there. Sarah couldn't really tell whether he was doing anything more than shuffling them around.

Martha cleared her throat, and he noticed them. "Can I help you?"

Sarah smiled and approached the man where he stood next to one of the several desks in the office. "Do you keep order records from as far back as the 1960s?"

"Yes, we keep all our order records. Why?"

"Excellent. Then I'm certain you can help me." She took the book out of her purse and put it on the desk.

The man eyed it. "There's no returns or refunds for anything past thirty days."

"Oh I don't want to return this. I want to know who commissioned it."

"How do you know it was done here?"

"You're the only bindery in the area, and you were in business in 1963."

"You're sure this book was done in this area? It wasn't done somewhere else?"

"I'm sure." Although she had no reason to be so positive it was done locally. Perhaps the author went further afield in order to preserve anonymity. Well, if she couldn't find the record here, then she'd widen her search.

The man looked even more alarmed than before.

"I'm sorry, is something wrong?" Sarah asked.

"No, no." His head shook from side to side. "No, I don't care about letting you see the order records—I figure, you have the physical book, which is like a receipt. I just don't have *time*. I have too many other things to do!" His voice was like a wail.

Sarah finally realized. This man was seriously overworked.

"If you're willing, we can look for the record," she said.

The man became still and unmoving. "You will?"

She got a nod from Martha. Why not? "How are they filed?"

"By order number." His tempo slowed. "We give each book a unique number printed under the paper glued to the inside cover. Normally you need to remove the paper to find the number, but the number always starts with the year and month of the order. If you know those, that'll get you to the right drawer." He seemed almost calm, in a squirrelly way.

"Well, we know the approximate date. Where are the cabinets?"

He led them between two or three desks piled high with papers and through an unmarked door in the back wall of the office. Inside was a room twice as large as the front office, filled only with file cabinets.

Martha seemed for a moment like she regretted her decision, but Sarah had already taken a look at the numbering system, and had figured it out. "Don't worry," she said. "I think this will be easier than we thought."

"You'll be okay?" the man asked, eyes blinking rapidly.

"Fine."

"Good." And in a flash he had zipped out of the room, leaving the door open, and was back to rushing to and fro in between the loaded desks.

The top drawer in the cabinet closest to the door was labeled, "2011010001-2011069999."

"Look," Sarah pointed to the label. "I'll hazard a guess the first four numbers mean the year 2011, then January or 01, and then the book number 0001. This looks to go through the year 2011, June or 06, and book number 9999."

Martha squinted at the numbers. "You figured that out pretty quick."

"So our book would be 1963, and..." What had the book's donation record said? "November or earlier, so 11 or 10, or maybe even 09."

"But what about the last four numbers? There could be 9,999 records. In each month!"

Sarah doubted there would be that many, but she quelled a rising worry that she was wrong. "Well, let's find the drawer and see how many records there are for November 1963."

They spread out and it was Martha who found the drawer labeled, "1963070001—1963129999." They heaved it open and found hanging file folders neatly marked by month: 196307—, 196308—, and so on. Some months had more than one bulging folder, but some months had only a single slim folder.

There were three folders for November 1963, each about an inch and a half thick. There were no chairs in the room, so Sarah and Martha sat down on the industrial-strength gray carpet, leaning against the filing cabinets, and each took a folder.

Sarah sifted through order form after order form, but most were large orders for libraries—local private libraries, public libraries, college and high school libraries. This was apparently the main bindery for many state and privately owned collections.

Most of the orders Sarah found were several pages stapled together, so when she found an order that was simply a lone sheet of paper, it immediately caught her attention. The order was for one manuscript to be bound. The color of the binding was up to the binders—"No preference" had been checked on the form.

The book description was: "Self-printed manuscript. 78 pages." That was the number of pages of the book.

Sarah's eyes eagerly scanned down the page. Where was the customer information? Who had commissioned this book?

There, at the bottom, was a signature on the line for the customer name:

William Drayton.

Because of the long drive back to Maple Hill, it was nearly supper time by the time Martha dropped Sarah off at her house. During the two and a half hour car trip back, they had discussed how in the world Sarah's father could be involved in Debby's story but didn't come up with any answers. Only more questions.

"First I find out my mother is the one who donated the book to the library, then I discover my father had the book bound."

"Maybe one of them is the author."

"I don't know. I can't dismiss the possibility, and yet I don't remember either of them being close to Debby, and no one who remembers Debby talked about my mom being friends with her. I didn't know to ask about my dad."

"Even if one of them isn't the author, they must have known the author. Your father, at least, helped make the book," Martha said.

"That's true." A thought occured. "At the Chamber of Commerce, that magazine press had been owned by Jerry Hobbs, Dad's friend."

"So maybe your dad had something to do with printing it too."

"There's one way to find out," Sarah said. "I'll go to Bradford Manor tomorrow to talk to him."

And she prayed he would be having a good day, memory-wise, or she might get nothing but more baseball stories. It seemed so strange, and yet the clues seemed to be pointing more in her dad's direction than in anyone else's.

She felt like she didn't know her parents as well as she thought she did. And there didn't seem to be any direct way to find out the truth—her mom was gone and her father's lucidity went in and out.

She had a feeling there was some important secret tucked away in his mind that might just be the key to solving everything.

CHAPTER FIFTEEN

T he first thing Sarah saw when she entered the nursing home sitting room was Olive, again in front of the bird cage. "Hello, Olive."

"Oh hi, Sarah." Wielding a pair of scissors, Olive was once again cutting scraps of fabric into slender strips. "You really need to stop stalking me like this."

Sarah laughed. "But you live such a wild and fascinating life. I can't help it."

"You want wild and fascinating? You should have seen Aaron McCarver try to steal Diane Ashley's blueberry muffin this morning. The World Wrestling Entertainment couldn't have staged a better fight."

There was a question that had popped into Sarah's head as soon as she saw Olive, and while she didn't want to put a damper on Olive's good mood this morning, she wanted to know the answer. "Olive, did you think Debby Neely was innocent?"

Olive's scissors paused in their motion, and she looked at the colorful birds in the cage. "Yes. Yes I did." She gave Sarah a steely glance. "And that's all I'm going to say on it today."

Sarah smiled, raising her hands up in front of her. "I wouldn't dare incur your wrath."

"Oh hi, Mrs. Hart." Tiffany Henderson came up to the two of them. "I just wheeled your dad out to the back patio. He's playing checkers with Mr. Blodgett."

Sarah had hoped to be able to talk to her father alone. Would he be willing to talk about Debby with another person there? "Thanks, Tiffany."

When she entered the back patio, she noted the slight chill from the concrete floor and the fact that this side of the building faced west, still in shadow despite the feeble morning sunlight. Her father sat at a low chess table set up in a corner.

His opponent was the same deaf man he'd been chatting with the last time Sarah came. "Hi, Dad."

He looked up. It took a few seconds, then he recognized her. "Sarah! How are you doing, my girl?"

"I'm fine. How are you feeling?"

"Victorious. I'm playing checkers with Chuck, here." He pointed at the other man, who looked up at Sarah and nodded. "I've got him cornered."

It actually looked more like Mr. Blodgett had her dad cornered, from the positions of his king'ed pieces. "You're a good player, Mr. Blodgett."

But he was staring at the board and didn't look up as she spoke.

"Oh he's deaf as a doornail," William Drayton said cheerfully. "He has a hearing aid, but he keeps losing it. Tiffany found it in his pot of marigolds the other day."

Maybe she'd be able to ask him about Debby after all, if Mr. Blodgett really couldn't hear. "Dad, I have a question for you."

"Hang on...." He made a move on the board.

"Do you remember a young woman who used to live in Maple Hill named Debby Neely?"

"Who?"

"I think Mom might have known her. She made quilted dresses at the old Pleiter's gift shop in the early sixties."

"Pleiter? Al Pleiter's a fine man. But your mom says his brother could use a little sugar."

"Debby worked for Al Pleiter at his shop."

"Shop? What shop?"

Sarah tried to bring his thoughts back to her real objective. "Debby Neely was arrested by the FBI back in 1962. Do you remember that?"

"Nope, don't know her."

"You...you don't remember her?"

"Never knew her. Is she a friend of yours?"

"Dad...," Sarah faltered, wondering if she should continue with her questions. "Do you remember going to a bindery and placing an order for a book to be bound? It would have been in November 1963."

He didn't answer, but proceeded to make another move on the checkerboard, prompting Mr. Blodgett to jump two of his pieces.

"I found an order form with your name on it," Sarah said.

"Is that right?"

Sarah pulled the book out of her purse. "Dad, I found the book in the library. Mom donated it in November 1963." He stared at it for a long moment. Then he smiled up at her. "Put that away, Sarah. Don't read at the table."

Maybe her father just needed a little nudge to get him back to 1963, put him in the mind frame of that time of his life. She concentrated hard on long-forgotten history lessons. "Dad, where were you when you heard about Kennedy being assassinated?" Not the most cheerful topic, but it was one of the major events of the year.

He tapped his chin, and at first Sarah thought he was only contemplating his next checkers move, but then he said, "I was driving down the highway. Came on the radio."

"Were you alone?" she asked.

"You and your brother were in the backseat. But your mom wasn't there. She was home."

"Why didn't she come with us?"

"Oh she had to work."

Work? She hadn't even realized her mother had been working in the early sixties. "Where did Mom work?"

"Secretary." Her father made a surprising jump of two of Mr. Blodgett's checkers pieces. The deaf old man just sat there, staring at the checkerboard.

"Mom worked full-time as a secretary?"

"No, only a few hours a day. While you kids are at school."

So that explained why Sarah didn't remember her mom going to a job. "How many years did she work?"

"Only a couple of years. We were saving up for a new refrigerator, and a new washer and dryer set."

She was amazed he remembered such details. "Do you remember where she worked?" she asked him again, although not hopeful for an answer.

"Don't forget to brush your teeth," he told her, and made another checkers move. "And no cheating this time—remember to use toothpaste."

She couldn't believe it. She had the distinct impression that this wasn't her father's normal forgetfulness, that he was deliberately stonewalling her. Her dad wouldn't do this unless...was he hiding something?

And Sarah couldn't be sure he even remembered what he was hiding or who he was protecting. It was probably time to give Dad a little rest.

Mr. Blodgett took another two of Dad's checkers pieces and Dad huffed.

Sarah bent and kissed his cheek. "Bye, Dad."

"Good night, sweetheart."

Sarah drove home from Bradford Manor feeling like a cold, heavy blanket had been draped around her shoulders. The bookbinding clue seemed to have reached a dead end. She intended to visit her father again another time to ask him, but his emphatic denial made her wonder if he really would answer her, or if he might stonewall her again. If he had been asked to keep some information in confidence, William Drayton would carry that secret to his grave. He might not quite remember what secret he was keeping, but he had seemed to react to Debby's name and the sight of the book, and clearly they were forbidden topics.

Both he and Mom had been involved somehow with this book. It could be that William had had the book bound and Ruth had donated it to the library in order to keep the author's identity secret. But why would they do that? For whom?

Sarah parked her car in her driveway and paused a moment to think. The bookbinding had led her down a fruitless trail to new questions and no answers. But her father had also given her a surprising clue—her mother's secretarial work. Sarah had wondered about the connection between Debby Neely and the author and her parents—and maybe her mom's workplace was the key component.

But how to figure out where her mother had worked in the early sixties?

In the same place she'd gone before looking for clues about her mother—the attic.

Martha joined her in the search, and the attic was cooler than it had been the last time they had been up there. A cold front was coming in and the weather lately had been cloudy and blustery. Sarah headed for the corner where she had been working and started looking at the boxes stacked there. "Here they are, the things from Mom's desk," she said to Martha. "I think there are three boxes full."

It was a bit tricky getting the boxes down the narrow, steep flight of stairs, but they managed to carry them into Sarah's dining room.

They each took a side of the dining room table and a box, with plenty of space on the table to look through the contents.

"This should go pretty quickly." Sarah took the lid off her box and dove in.

"I've got nothing but books." Martha set a stack of them on the table.

"I've got lots of papers." Sarah picked up a few folders and discovered some paid bills, a few receipts for large items her dad had purchased, and even a couple of to-do lists. She dutifully looked through each folder and laid it on the table, stacked to the side. "Look to see if anything can be donated or thrown away," she said. "Maybe we'll have only one or two boxes to return to the attic rather than three."

"I'm all for that," Martha said, "but I think you'll probably want to keep some of these. Look, Sarah, this one has your mother's handwriting in the margins." She passed her a copy of *Streams in the Desert*.

Sarah flipped it open and saw her mom's delicate scrawls next to some of the daily devotions. Some were short prayers—"Lord, make me more like you." Some were notes to herself—"Remember that the Lord sees that leak in the bathroom pipes. He will take care of you, little sparrow."

"Oh Martha, this is wonderful." Sarah flipped to more devotionals, each one on a separate calendar day.

Martha came around the table to look over her shoulder at the book. "Look at that, she put the year next to each note."

Some devotional days had multiple notes, and the year written next to each note differentiated them from each other, even though they were on the same day. Sarah turned to her birthday and saw five different things:

"Lord, grow my daughter into a woman who will bring you glory. 1947." The day Sarah had been born.

"Only you can heal her hurt, God. 1955." Sarah didn't even remember why she'd been in pain, or if it had been physical or emotional, but her mother's prayer touched her even years later.

"Bless the work of her hands. 1964." The year she graduated high school.

"Remember, SHE'LL GROW OUT OF IT. 1965."

Sarah and Martha both burst into laughter at that last one.

Curious, she turned to the November devotionals, since the book had been printed and donated to the library in that month. There was only one note dated 1963, scrawled next to November 12: "All things work together for good for those who love God."

Sarah started to page back toward her dad's birthday, but Martha stopped her.

"Wait." She stabbed her finger in between the pages and turned a few back to October 9. "Look."

"Let me be a blessing to my co-workers. 1963."

"Dad's memory was spot on. Mom really was working that year. But where?"

"Well, what are we waiting for? Let's get moving." Martha went back to her side of the table and her box.

How precious this book was. Sarah put it down reluctantly but promised herself she'd look through it at her leisure later, when she could dwell on each small notation.

She returned to her box of papers. It was probably for the best that she had this box, because she could best decide which papers to keep and which to throw away. She picked up a file that was stuffed to bursting with paper and flipped it open.

It was all typewritten sheets.

I'm telling this story because I can't get the picture of her face out of my mind. When I go to sleep, I can still see her eyes on the day the FBI came to Maple Hill to take her away.

This was the book, in a typewritten manuscript format.

"Oh my goodness."

"What is it?" Martha asked.

Sarah handed her the paper.

Martha read it closely and gasped. "This is the book! Why is it in your mom's boxes?"

"I ... I don't know."

"Who typed this out? Your mom?"

"Your guess is as good as mine. I think ... maybe it could be Mom's typewriter ... "

"Do you still have it?"

"I should. We'll have to look through more boxes in the attic."

Martha grinned. "We'll find it and compare typewriter sample pages, just like on those crime-solving shows."

Sarah laughed, but her laughter slowly shifted into a sigh. Maybe she had been wrong all along and the author was Ruth Drayton after all. This might be the proof, right here.

CHAPTER SIXTEEN

Sarah settled into her stained oak Mission-style rocking chair in the living room, a steaming mug of Annie Harper's chamomile tea next to her on the small circular lampstand, and a bright lamp illuminating the book in her lap. The blustery evening had chilled her, so she had lit a fire in the fireplace. She was only a few pages from the end, so she hoped to finish the book tonight.

When Debby told me about the bombing of the federal courthouse, I admit at first I was shocked. I didn't know what to do. I didn't know what to think. I even wondered if maybe I should march her down to the police station right at that moment.

And I'm ashamed to confess it, but I was also a bit skeptical when she insisted she didn't do it. After all, she'd been there, she'd been seen running away from the scene of the crime.

But I remembered that I knew her, that we were friends. She had trusted me with her confidence.

The pastor said that we're known by our fruit. Well, Debby was accused of making and setting off that bomb, but she didn't do a single violent thing in the entire two years she was in town. She was gentle, kind, compassionate. She loved children and animals and did nice things for them. People couldn't say enough good things about her. This wasn't the fruit of a bomber.

She insisted she was innocent, and so I believed her, because I was her friend. I had known her for two years. I had seen her fruit. She told me about how she hadn't known what was going to happen until it was too late, how she tried to stop Josiah from setting off the bomb. She told me about running away from the building just before it blew up.

I wanted to get help for her. I talked to a town lawyer, to see if there were any legal options. I tried to get her to talk to me more, to see if maybe I could catch some clue that would help prove her innocence.

But there wasn't any proof. And then suddenly the FBI came to town and found her.

The shrill ringing of the telephone startled Sarah. She hesitated, caught up in the book's narrative, but then she remembered she'd left a message on Jenna's answering machine earlier that day.

Sure enough, it was her daughter. "Hi, Mom! Sorry we missed you when you called earlier. The boys are in soccer this season and cell phone reception at the field is non-existent."

"Soccer? Already?"

"They're pretty cute. A bunch of little boys running around like crazy. The coaches are great."

"How do they like it?"

"Thomas is pretty good for his age, actually. Jonathan is still feeling out the whole 'How fast can I run without falling and skinning my knee?' thing, so he doesn't quite get that there's a ball involved too."

Sarah laughed. "As long as they're having fun, right?"

"Oh trust me, they're having fun. It rained a couple of weekends ago and they were told they *have* to play their games in the mud. They thought they'd died and gone to heaven."

In the background, Sarah could hear "Gramma, Gramma."

"Okay, here you go," Jenna said, and then Jonathan's breathy voice sounded in her ear.

"Gramma?"

"Hello, darling. How are you doing?"

"Gramma, I falls down in tha mud! An' run an' run an' run!" Sarah listened closely as Jonathan continued on in his four-year-old semicoherence, until she heard, "An' it goes vroom-vroom. So now I go sleep g'nite."

Sarah was hard-pressed not to split her sides laughing. The twins had started talking quite well rather early, but Thomas and Jonathan had been slower on the language skills. Jonathan always made an effort to talk to her although she understood less than forty percent of what he said, and he had a concise telephone conversational style that consisted of one garbled sentence ending with "So now I go sleep g'nite," even when it was the middle of the day.

There was a ruckus on the other end of the phone, then Thomas said, "Hi, Grandma."

"Hi, sweetie. I heard you're having fun at soccer."

"I wish you had been there, Grandma, 'cuz the goalie gave me the ball 'cuz his name is Chas and he's supernice. But then this guy Roger, he comes running and I think he's going to tackle me 'cuz he's a big bully at school too. So Roger tried to get the ball but I went *zing!* and then did *zing-zang!* and *Watch out!* and I got it so far away from him he had to get on his rocket to the moon to find me."

"Wow. I take it that means you were really fast."

"Grandma, I was extraspecial crispy fast and my feet went *Yabong!* and the ball went *bouncy-bouncy-bouncy.* I didn't get it into the goal but I was sooooooo close and Mommy screamed like a girl. Daddy said she is a girl so that's okay."

"Time for bed," their father David called in the background.

"Okay, good night, Grandma. I'll call you next week after our next game so I can tell you all about it."

"I definitely want to hear all about it. Good night, Thomas."

Jenna came back on the line. "Hi, Mom. So how are things out there?"

"Well, I found a pretty strange book at the library and I've been spending some time looking into it."

"What's strange about it? Are you on a new adventure?"

"I guess you could call it that." She told her about her efforts to find the identity of the book's author, and how she had also been learning more about Debby Neely's character. "And she made the most astonishing quilted dresses I've ever seen...."

"Quilted dresses? No wonder you're so eager about this. Mom, you get more excitement in your life than we do." She laughed.

"I'm sure you get enough excitement from the boys. Your job is going okay?"

Jenna launched into the ups and downs of her newest marketing campaign, punctuated by a story David had told her about a patient of his who brought in his entire family in order to find out if his shovel-shaped incisors were a family trait or not.

"I'll let you go, Mom, I've got to get the kids into bed. Take care! Love you!"

"Love you too."

As she hung up the phone, she paused a moment. *Lord, watch over Jenna, David, Thomas, and Jonathan.* Sarah remembered the prayer her mother had written down for her in the devotional book, and she prayed, *Father, grow Thomas and Jonathan into young men who will bring you glory. Help Jenna and David make decisions that please you. Help their relationship grow in love and communication. In Jesus's Name, Amen.*

She took a sip of her cooled tea before picking up the book. It was about time for bed, and she wanted to finish it tonight.

I was with everyone else at the church when those men came, dressed all smart and wearing big guns. They had the gall to come right after Sunday service, when everyone was outside enjoying the sun. Their fancy cars almost ran over Mrs. Griggs.

Debby had been playing with some of the children on the part of the green right in front of the church, but as soon as she saw the men and the cars, she handed the kids off to their parents. The men surrounded her—it seemed like there were so many of them, all for one small girl.

Debby was so brave. She had told me she didn't want to get me, or anybody else, involved in everything, and that I shouldn't do anything if they came for her. But inside my heart, I told myself I'd fight for her because she was my friend.

But when the moment came, I froze. I couldn't run out in the midst of them and rip their hands from her arms, and try to stop them. I was just one person, and it looked like they'd brought an entire army. They were big and tall and angry-looking, maybe because Debby had evaded them for so long.

So I didn't do anything because I was afraid. I'm ashamed of myself to this day.

When they came for her, she didn't resist. Just stood with her eyes cold and empty. She looked defeated and numb. I tried to get her to look at me, but I think she deliberately didn't look my way.

I try to tell myself that it was inevitable that she would be caught, but it doesn't make me feel any better. I keep thinking I was not a good friend, that I shouldn't have been such a coward. I should have worked harder to try to find proof she was innocent. I should have been more careful in my efforts to aim to help her. Then maybe she wouldn't now be in jail for something she didn't do.

This isn't just a confession, but also a long-lasting record of the truth. This is a reminder of my own guilt and cowardice. It's been gnawing at me, and I needed to get it all out of me. I needed to have something written to remind me so I wouldn't forget.

And that was the end of the book.

Sarah sat in her chair. What an incredible ending to this story. It was almost as if the writer was rushing to get it all out because it was too embarrassing, too shaming.

She understood the author's initial skepticism about Debby's innocence. Sarah was still a bit skeptical herself. Debby had seemed like a nice person, but so far, there was nothing to prove she was innocent, and a few things that made her seem not innocent at all.

Had Josiah, her ex-boyfriend and the witness, had some sort of proof against Debby? There had to have been something more than just people seeing her run away from the explosion and a single witness—an ex-boyfriend, no less—saying she was involved. Why would she have fled from the FBI because of only those two pieces of evidence? Her running away just didn't seem to Sarah like the action of an innocent woman.

Then again, the author had a good point about being known by your fruits. It was in the Bible, and Sarah had seen evidence of this in her own life. Debby's "fruit" seemed to have been compassion for children, friendliness to adults, a hard work ethic at Pleiter's and in her own garment sales. Could Debby really have hidden violent or extremist tendencies for the two years she had been in town? Had everyone been deceived by her?

There was a passage that stood out for Sarah:

I should have been more careful in my efforts to try to help her. Then maybe she wouldn't now be in jail for something she didn't do.

If the writer was somehow at fault for the FBI arriving, Sarah could better understand the remorse that dampened each page.

She could imagine herself as a bystander when Debby was arrested, seeing government officials roll into town. They would have been completely foreign to Maple Hill. And Debby would have been in the center of it all, a young woman who had betrayed the trust of the people who thought they knew her.

Sarah pictured the scene and wondered if she would have stepped forward to say or do something, even if she felt without a shadow of a doubt that Debby was innocent. She couldn't say for sure that she would have done something, and that made her feel a little ashamed. She could understand the author's fear in the situation.

She also knew that the scene of a federal arrest wasn't the place for protests or heroics. It probably would have only made things worse for Debby. The author seemed a little harsh on him- or herself, but she could understand the desire to do something, as well as the fear that could hold one back.

But there had been one key clue she'd picked up on in these last pages—the author had spoken to a lawyer. In contrast to finding a woman whose name began with the letter C and who had gone to the Congregational Church, figuring out who had been a lawyer in Maple Hill in 1962 would be a cakewalk.

Well, assuming you had a son who was a lawyer in Maple Hill.

Early the next morning, Sarah dialed her son at his office.

"Hi, Mom," he said when his legal secretary transferred him over. "What's up?"

"I hope you don't mind, but I want to ask you to do something for me."

"Sure."

"Do you remember that book I'm looking into?"

"Hmm, let me think...you mean the book you couldn't stop talking about at Sunday dinner with us?" he teased.

"You have to admit it's intriguing, and you'll be even more intrigued when I tell you what I discovered."

"Let me guess. Grandpa William's an FBI agent."

"Actually, Grandpa William is the one who had the book bound in 1963," she said.

"What? I was kidding about his being involved in this."

Sarah explained about the trip to the bindery, her visit to her father, and also finding the manuscript.

"Wow, now I can understand why you really want to know who wrote this book."

"I'm hoping you can help me with that," Sarah said. "There are very few people mentioned in the book, but one is a lawyer who was in town in 1962."

"And that's where you call your brilliant detective son." Sarah could hear the smile in his words.

"I don't want to violate any attorney-client confidentiality, but if he knew Debby and can tell me about her or her friends, it would help a lot."

"What year would this be, again?"

"Debbie came to town in 1960 and was arrested in 1962."

"When we moved to Maple Hill, I bought the practice from a lawyer named Joshua Rosenthal. Joshua had started practicing in Maple Hill in the late sixties, so he's not your man, unfortunately. But I can introduce you to him and we can ask who the lawyers were in Maple Hill before he started his practice."

"Thanks. I appreciate your help."

"I've got a free lunch hour today. Do you want me to call him to see if we can come by?"

"If it's not going to put a crunch on your work schedule, or his."

"He's retired, Mom. His only appointment is probably sleeping next to his fishing line out on the lake on his property."

"What a tough life."

"Let me call him to see if he can chat with us today. Can you be at my office around eleven thirty?"

Sarah was actually ten minutes early, and Jason drove them to the outskirts of Maple Hill. They entered a lonely country road that wound between the trees before it meandered in front of a large farmhouse on a vast cleared acre or two of land. A lake stood on the far end of the property with trees surrounding part of it.

Rather than pulling up in front of the farmhouse, Jason drove down a rutted dirt track toward the lake. "I promised Joshua you wouldn't mind talking to him while he's fishing," he said.

The track got progressively worse, until Sarah felt like a shaken can of soda by the time they parked beside the lake. She gratefully got out of the car and stood beside the stream that wound down the rolling hillside to feed the lake. A second stream cut through the field into a forested area to carry the water away.

Joshua Rosenthal had a full head of thick, curly white hair, which looked a little like a Q-tip contrasted with his ultralean frame. He stood at the edge of the lake casting his line and reeling it back, casting it out and reeling it back. The last time he reeled it in, he picked it up between two thin, tanned fingers and shook his head. "Crankbait just isn't working today." He turned and asked Sarah, "What do you think? Crawlers, instead? Or crayfish?"

She figured she had a fifty-fifty chance of getting the answer right. "Crayfish."

He went to work undoing his bait from this line. "Smart woman. You're probably a pro at largemouth bass."

Jason said, "Joshua, this is my mother, Sarah Hart."

Sarah wasn't entirely sure if she'd even seen a largemouth bass, but she smiled at him anyway. "Nice to meet you."

"Joshua Rosenthal. You had some questions for me?" He reached into a tackle box on the ground next to him and pulled out a brown-colored something that looked a little like a gummi worm.

"I'm looking for the names of lawyers who practiced in Maple Hill from 1960 through 1962."

"That's pretty specific."

Sarah waited.

He seemed to have finished tying some complicated knot in his fishing line, and now he cast it way out in the lake. "When I started my practice in 1968, there were two lawyers in Maple Hill. Thing is, one of them hadn't been in good health since he fell and broke his hip in 1960, and he'd been hiring the other lawyer to take any of his clients who needed help. So even though there were technically two lawyers in town, Tom Amsden would be the one to talk to rather than the other lawyer."

"Do you know where he is now?"

"He retired in 1989, but I'm afraid I don't have any contact information for him."

Sarah began mentally sifting through other ways she could find out where Tom Amsden had gone after he retired, but Jason spoke up. "Do you know who his legal secretary was?"

"That's a good idea." Joshua thought a moment. "I don't know off the top of my head, but my wife would. She worked with me, you know."

"I'll give her a call. Thanks." Jason said.

Joshua nodded slowly. He was reeling in this new bait slowly, in very delicate jerks. "Did you have any other questions?"

"No. Thank you so much for your time," Sarah said.

As they walked back to the car, she said to Jason, "Thanks for driving me out here."

"Are you kidding?" He gave her a one-armed hug. "I wouldn't pass up a chance to spend time with my favorite mother."

She laughed. Jason had used that one on her from time to time, ever since eighth grade, when he had asked Sarah who was her favorite child. Sarah had diplomatically, and honestly, said that Jason was her favorite son.

"What are you going to tell the twins when they ask you who your favorite is?" Sarah asked.

"I haven't figured it out yet." He grinned at her as he started the car. "I guess I'll just tell them to ask their grandma."

CHAPTER SEVENTEEN

Later that afternoon, Jason called Sarah with the name and home number of Tom Amsden's legal secretary. Sarah was surprised to discover it was Annie Harper.

But then she realized she should have assumed Annie had had some other career before embarking on her herbal Internet business and her New Age shop downtown, and it was obvious she was very intelligent.

"Hello?"

"Hi Annie, this is Sarah Hart."

"Oh hello. How did you like the chamomile?"

"It's absolutely wonderful," Sarah said. "But my reason for calling is to ask if you have time to talk to me in person today. I wanted to ask you about your old boss, Tom Amsden."

There was a brief pause, then Annie said, "That's fine. Would you be willing to come by my place? I closed the shop early today and I'm working on a few things here."

Sarah jotted down the address and driving directions and headed out. Annie lived just a couple of blocks from downtown in a charming white clapboard house. Just beyond it, the panes of a small greenhouse gleamed dully in the indifferent light from the overcast skies.

The large front garden was filled with different types of plants and flowers. The daffodils were up, and Sarah recognized some potted herbs sitting next to Swiss chard and a rosebush. A blackberry bramble twined itself along the white picket fence, stopping at the wide gate.

What an interesting garden. Sarah picked her way along the path through a plot of what she thought was corn on one side and pansies on the other.

The door was bright red, and after knocking, Sarah couldn't resist peeking at the wide picture windows that faced the garden. They were hung with what looked like colorful silk streamers instead of drapes.

The door opened to reveal a gypsy. Sarah didn't recognize Annie at first. At the store, Sarah had always seen her with her straight, silver-streaked dark hair in a low bun, but now she had let it loose around her shoulders. Sarah knew Annie was close to her own age, and now Sarah could see and envy—just a little—Annie's dark locks. Sarah's own hair, unfortunately, was becoming more gray than blonde.

Annie's pale skin contrasted with a red silk scarf tied around her head that matched her red lipstick, a brighter shade than she used when at her store. She had on a white peasant blouse over a full, dark green velvet skirt, and she was barefoot.

"Come in, come in." Even Annie's voice seemed different. She stepped aside and let Sarah enter her tiny living room, Sarah guessed, although it was unlike any other living room she'd ever seen. Instead of sofas and chairs, there were giant pillows on the floor for people to sit on. The walls were hung with more silk streamers to match the window hangings. There were a few gilded side tables here and there, some holding lamps that had giant fringed shades. Sarah hadn't known what to expect from Annie's home, but it certainly wasn't this.

Annie sank gracefully onto one of the giant pillows, so Sarah joined her on the floor. "Would you like something to drink? I have St. John's wort tea steeping."

"No, thank you," Sarah said.

She sat a bit awkwardly on her pillow. Her legs weren't what they used to be, and sitting cross-legged was hard for her. At the same time, reclining like Annie seemed a bit too casual and rather awkward. She shifted until she found a relatively comfortable seat. "Um...so you used to be Tom Amsden's legal secretary?"

"Yes, I worked for him for nine years."

"Were you with him until he retired?"

"Yes. He had some other woman who had been with him for ages, but then she retired and he hired me. Then after Tom retired, my mother died and left me her house. I had saved up a lot since I'd been living with Mom, so that's when I started my mail order herbal business."

"Do you know where Tom is now?"

"Not exactly. I have a post office box, that's all."

"No telephone number?"

"He detests phones. He only tolerated having one in his law office, and he hated having one in his home when he lived in Maple Hill. He always said that when he retired, he wouldn't have a phone."

"That seems kind of strange."

"Not if you had met him. Tom liked his solitude. He liked talking to people only on his own terms, when he wanted to speak to them. He didn't like people interrupting him."

Sarah asked, "Would you mind giving his mailing address to me? I'd like to contact him."

"He values his privacy, even more so now that he's retired."

"I'd only send him a letter. He doesn't have to respond if he doesn't want to."

"I suppose you're right." She rose easily from the pillow and went to a tiny writing desk in the corner, searching through a drawer.

"When was the last time you heard from him?"

"Oh a long time ago. Maybe a year or two? He mailed me some old depositions to file away for him." She copied the address from an address book and gave the paper to Sarah.

"Thank you," Sarah said. The post office box was in a town she wasn't familiar with.

"Does this have to do with that woman you were searching for?" Annie walked to the far side of the living room to a small cherrywood dining room table. It had elaborately carved legs and molding along the outside edge. On it was a lamp, some pens in a cup, several stacks of books, and a laptop computer. Snugged up close to it was a black ergonomic office chair draped with more silk scarves. A teapot and an Asian-style teacup sat on a corner of the table, and Annie poured herself a cup of her tisane.

"Yes. I think Tom knew her. I just want to ask if he'd be willing to share more about what she was like, who her friends were."

"I don't think he'll answer you, but it's worth a shot," Annie said, sipping her tea.

"What was he like when you worked for him?" Sarah asked.

"He was a good lawyer," she said in an even tone.

Her neutral face intrigued Sarah even more than her strange quirkiness. "He worked primarily with Maple Hill residents?"

Annie nodded. "I think his most famous case was when he fought for justice for some old ladies over a land dispute once."

Annie didn't say anything against Tom, but Sarah got the distinct impression that she hadn't liked her boss very much. The carefully polite way she spoke of him, the short answers...what she didn't say told Sarah even more about Tom than what she did say. Sarah decided to push a little. "So Tom was a good man?"

Annie hesitated for a half a breath, and in that split second, her ruby red lips tightened. "He was a very smart lawyer and he loved what he did." Annie glanced at the desk at the far end of the room. "If you don't have any more questions, I need to get back to work. I have several orders to fill and ship tomorrow."

"Of course." Sarah pushed herself up to her feet. "Thank you so much for your time and for Tom's post office box number."

She walked out onto the front porch. Annie held the door open, and said, "Just a warning. He may not be the same man that he was."

Sarah stared at her, unsure what to say.

"In fact," Annie added, "he might be even worse." She then closed the door.

Sarah blinked at the red door for a second, tempted for a second to knock again and ask what she meant. Then again, the last time Sarah had asked Annie about one of her puzzles, Annie had been equally dramatic, and that had turned out fine.

Annie hadn't exactly gushed about her ex-boss. If he was already an unpleasant character, Sarah didn't know that she'd like to meet him if he was even worse.

CHAPTER EIGHTEEN

arah again called Ivan Hillman. His daughter Alana answered the phone. "Hello?"

"Hi, this is Sarah Hart."

"Oh hi, Sarah. No, he hasn't found the picture yet, although he's been hunting high and low."

In the background, Ivan said, "Hart? Is that Sarah? Give me the phone. Hello, Sarah. Haven't found the picture yet. Didn't realize I had so much stuff."

"I hope you do find it, although if you can't, that's fine too."

"I'd be able to look more if *someone* wouldn't keep trying to make me take naps."

In the background, Sarah heard Alana sigh. "I wouldn't nag about napping if someone didn't stop getting up at four o'clock and needing a nap by noon."

"Did you want me to come over to help—" Sarah said.

"No, no help. Whenever I get help, it just ends up being more of a mess."

His daughter called out, "Dad, no one can make it more of a mess because your photography room looks like a *bomb* has gone off inside it."

Sarah stifled her laughter.

"Give me a few days," Ivan said to Sarah. "I'm close. I can feel it."

"All you're feeling is arthritis, Dad," Alana said.

"There's no hurry," Sarah said.

"No hurry? Of course there's reason to hurry. I'm eighty-five years old. I might pop off tomorrow, and I still have so much I need to do!"

No wonder he got up at 4:00 AM and had to nap at noon. He sounded like he went nonstop for those few hours. "Well, thanks, Ivan."

"Don't thank me yet. I'll get that picture for you." They hung up.

Sarah sat down at her desk and finished composing a very polite letter to Tom Amsden, asking him if he'd be willing to write to her and answer her questions about Debby Neely. She had written several drafts, trying to figure out how to phrase things and what exactly to say.

The author had told Tom about Debby's situation, which meant he might know more about the situation than other people she had talked to. She really hoped he'd respond to her.

She finished a clean copy of the letter, reading it through one more time before she addressed the envelope and stuck a stamp on it, then dropped it off in her mailbox.

This lead on the lawyer was the only one she had now, until Ivan Hillman could find that picture of the choir. Using the picture to jog memories might give her more clues, but everything hinged on whether or not that picture could even be found. Until then, what did she have?

When she was puzzled about a quilt, she always wrote her thoughts out. Why not do so now?

Sarah got out her notebook and a pen, and sat at her desk. She started off by writing about everything she knew so far:

Book donated to library by Mom

Book pages printed on a magazine press owned by Dad's friend

Dad had book bound by bindery

Olive and Dad reluctant to speak about Debby—why?

Debby worked at Pleiter's Handmade Gifts/The Galleria and sold quilted garments there

Debby went to church at the Congregational Church

Debby was shy and/or trying to keep out of notice

Debby was accused of making and setting off a bomb at a federal courthouse that killed a judge and injured several people, but she claims she was innocent. Witnesses put Debby at the scene and ex-boyfriend Josiah says she did it—false witness?

Sarah made a list of what she knew about the author:

Debby's friend

Went to Debby's church

Feels guilty about Debby's arrest

Possibly one of the people mentioned in the book—Debby's landlady, Olive, lawyer

As she scanned her handwritten lines, she suddenly realized there was one unorthodox way to find out more about Debby—her dresses.

A quilt revealed a lot about the quilter's personality and preferences. Whether she was practical or flamboyant, whether she was sentimental or fashionable, how she felt about the person for whom she had made the quilt. If Sarah was lucky enough to see several quilts made by the same person, she could find out about the quilter herself: the types of fabric she tended to choose, the patterns she liked, how neat her stitches were, the kinds of stitches she used, the colors she liked to place next to each other. These variables differed from quilter to quilter. Sarah had already looked at the dress her mother had bought, but there were patterns she might discover if she could see a range of Debby's work. Sarah could find out about Debby's personality, and maybe even figure out what kind of person Debby's close friend— the author of the book—would be.

She dialed The Galleria, and asked to speak to C.J.

"Hello?"

"Hi, C.J., it's Sarah Hart."

"Oh hi, Sarah. I heard from my mother that you got the name of Debby's co-worker."

"Yes, your mom was wonderfully helpful."

"What can I do for you?"

"You mentioned something about how your grandfather never threw anything away?"

C.J. laughed. "He was a notorious packrat. Mom says he drove my grandmother nuts."

"Does the store still have old sales receipts from 1960 through 1962?"

"Yeah, I'm pretty sure it does. What are you looking for?" There was the sound of file cabinet drawers opening.

By the end of this mystery, Sarah would never want to look at another file cabinet. "I'm hoping to find the names of the women who bought the dresses Debby made. Some of her customers might be in town and still have the dresses. I'd like to look at them."

"Yup, here are all the sales receipts, in folders separated by month and year. What months did you want?"

"Spring 1960 to . . . actually, I don't know when in 1962."

"I'll give you January 1960 to December 1962. Sound good?"

"That would be wonderful. Are you sure you don't mind my looking at your store's records?"

"I don't mind at all. The amount Pleiter's made in 1960 isn't exactly a state secret I need to keep. Tell you what. I'm about to leave the store, so I can swing by your house and drop these off for you."

"I'd so appreciate that." She gave him her address, and in fifteen minutes, he was on her front porch and handing her a small box filled with manila folders.

"Have at it." He gave a cheery wave and headed back to his car, which was idling in her driveway.

Sarah certainly did have at it, taking the box to her sewing room and delving into the folders. In those years, Pleiter's gift shop had mostly sold small or handmade items rather than the large art pieces that dominated The Galleria now. Pleiter's had done well in selling hand-tooled leather bags, crocheted and knitted lace doilies and tablecloths, a few quilts, and some mantle clocks.

And every month from June 1960 through April 1962, there were several dresses and later vests sold that had been made by Debby Neely.

The receipts described each one as "quilted dress" or "quilted vest" on the description line. She was delighted to find the purchase receipt for her mother's blue dress. On the receipts, Sarah recognized two different handwritings—one lacy and loopy, the other small but neat.

The dresses secured a rather high price that made Sarah raise her eyebrows. Some of the dresses had been custom ordered, it seemed, for throughout 1961, some of the receipts would give a name, like one from May that said "green quilted dress for Imogene Smythe."

The name gave Sarah pause. She couldn't remember the maiden name of her neighbor Imogene Dowling, but this might be the same woman.

She recognized several names as belonging to women from church, and she hadn't dreamed that so many of Debby's customers would still be here in town. Sarah was anxious to call these women to see if they still had Debby's dresses.

The first thing Sarah did was make a list of the women who had bought Debby's garments, what each of them had bought, and the date on the receipt. Then she started looking up names and telephone numbers in the phone book.

For some names, the last name was listed in the phone book but with a different first name or a different first initial. Sarah wrote down the number and the different name so she could call, just in case the garment had been passed down to a child or in-law.

She couldn't find listings for a few other names in the telephone book at all. Several may have been tourists. She had also expected that some must have married or moved away by now.

Armed with the list, she picked up her telephone and started her cold calls.

It was easier than she had expected. Most of the women whose names she had found in the telephone book were more than happy to talk to her and promised to look for their dresses. Several knew where their garments were stored because they had been carefully preserved to protect the exquisite stitching.

For the customers whose last names but not first names she had found in the phone book, she had a few "wrong number" calls. But she was also gratified to find a few women who were daughters or granddaughters of the women who had originally bought Debby's dresses. They were eager to ask their parent or look for the garment in their attics and storerooms. Sarah left her telephone number with each woman she spoke to, and they all promised to call her if they found the dress so that she could come over to look at it.

While she was heating up some soup for supper, she called Martha and updated her on her visit with Annie and about Debby's dresses.

"How neat! When are you going to go see the dresses?"

"Several women called me back while I was still going down the list. I have two appointments tomorrow to see Debby's dresses, and one more on Sunday."

"Well, I'm going with you. I'd love to see them too."

"Come on over for breakfast tomorrow, then."

She said goodbye to Martha, but as soon as she hung up, the phone rang again. "Hello?"

"Sarah? It's Imogene Dowling."

"Thanks for calling me back, Imogene. Did Elmer give you my message?"

"About the dress? Yes, it was in the back of the spare closet, covered with a linen sheet. Do you want to come over right now to look at it?"

"I'd love to." Sarah walked next door.

Imogene stood holding the front door open, and the kitchen light behind her turned her ash-blonde curls golden. "Hi." Imogene was a lovely, round woman who always gave terrific, warm, strong hugs—she gave Sarah one now. "I hadn't even thought of that dress in so long. It brought back memories to see it again."

"When I saw your name on the receipt, I wasn't sure if it was you because I couldn't remember your last name before you married Elmer."

Imogene nodded. "Smythe." She led them into the living room, where she had cleared off the coffee table and laid the dress out.

It was a rich plum color. The entire dress had been created from strips of varying shades of purple and bluish burgundy, making the surface shimmer in the lamplight.

"Look at all the different fabrics she used," Sarah breathed. "I'm counting at least fifteen different ones."

Just like her mother's dress, the strips on Imogene's dress had been cut and shaped to the wearer's curves, smoothing out at the bustline and nipping in at the waist. Sarah wasn't a dressmaker, but she could tell that the construction was complicated and graceful. The skirt had larger strips that flared out slightly to create a lovely drape. On the top, the seamed edges of the pieces of fabric were flowing and straight, nothing crooked or out of line. The quilt stitching was delicate and embroiderylike, enhancing the graceful lines.

With Imogene's permission, she gently turned the garment inside out to look at the quilting stitches on the inside. Also like her mother's dress, the inside stitches weren't as neat as the outside stitches.

"Would you look at that," Imogene said, peering at the fabric. Being very skilled at embroidery herself, Imogene recognized the odd stitches. "I've never noticed that before." She actually gathered a portion of the skirt so she could peer closer at it. "My goodness. This is absurd. But the stitches on the outside are perfectly fine." For some stitches, the needle had cut into the fabrics at an angle rather than piercing straight down, and some of the running stitches had actually been done out of order.

"Maybe it was just her style," Sarah said. "Some quilters have odd ways of going about making a quilt, but the finished object is the same as any other quilter's. Still, Debby's stitches are a bit eccentric."

"Well, she was rather quiet," Imogene said. "She had the sort of personality that wouldn't say boo to a mouse. At least, that's the impression I got whenever I spoke to her."

"Did you know her well?"

"I spoke to her sometimes. She liked having her lunch out on the village green, and I'd see her there. That's how I got my dress," she said. "My cousin Rosemary had just snatched up a dress that Debby had put out in the store that day, and I saw Debby at lunch. I asked her if she'd make a dress on commission. The other one had been a little too short for me, anyway. It made Rosemary so mad because the dress was a little short for her too, but mine fit like a glove."

Sarah had brought her digital camera with her, and so, after asking permission, she spread out the fabric in certain places and she took lots of pictures.

"You can borrow it, if you like," Imogene offered.

"You don't mind?"

"Of course I don't mind. I know where you live." She winked.

With the dress rewrapped in its sheet and gently cradled in her arms, Sarah headed home. She put the dress in her sewing room while reheating her cold soup. She finally sat down to her meal with a contented sigh.

When she got more dresses—or more pictures of dresses—she would look at all of them side by side and search for any patterns she could see. She couldn't help grinning. This weekend was going to be fun.

CHAPTER NINETEEN

That weekend, Sarah actually did work Martha rather hard. On Saturday morning, her phone started ringing at 7:30 AM, and she ended up having six appointments to see Debby's dresses on Saturday, with three appointments set for Sunday.

At the first appointment, the owner was more than happy to let Sarah borrow the dress to look over at her leisure. However, some of the other women weren't so accommodating.

Eloise Dubois had been appalled that Sarah hadn't intended to use latex gloves before touching her pale pink dress. Eloise also insisted on masks for all of them—including herself—making Sarah think of nurses at the hospital. However, the mask did filter out some of the overpowering bleach smell from the freshly cleaned kitchen floor, and the pungent glass cleaner that Eloise had apparently just used on the windows and the crystal chandeliers.

Eloise flinched every time Sarah touched her dress, which had been laid out on the dining room table. The woman stood hovering behind Sarah, her hands half-raised as if poised to stop her at any moment.

"May I turn the dress inside out?" Sarah asked her.

"Oh don't do that!" Eloise said. "It might tear."

"Mrs. Dubois, I restore antique quilts, and I'm very familiar with fragile fabrics. I can assure you that it won't damage the dress to turn it inside out. I'll be very careful."

She grudgingly allowed Sarah to look on the inside, though she winced every time Sarah moved a pink fold. As expected, the inside stitches were irregular like the stitches on her mother's dress.

When Sarah brought out her camera, Eloise quickly stepped between her and the dress. "You're not going to take pictures, are you?" She asked.

"Yes, I was. You don't mind, do you?"

"Well . . . well, won't the flash damage the dress?"

"Not at all." Sarah glanced at the dining room windows, which were covered by heavy drapes that had been pulled tightly shut. "But I could take pictures just using natural sunlight, if you'd like."

"That would be even worse!" Eloise said.

"Oh but Eloise," Martha chimed in, her voice sweeter than honey, "sunlight is a natural disinfectant. And who knows what kinds of germs can fester when a dress has been tucked away for so long."

"Germs?"

"Nothing a little sunlight won't cure." Martha tugged the drapes open.

Eloise still fluttered nervously as Sarah took her pictures, and Sarah didn't even bother to ask her if she'd let her borrow the dress for further study.

"I had an aunt like that," Martha said as they headed to Sarah's car. "She wouldn't visit her son's horse stables. It gave her heart palpitations."

Sarah was again glad for Martha's presence at the next appointment, because Gloria Hampshire peppered Sarah with questions. Sarah thought it was rude to continue staring at the dress when answering Gloria's questions, so she had to glance up every time Gloria asked her something. It made it difficult for her to study the stitches.

"My aunt bought this dress," Gloria said. "When she died, you wouldn't believe how my sister and I fought over who would get it. Do you have a sister?"

"No, I don't."

"Our husbands finally made us draw straws. I got the dress but she got the Royal Albert tea set. You're married?"

Sarah dragged her eyes from a particularly interesting line of stitches. "Widowed."

"Oh that's too bad. What was your husband like?"

"Gerry was a very kind man. He was an accountant, but he also liked doing woodworking." Then it occurred to her that she could turn the tables. "What's your husband like?"

While Gloria chatted about her husband, Sarah searched for that interesting line of stitches again. She had just found it when Gloria said, "So your husband was an accountant? He did investments? Taxes?"

Sarah was about to answer her when Martha broke in. "Gloria, you have such interesting chickens all over your living room." She gestured to the chicken motif that dominated the tiny room, from the chickens prancing on the wallpaper border to the chicken figurines on the mantelpiece. "Where did you get them all?"

Sarah had never been more grateful to her friend. Martha plied Gloria with questions about each porcelain chicken figurine, of which there were sixty-five in the room, the chicken paintings on the wall, the chicken pillows on the sofa, and the chicken tea set. Martha asked Gloria about the chicken coasters and the chicken afghans even while she helped Sarah by holding the dress as she took pictures.

Sarah managed to slip in a question. "Would you let us borrow your dress for a little while?"

"I don't know." Gloria said. "It took so much to get it from my sister, I'd have a hard time giving it up for even a little while."

"Sarah will take good care of it," Martha replied. "She restores antique quilts, you know, and she'll return it to you safe and sound."

"Well, if that's the case, then go right ahead. So you restore—"

"Gloria!" Martha said. "Is that chicken design on those place mats exactly the same as the one on your throw pillows?"

After Gloria told them how she got the place mats, Sarah said, "Thank you for letting us look at the dress and your lovely house." They headed toward the door.

"Oh anytime." Gloria beamed, waving to them from her doorway. "It's so nice to have company."

On Monday, Sarah was surprised by a knock at the front door just as she was making morning coffee.

Janet Dean stood on her front porch. "Hello, Sarah. I hope you don't mind my dropping in this way."

"Not at all. Come on in. Coffee?"

"Is it the real stuff or decaf?"

"The real stuff."

"Then pour me a big mug and don't tell Tiffany," Janet said.

They sat in the living room, and Janet sniffed the aroma of the coffee for a moment before taking a sip. "Mmm."

Sarah smiled. "I hope I won't get in trouble with Tiffany. She's my father's nurse too, you know."

"It'll be our secret," Janet said. "I came by because I wanted to give you this." She handed her a soft parcel wrapped carefully in brown paper and tied with string.

It was light, and obviously some sort of fabic. "Thank you. What is it?"

"Open it and find out."

Sarah found a pair of scissors and carefully snipped the string tying the parcel together. She pushed aside the paper.

Inside, cloaked in tissue paper, was an amethyst-colored vest, quilted from scraps of different purple-patterned fabrics. Sarah caught her breath. "You bought this from Debby Neely?"

"About a month before she was arrested. By the time I bought this, she had stopped making dresses—I suppose they took her too long, and vests are smaller and faster. But the workmanship is still beautiful, isn't it?"

"Most definitely." Sarah smoothed the folds of the vest in her lap.

"I heard from people at church that you've been looking at all of Debby's dresses—well, the ones that people have been able to find." Janet suddenly smiled. "It's probably caused a rash of spring cleaning all over Maple Hill."

But as Sarah glanced at the vest, she realized she didn't remember seeing the receipt for it. "Did you buy this through Pleiter's?" she asked Janet.

"No. I wasn't supposed to tell anyone, but Debby did this one for me for a reduced price, so she didn't sell it to me through the store."

"That was nice of her." Janet's missing purchase receipt reminded her of something Olive had said the first time she spoke to her about Debby. "Do you happen to know a woman named Myra Johnson?"

"Of course. Myra goes to our church. Why?"

"Olive Cavanaugh mentioned her name to me once, saying that Myra was the one who got Debby to start selling her dresses at Pleiter's."

"I believe that. Myra had one of the first dresses Debby made."

"She did?" Sarah asked. There wasn't a purchase receipt for Myra either.

"It was red, and it was amazing."

"Do you know if Myra was close to Debby?"

Janet paused to think. "Well, Myra's the type of person who's friendly with everyone. I really couldn't say. But I can give you her phone number, if you want to chat with her. She uses a walker now and has to rely on her granddaughter to help her around, but she's fun to talk to."

Sarah got a chance to speak to Myra the very next day. Myra and her granddaughter Missy offered to drive to Sarah's house, with Myra's dress.

"Hello," Sarah called as they got out of the car. "Thank you so much for coming. I wouldn't have minded going to your home, though."

"It's actually good for Grandma." Missy unfolded Myra's walker. "Otherwise, she doesn't get out much."

Missy helped her grandmother up the steps into the house and brought the walker in after settling her in a chair in the living room.

"I heard from several women at church on Sunday that you had come by to look at Debby's dresses," Myra said in a soft, spidery voice. Her hazel eyes were so light, they looked like white gold.

"Yes, I was grateful the owners let me look at them. The dresses are beautiful." Sarah offered refreshments, which Myra and Missy declined.

"I overheard one of them talking to Grandma," Missy said. "They were discussing their dresses and describing them. But I think Grandma's is still the most beautiful. See for yourself." She handed Sarah the paper grocery bag she had been carrying.

Sarah removed the tissue-wrapped object inside and suddenly had to remind herself to breathe. The tissue had drifted apart to reveal the most magnificent quilted dress she had yet seen. It shimmered like a ruby, made of fabric pieces in shades that ranged from wine-colored burgundy to crimson rose to dark pink. The quilting stitches were more like embroidery, much more detailed and complex than on any of the other dresses.

"This is . . . ," Sarah couldn't find words to describe it. "It's amazing."

Missy and Myra were grinning with identical smiles. Sarah could see how Myra would have looked almost exactly like Missy at her age.

"I hadn't even remembered I had bought it," Myra said. "My memory's just not what it was. But I'm pretty sure I was the first person to buy a dress from Debby."

"How do you know?" Sarah asked.

"I bought this from her before she started selling her dresses at Pleiter's. I remember when I ordered it from her. She was in the village green sitting on a bench, and she was wearing this pretty green dress. I asked her about it, and she said she had made it. I asked her how much she'd charge if she made me one in red."

"It's more than just red," Sarah said. "It's like stained glass."

"I was astounded," Myra said. "It took her a little longer than she thought at first it would. I remember her apologizing for that."

"Did you ever wear it?" Sarah asked.

Myra's eyes glowed as she cast back in her memory. "Oh my, yes. I wore it to a Christmas party, and a Valentine's Day dance, and let me tell you, I definitely turned heads. But then I got pregnant and gained weight, and never fit into it again."

"Grandma was smaller than me," Missy said, "but I'm going to try to lose a little weight so I can fit into the dress for my husband's annual Christmas party. It's always at a nice restaurant in the city somewhere."

"You'll be a hit." Sarah ran a hand over the seams between the quilted pieces. There must have been more than twenty different fabrics used for this dress.

"What exactly are you looking for when you look at the dresses?" Missy asked.

"I'll show you." Sarah carefully turned the dress inside out to reveal the underside of the quilted pieces. She was surprised to find that the stitches were neater than on any of the other dresses. There were a few places where the stitches were a bit irregular, but there were other places where the stitches were almost normal—almost, but not quite.

"I do some embroidery myself," Missy said. "Those kits I buy at the craft store. I understand a little bit about it."

"Oh good. You'll probably see what I'm talking about." She pointed to a series of stitches. "Do you see how the thread seems to enter the fabric at a strange angle?"

"Yes, rather than going straight through." Missy peered closer. "And she sewed some of the stitches out of order too, rather than one after another in a line. That just isn't done in embroidery. How odd."

"Not all the stitches are that bad." Sarah pointed out a section where the stitches were a bit neater. "Although you can see that the stitching is still not quite what you'd expect from a quilter."

"I saw the other dresses Debby sold at Pleiter's," Myra said. "I remember thinking none of them were as pretty as my dress. I was so sad when I couldn't wear it anymore."

Sarah turned the dress right side out again to look at the exquisite patterns Debby had quilted into the fabric. In the other dresses, the combination of different fabrics had been the most beautiful aspect of the garments, but here, Debby had added more complex designs when she quilted the two layers together. It was masterly.

"None of the other dresses are as exquisitely made as this one," Sarah said. "This is definitely the most beautiful out of them all. And it has the neatest stitches too."

Then she realized something she hadn't thought of before. "You mentioned this was the first dress Debby made?" she asked Myra.

"She hadn't started selling anything at Pleiter's yet. Only after she made my dress did she start selling them in the store."

"And all the dresses I saw were sold at Pleiter's...*after* this one. I can't believe I didn't think of it."

"Think of what?" Missy asked.

"I haven't been paying attention to *when* each dress was made. Debby fashioned garments over a two-year period in Maple Hill, and it's obvious that on this dress her stitching isn't as uneven as on the dress my mother bought, or on Janet's vest, and they purchased those items only a few months before Debby was arrested."

"So her stitching may have started off better...," Missy said.

"But then got worse," Sarah finished. "I'll have to map out when each dress was made and look at the stitching again."

"You're welcome to borrow this," Myra said.

"Thank you so much. I'll take good care of it."

"It sounds like quite the intricate mystery."

Sarah traced an embroidered leaf on the red fabric. "And you have just helped me discover a crucial pattern."

CHAPTER TWENTY

When Sarah stopped in at the Wild Goose Chase fabric shop to speak to her good friend Vanessa Sawyer, she couldn't wait to tell her all about the dresses.

As she entered the shop, Sarah's eye automatically went to the mural running around the store just below the high ceiling, picking out the lone gosling trying to keep up with the flock of Canadian geese.

"Sarah!" Vanessa looked up from the front counter, where she had been plugging in numbers on a calculator.

"I don't want to interrupt you," Sarah said.

"Oh, I'm just calculating how many yards I need for a new skirt. How have you been? I wondered if you'd been abducted by aliens."

Sarah laughed. "What?"

"Well, I couldn't think of any other reason you haven't been in my shop for more than two weeks."

"I have so much to tell you." Sarah told her all about the book, Debby Neely, and the dresses. As she described them to Vanessa, the petite woman was practically drooling.

"I have got to look at these dresses." Vanessa said. "Let me arrange for babysitting for the kids, and I'll come over tonight after the store closes!"

"Sounds great."

Vanessa arrived at Sarah's house just as she and Chloe were finishing dinner. Sarah had cooked for Chloe this time—she'd had a small tater tot casserole in the freezer, and after popping it in the oven, she'd made a big salad.

"Hello," Vanessa called out as she simultaneously knocked and entered the house.

"In here," Sarah called from the kitchen table.

"Hi, Chloe. How's your leg doing?" Vanessa and Chloe had bonded over their love for spinning wool. Vanessa sold wool roving at the Wild Goose Chase, although it hadn't quite taken off yet.

They chatted for a bit, but then Chloe went upstairs to get some work done on her computer.

"Now where are those dresses?" Vanessa asked, and Sarah led the way to her sewing room.

On her quilting frame, she had laid out the dresses. She had also downloaded the pictures from her camera onto her computer so they could see pictures of the dresses she hadn't been able to borrow. She and Vanessa pored over the dresses, sometimes with magnifying glasses to see the stitches. For the digital pictures, they were able to zoom in to see the details. They "oohed" and "aahed" over the colors and patterns, turning the dresses this way and that.

At last, Vanessa sat back, shaking her head. "I just don't understand why the stitches are so irregular inside the dresses."

"If she had been filling orders and trying to hurry, the stitches would have been sloppy on the outside as well as the inside. But the outside stitches are meticulous," Sarah said.

"Maybe she had inconsistent lighting for her work?"

"Then the stitches would be neater in some areas and irregular in others, depending on the type of light she had."

"I can't believe she didn't do some of her needlework while minding the store," Vanessa said. "And the counter in The Galleria is near the front of the store, right by those large picture windows. The light in there is fine even without electrical lights."

"I agree."

"I can see how the stitching deteriorates the longer she was in Maple Hill." Vanessa paused at a picture on the computer screen and scrolled down so she could see the line of stitching. "Do you think she had some type of trouble with her vision?"

"If that were true, wouldn't she have produced irregular stitches on the outside as well as the inside? And she was only nineteen or twenty years old at the time. That seems too young to have any problem with her sight that glasses couldn't correct."

Vanessa shrugged. "I suppose you could ask a doctor, but there are so many possibilities of what could have been wrong."

"Even then we wouldn't know for sure."

"I guess the only way to find the truth is to find Debby Neely," Vanessa said.

"I've looked for her online and I simply can't find her. I can't find anything about the bombing itself. And I still have no idea which prison she was sent to. I even wonder if Debby Neely was this woman's real name."

The soft thump of Chloe's crutches outside the sewing room made Sarah look up. Chloe held out an envelope to her. "When the mail came today, I grabbed mine, but I accidentally took this with it."

"Thanks, Chloe." Sarah absently took the letter and set it on her desk.

"I better go," Vanessa said, rising. "Tomorrow's another school day. The kids are already counting down the days until summer. I'm sorry I wasn't much help, but I'm so glad you let me see Debby's beautiful work."

"You were a lot of help. You always are. It was so nice to talk this out with someone who understands quilting and garment design."

Vanessa patted the gold-colored dress laid out in front of her one last time and helped Sarah put the dresses carefully away, then headed home.

After Vanessa left, Sarah went back into her sewing room to turn off the gooseneck lamp when she remembered the envelope Chloe had given to her.

It was the one she'd sent to Tom Amsden, but it had been returned to her. The postmaster had stamped "Return to Sender" next to Tom's address. There was no other explanation.

Had he passed away? Annie had said that she hadn't heard from him anytime recently. Or maybe he had simply decided to give up his post office box, for whatever reason. She sighed. She had counted on getting in touch with him.

She was about to throw the envelope away when something on the back seemed odd. Sarah peered at it.

The edges of the flap were uneven and rough. When she had sealed the envelope, the flap had lain smooth against the paper. Now the edges were bumpy and hard to the touch.

It had been glued shut.

She peered closer at the edge of the flap. There were some fuzzy spots where it looked like the flap had been torn open. Someone had opened it and then resealed it.

Sarah got a letter opener and carefully slit the top of the envelope. She pulled out just her letter, nothing more. But suspicious now, she opened the letter and studied the paper closely. There was what looked like a few drops of coffee splattered in a fine mist on the top half of the first page, and then a faint smudge mark on the right edge of the second page.

Someone had read her letter and then sent it back.

No, she was jumping to conclusions. Maybe someone else had gotten the letter, opened it, realized it wasn't for him, and had it sent back. She had done that by accident with mail meant for her neighbors that was mistakenly put in her box.

Sarah laid the letter next to the envelope on the coffee table. She wasn't sure what to do next. If a stranger had mistakenly read this, she had hit another dead end. But she didn't think that's what had happened. She was more and more certain that Tom Amsden had received the letter and read it, and he obviously didn't want to talk to her.

She wanted to go visit him. A part of her felt that would be too pushy. But another part of her was determined to find out the truth about Debby Neely and who the author of the book was. After all, the author had involved both her parents in writing that book. And she wanted to know why Tom would open the letter and then return it.

No, she'd forgotten—she had only a post office box number, not a house number. She couldn't just drive into Drysdale and go knocking from door to door. She didn't even know where Drysdale was—if it was within driving distance or not.

Curious, she went to her computer and searched for Drysdale. It was less than two hours away by car, apparently a small mountain town. The online map showed it to be in a forested area, with a few lakes and some nice hiking trails.

And a sheep farm. Babette Woolery.

Sarah stared at that name for a few seconds as an idea sparked in her mind. She grabbed the envelope and headed upstairs.

At her knock, Chloe said, "Come in." The girl had her leg propped up and was doing work on her laptop.

"Got all your work done?" Sarah asked.

"No matter how much I get done, my uncle just gives me more, so technically, I'll *never* get my work done." She rolled her eyes, but it was followed by a smile. "What can I do for you?"

"Are you familiar with Babette Woolery?"

"Of course. Great farmers. Very clean pastures. I bought two sheep from them. Why?"

"Did you visit Drysdale too?"

"Sure. It's right next door, plus it's a really small town, barely a hundred people."

"Great." Sarah showed her the envelope and explained about it.

"I can't believe that. It's so rude."

"My problem is that I don't know for certain if Tom still lives there, if he's moved away, or if he's deliberately ignoring me. So I'm wondering if you could do me a favor. Do you think you could talk to that sheep farmer and find out if Tom's in the area?"

Chloe gave her a broad grin. "I can do better than that. I can find out where he lives."

CHAPTER TWENTY-ONE

C hloe's injured leg prevented her from making the car ride to Drysdale, but she had called the farmer who ran Babette Woolery and gotten precise directions to Tom Amsden's house, which she'd given to Sarah. The farmer had mentioned seeing Tom at the post office only a week before, which meant they could rule out the possibility that Tom had passed away.

"For all we know, Tom never got the letter, so you're simply coming by to talk to him in person instead," Martha said as she drove them down a country lane. They were almost to Drysdale.

"You make it sound so reasonable," Sarah said. "I hope we're not intruding."

"You're not."

"I wish I knew why he returned the letter."

Martha turned left at a large oak tree, following the sheep farmer's instructions. The lane was gravel and very rough, and the minivan bounced around so much that Martha had to slow the car to a crawl. They passed more oak trees, these overgrown with mistletoe and nestled among three-foot-tall weeds. After a few more yards, they came in sight of a house.

It was a typical two-story farmhouse, but it seemed to sag in the dim afternoon light. Gray white paint peeled off in ribbons from the exterior walls, and the roof was missing shingles. Grime coated the windows while the wraparound porch railing was missing some rails, making it look like a gap-toothed leer. A beat-up Ford pickup truck stood next to the short flight of crooked steps leading up to the porch and the front door.

They parked and got out of the car. "I wonder if we got the directions wrong," Martha said. "It looks like nobody lives here."

"Someone does." Sarah pointed to the truck. "The registration sticker is current, and there aren't any weeds growing up around the tires." If the truck wasn't being used, it would have been engulfed in weeds, like the three-foot-tall monsters they'd seen encircling the oak trees when they turned into the lane.

They walked up to the front door, avoiding a step that had broken down the center, and Sarah knocked on the door. From inside came the faint sound of a game show from a television set.

No answer. Sarah knocked again, louder and longer. Still no answer. "Maybe he's not home."

"He's home." Martha stepped forward and rapped hard on the door, and she kept pounding until they heard footsteps approaching.

"Go away," snapped an irate voice just as the door opened. An old man about the same age as Sarah's father glowered at them with eyes still piercing and dark despite his age. His face was a mass of vertical lines and shapes— deep grooves ran down the sides of his mouth, his narrow nose was decidedly hooked, and deep furrows ran between his brows. There were wisps of white around the sides of his pointy bald head. He reminded Sarah of a picture of Ebenezer Scrooge from one of her kids' children's books.

"I already sent you a check," he said.

"Tom Amsden?" she asked.

"Yes, yes," he said. "You people came last week already to hit me up for money. Leave me alone." He started to close the door on them, but Martha wedged her foot between the door and the frame.

"I'm not with any group. My name is Sarah Hart, and I wrote you a letter last week."

The door remained mostly closed. "I told you I didn't want to talk to you."

"Actually," Martha said, "you didn't. You just returned the letter."

"That's not obvious enough?"

"I only have a few questions," Sarah said. "It won't take too much of your time."

"I don't want to give you a few minutes," Tom replied.

"We could stand here and knock on your door all day," Martha said.

The mere suggestion made Tom crack the door open a little wider.

"But if you give us five minutes, then we promise we won't bother you ever again," Martha added with a smile.

Tom hesitated, obviously weighing the value of his time right now versus being annoyed by them in the future. "Fine. What do you want to know?" He propped himself up against the door frame without asking them in.

Which was fine with Sarah. She didn't want to see the state of the interior of the house if it was anything like the outside. "Did you know Debby Neely?"

"Yes, yes, the little degenerate."

"Oh my. You didn't like her?"

"It didn't matter if I liked her or not. She was a fugitive from the law, taking refuge among good people, taking advantage of them."

This was a side of Debby that Sarah hadn't heard before. "She was guilty, then, of the crime she was arrested for?"

"Of course she was guilty. The FBI knew exactly what they were doing. They don't let people blow up courthouses and then get away with it."

"But she said she was innocent," Martha said.

"There was a witness who saw her there." Tom said. "You can't refute a witness."

Sarah believed you could refute a witness, but Tom seemed to be very black-and-white. There was no in between for him.

"Did you talk to the witness?" Martha asked.

"Of course not. An outsider can't walk up and speak to a witness."

"Then how do you know what he saw?"

"Because the FBI told me when I called them," he said.

There was a moment when Sarah's heart skipped a beat, then resumed. "You called the FBI?"

"I did my civic duty," he said. "More than I can say for other people."

"What other—"

"I'm done talking to you. I gave you a few minutes."

"But Debby—" Martha said, but Tom cut her off.

"You're wasting your time. That murderer was guilty." He slammed the door shut in their faces.

Sarah stood staring at it in shock for a moment, then shook her head. She told Martha, "Let's go."

As they drove home, Sarah said, "That was not exactly what I expected. But it was curious. He almost looked ashamed when he said he had called the FBI on Debby."

"You thought so?" Martha asked. "He seemed pretty proud of 'doing his civic duty.'"

"He was so legalistic," Sarah said. "He talked about her being a fugitive from the law, and he put complete trust in that one witness—I'm assuming he means Josiah."

"He had no way of knowing whether that witness was telling the truth."

"Exactly. But what if, deep inside, he wondered if maybe she wasn't guilty? But he couldn't see past his right-or-wrong tendencies, so he turned her in."

"And then he wrote the book, to confess that he believed she was innocent? I don't know if I buy that," Martha said.

"Well I do think he's hiding something."

"I do too," Martha said.

They were interrupted when Sarah's cell phone rang. Alana Marquez's name on the caller ID was like an instant boost to Sarah's spirits. "Hi, Alana."

"Dad found the picture."

"That's wonderful!"

"He also found the negative and is developing a couple more copies, but he said he wants you to have the one he found. Do you want to come by to pick it up?"

"I would love to. I'm heading back to Maple Hill now, so in two hours?"

"Sure thing." Alana gave Sarah directions to the house and hung up.

Ivan's house was in an older section of Maple Hill, where a lot of the houses were made of bricks in muted shades. Ivan's home had two floors, and basement windows peeked out at the foot of the house, facing the street.

Sarah knocked on the door, which was a freshly painted spring green color. Alana answered, running her fingers through her ash brown hair to push it back from her face. After Sarah introduced Martha, Alana gave them a friendly smile. "Come on in."

Ivan Hillman sat in an overstuffed recliner in the living room. He was a bag of bones with a wide, toothy grin that mirrored his daughter's more feminine version. "Thought I'd never find it, did ya?" He handed her a black-and-white photograph.

"I had complete faith in you," Sarah said.

The photo was of a group of perhaps thirty people, standing in the choir area behind the podium in the Congregational Church. Most of the choir looked to be in their early twenties. They smiled at the camera, arrayed in festive dresses and suits rather than choir robes, with a few sporting tinsel necklaces or sprigs of mistletoe in their hair or on their lapels.

"Which one is Debby Neely?" Sarah asked.

Ivan shrugged. "Beats me if I know. I asked Janet Dean to come over, since she's the one who told you about the picture. She should be here soon."

Sarah and Martha studied the picture, searching the faces of the choir members. Sarah saw one cheerful face and immediately recognized a much younger Janet, not far out of her teens. She stood next to a timid-looking young man who looked like a stick with big ears and bony shoulders. Next to him was a tall thin woman with a narrow nose and pointed chin, but her eyes were soft and warm.

On the row behind them were some older women and a small young woman with a heart-shaped face and olive-tinted skin. She had a small smile and clear eyes. Something about her made Sarah think she was Debby, but her memory of Debby's face was so hazy, she couldn't be sure. "Do you think that's Debby?" she asked Martha.

Martha shook her head. "I don't remember Debby well enough to say for certain."

Before they knew it, there was a knock at the door and Alana opened it for Janet, who sat down on the red and brown striped couch and eagerly reached for the picture Sarah held out to her. Sarah and Martha sat on either side of Janet.

"Which one is Debby?" Martha asked, unable to contain her excitement.

Janet pointed to the young woman with the heart-shaped face and clear eyes. Sarah studied her image. It was hard to believe she was the murderer Tom Amsden had accused her of being.

Janet squinted at the photo and brought it closer to her face. "Ivan, you need to learn to focus better. Everyone's blurry."

"It's your eyesight, not my photography," Ivan said.

"Oh you." Janet ran her finger across each choir member. "There's Dale, I had forgotten how skinny he was. Lorna Bond, Lew Columbia, Francis Corriedale...they've all passed away," she said sadly. "Oh." Her finger paused on the thin young woman. "I think that's Carolyn Amsden."

Amsden?

And Carolyn with a C?

Janet brought the photo closer. "It's hard to tell, but I think it is. I had forgotten about Carolyn." She smiled at Sarah. "I forget a lot these days."

"Don't we all," Sarah said. "Who's Carolyn?"

"She and Debby were friends. At least, I think they were. I saw them together a lot after church, and Debby didn't spend much time with anyone else that I could see."

"Is she related to Tom Amsden, the lawyer?"

"Yes, poor girl."

Sarah was tempted to ask why Janet had such sympathy for Tom's daughter, but after having met the man herself, she assumed he must have made a similar impression on others too.

"Do you know where Carolyn is now?"

"In Arizona, I think. She became an airline stewardess. We thought she was so glamorous, traveling everywhere. She married a businessman she met in Phoenix."

"Do you remember her married name?"

Janet stared at Carolyn's face in the photo as if the image would help the name appear. "I'm sorry," she said finally.

Sarah knew she'd have some work ahead of her to find Carolyn Amsden now that she was married. But it would be a lot easier than finding a woman whose first name began with a C.

And with God, everything was possible. She was trying to rely too much on herself.

Lord, please help me find Carolyn. I know you can do it, even though I can't.

And then, she wasn't sure why, but she added, *I'll go where you lead me.*

CHAPTER TWENTY-TWO

T hanks so much for watching the girls, Sarah,"
Maggie said as the twins and their classmate Zoe
filed into Sarah's house. Jason and Maggie followed
but kept their coats on.

"I love any excuse to spend time with my granddaughters," Sarah said.

Zoe cleared her throat and grinned.

"And their friends," Sarah added. "You two enjoy your
date night."

"Don't get into any trouble we would get into," Amy said.

Jason laughed. "Is Grandma's house still going to be
standing when we get back?"

"Dad," Audrey said, "we're almost thirteen, not three.
We've gotten past the 'burning down the house' phase."

"Speak for yourself." Amy gave a grin.

Sarah and the three girls waved good-bye to Maggie and
Jason and closed the door.

The twins had brought the project they had been working on with Zoe, a bridge they were designing themselves, constructed of toothpicks and school glue. They worked on it around Sarah's dining room table, while she sat in her sewing room and kept half an eye on them.

It was a blustery night. The temperature had dropped quite suddenly, and the Queen Anne house creaked in the wind. Stray drafts whistled around them from time to time, but the girls were oblivious as they worked on their bridge. It was halfway done, but they had to be careful they didn't ruin what they had already constructed.

Sarah sat in front of her computer trying to find Carolyn Amsden. She tried social networking sites, and she scrolled through pages and pages of results from doing a Web search.

It was the advertisement for finding your classmates that gave her the idea. Wouldn't Carolyn's high school reunion coordinator have the updated addresses of everyone from the graduating class?

It was amazing what was now available on the Internet. Sarah was able to search an alumni database on Maple Hill High's Web site. She discovered Carolyn Amsden's graduating class and was able to dig a little deeper to find the class reunion coordinator.

It was Linda.

The same Linda from the Congregational Church who had been so rude to Sarah, who had insisted Debby had not attended services there, who believed Debby was a murderer.

Sarah stared at the alumni site on her computer screen for a long moment. There was a telephone number listed, but her hands weighed fifty pounds each, and she couldn't move them, couldn't pick up the telephone.

But hadn't she just prayed, *Lord, I'll go where you lead me?*

She closed her eyes and prayed again, *Lord, give me the strength to obey.*

She dialed Linda's number.

And got an answering machine.

Sarah left a message, telling Linda she had been hoping to get Carolyn Amsden's contact information and set the telephone down.

"Oh no!" One of the twins groaned.

"What is it?" Sarah asked.

"My hands are shaking too much, and I made a mistake."

"My hands are steady as a rock," Zoe said. "Do you want me to help you with your section?"

Sarah glanced into the dining room and saw Zoe bent over, patiently and painstakingly gluing one section of the bridge to the other while Amy rubbed her hands together briskly.

"I'll turn up the heat." Sarah made her way to the thermostat and raised the temperature a notch.

Hmm, it was rather cold. Her own hands were icy. Good thing she didn't have a quilt project tonight, or she might lay down uneven stitches that she'd only have to pick out tomorrow.

She stopped to listen to herself. Uneven stitches.

"Oh my goodness," she said.

Amy and Audrey looked up at her, their blue eyes identical in concern. "Grandma, are you okay?" Amy asked.

"Sorry, girls, I didn't mean to alarm you. I just realized something very important that has to do with that book I've been investigating."

"What about it?" Audrey asked.

"Debby made some very uneven stitches, and at first I thought it could have been something wrong with her eyes, but now I'm thinking it was because her hands were shaking."

Amy looked at her own hands. "Was she cold all the time?"

"I don't think so." Sarah thought back to the dresses she had spent hours poring over. "Her stitches were getting progressively worse. It couldn't have been because of the change of seasons."

"So why would her hands be shaking all the time?" Amy said.

"Is it kind of like Mr. Maplethorpe's hands?" Audrey asked.

Sarah's mind raced. Ernie Maplethorpe's shaking hands were due to a neurological disease. What if Debby had also had some type of neurological disease? Not Parkinson's, but something that affected her hands. Something that got progressively worse as she got older.

Sarah made a mental note to call Martha the next day and ask her for the name and number of Ernie's neurologist at UMass Hospital. The doctor might be able to tell Sarah if her theory was even possible.

And if Debby's hands had been shaking from some type of disease or disorder, would she even have been able to build an intricate explosive?

Her thoughts were interrupted by the ringing of the telephone. "Hello?"

"Hello, this is Linda."

"Hello, Linda. Thanks so much for calling me back."

"I'm afraid I cannot give out alumni contact information to nonalumni," Linda said.

Sarah had imagined some roadblock. "Well, I didn't graduate with your class, but I *am* a Maple Hill High alum. Well, Maple Hill Central back then."

"Why do you need to speak to Carolyn?" Linda asked.

"She apparently was good friends with Debby Neely, and I want to know if they still kept in touch."

"I doubt they stayed in touch once Debby went to jail. She was that murderer who made the bomb."

"Actually, she might have been physically incapable of making a bomb."

There was a thick, tense silence that began to make Sarah uncomfortable. Then Linda asked, "What are you talking about?"

"I've been looking at Debby's sewing, and it shows that there's a chance she has some sort of disease or disorder that might have prevented her from being able to make a bomb."

"She might be innocent?" Linda asked.

"I don't know for certain. I'm waiting to speak to a doctor to confirm the possibility."

"And what does this have to do with Carolyn?"

Quite a bit, not the least of which was Sarah's own curiosity about who the book's author was. But at the top of her list was Debby. "Carolyn might know something that could prove Debby's innocence."

Again, silence. Sarah began to wonder if Linda had hung up and was about to do the same when she heard, "Carolyn's married name is Rodriguez, and here's her e-mail address."

At first, Sarah was almost too surprised to grab a piece of paper and pen. Eventually she tore off a page of scrap paper and wrote down the mailing address. "Thank you so much, Linda. I really appreciate it."

"Well," Linda growled, "you should."

Sarah had to hold back her laughter. "Good night, Linda."

"Good night."

She hung up the phone. What an odd conversation. But Linda had seemed surprised at the possibility that Debby might be innocent. Sarah wondered what Linda had been thinking at that moment. Had it somehow changed the way she had been thinking about Debby for the past fifty years?

Sarah moved to reseat herself at her computer, mentally working on an e-mail message to Carolyn, but her knee accidentally knocked into the ironing board. She hadn't any fabric on it, but she had been using it as extra space to store things like her mother's devotional and the typewritten manuscript. As her knee jarred the board, the manila folder with the manuscript pages slipped and pages cascaded to the floor.

"Oh bother." She bent down and scooped the pages up, not too concerned about page order. After all, she already had the hardcover book. She wasn't sure what she ought to do with this manuscript. Maybe Irene would be interested in it for the historical society.

In the act of sticking the pages back in the folder, she froze. There was writing on some of the typewritten pages.

And the handwriting wasn't her mother's or her father's.

After that day, Debby and I became closer friends, but it took six months before she confided in me that she was running from the law.

The words "six months" had been crossed out in blue pen and "more than a year" was written above them in a cramped hand—a correction to the manuscript.

Her mom had taken an administrative course before she was married, and from what her father had said, she had also worked temporarily as a secretary. She would have been qualified to transcribe someone's words as they dictated, or even from a recording.

And then the author made corrections to the transcript.

Sarah flipped through the rest of the stack of papers. There, and there ... places where words had been crossed out and corrections made in that same cramped handwriting. The lowercase g's had an odd slant to the tail, and the s's looked like lightning bolts.

This would explain why her parents had been involved in the book. The author may have asked her mom to type the manuscript. The book was typeset and printed by Jerry Hobbs, Dad's friend who owned the magazine press. Dad had the book bound at the bindery, and Mom donated the book to the library. All to protect the identity of the author.

But now the question was, whose handwriting was that?

An e-mail from Carolyn Rodriguez showed up in Sarah's in-box the very next morning. Carolyn had responded to her message late last night, but since Phoenix, where Carolyn lived, was in a different time zone, Sarah had already been in bed.

Sarah had to remind herself to be patient now as she waited for it to be a decent hour to call Carolyn. She was about to pour herself another cup of coffee when the phone rang.

"Hello?"

"Hi, Sarah, it's Liam."

Just the sound of his voice made her smile. "Hi there. How are you?"

"Ah, Sarah," he said in a woeful voice, "my masculinity is at risk."

"What?"

"Yesterday, Vanessa was in the café chatting with one of the knitting ladies from that investment group I told you about. The two of them were thick as thieves at a table, working over some knitting thing. Did you know Vanessa is learning to knit? Is there any crafty thing that woman doesn't do?"

"Doesn't seem like it, does it?"

"Well I, the unsuspecting fool, went over to their table to see what they were doing and to possibly rib Vanessa. After all, isn't it considered 'betraying' her fabric store if she starts playing around with string and two sticks?"

Sarah smiled as he warmed up to his story.

"Vanessa promptly challenged me to know what I was talking about before teasing two helpless women. Helpless? Ha! I was beguiled into their schemes, I tell you."

"What did she challenge you to do?" Sarah asked.

"She dared me to learn how to knit! Out loud, in my own store."

Sarah burst into laughter. "And did you?"

"I am now the proud owner of two skills—knitting and cusping on."

"Cusping on? Like ... a tooth?"

"Not a bicuspid. It's the first row of knitting, or some such like that."

Sarah's laughter gave her a stitch in her side. "Liam, it's 'casting on,' not 'cusping on.'"

"Do you see? I've been so traumatized, I no longer have control of the English language."

"Well, at least you survived. And don't worry, I'll watch you in the next few weeks to make sure you don't start looking at sweater patterns."

"At least I have one friend looking out for my welfare. So how are things going with you? How's the research about the book going?"

Sarah caught him up with everything she'd learned recently, including her very latest find of the handwritten notes on the typed manuscript pages.

"So now you only need handwriting samples of everyone who knew Debby to compare to the manuscript?" Liam asked.

"Well, I have to admit it's probably a bit of a long shot. Handwriting can change over fifty years." She also told him about discovering that Tom's daughter Carolyn had been friends with Debby. "I'm only waiting for a good time to call her. Arizona's two hours behind us."

"Well, I'll let you get back to sleuthing, then. I just wanted to see how you were doing. Are we still on for dinner next week Friday?"

"I can't wait." After saying good-bye, she sat there smiling at the telephone for a moment.

She checked the time and thought it might be okay to call Carolyn now. She punched in the telephone number from

Carolyn's e-mail. There was ringing, and then a woman's voice said, "Hello?"

"Hello, this is Sarah Hart."

"Hi, Sarah, this is Carolyn Rodriguez." Her voice was smooth and melodic, which belied her sharp features in the photograph.

"Thank you so much for writing back and giving me your number," Sarah said. "I've been so eager to talk to you about Debby."

"Your e-mail last night was such a surprise. What exactly did you want to know about her?" Carolyn asked.

"Were you good friends with Debby?"

"I would say so. We became close after she joined the church choir."

"Did she tell you about the FBI being after her?"

Carolyn sighed. "Yes, although she never really told me what she had done. That whole business was truly sad. I can't believe my own father turned her in."

"I spoke to him. Well, for about five minutes."

"That sounds like him," Carolyn said.

"He insisted Debby was guilty."

"He's lying. He knew Debby was innocent."

"How did he know?" Sarah asked.

"He always told me how inaccurate polygraph tests were back then. Even said he had clients who had passed while lying through their teeth. He would always tell me how easy it was. But he *chose* to believe Josiah's testimony and his lie detector test results because Josiah put up this conservative front, hiding behind his family, and Debby and her brother were painted as 'radicals.'"

"Are you saying that in your father's mind, it all came down to politics? Even though Debby might not have had anything to do with the bomb?"

"You have to remember the time period. People were taking sides. My father follows the system. He doesn't deviate. He didn't want social revolution, but that was what Debby's brother stood for, and since her brother was a 'dangerous radical,' then Debby must be too. After all, a man was killed and people injured, and she was at the scene."

"There might be a way to prove she couldn't have made the explosive device," Sarah said slowly. She explained her theory about Debby's hands. "A friend of mind knows a neurologist at UMass Hospital and gave me his number. I called and left a message. I'm waiting for him to call me back so I can talk to him about Debby."

"I didn't even know about her hands. I wonder why she didn't tell me."

"I don't think she told anyone."

"Maybe with all the advances in science over the last few decades, she can be exonerated." Carolyn said. "I hope it's not too little, too late. She's been in prison for fifty years."

"Do you know where Debby is now?"

"No. I wasn't even there when the FBI came to Maple Hill. I had been visiting my grandparents for a month. When I got back, I found out Debby had been arrested only the day before I returned. I never got a chance to say good-bye." She sighed heavily. "I tried calling the FBI to find out where they had taken her, but I just didn't have the knowledge or the connections to find her."

"I can't imagine how helpless and frustrated you must have felt," Sarah said.

"I admit, I took it out on my father for a long time," Carolyn said. "I haven't spoken to him for about forty years."

"I'm so sorry."

There was a moment of silence, then Carolyn asked, "Is there anything else I can tell you about Debby? I don't know if I'm much help, but it does make me feel better to talk about her after all these years."

Sarah didn't want to take up too much of her time, but she did have a couple more questions. "Actually, I was wondering if you knew my mother, Ruth Drayton, or my father William?"

"No. I might recognize their faces, but the names don't ring a bell."

Sarah couldn't be sure, but it sounded like Carolyn was telling the truth, which meant she wasn't the author of the book. If she could compare Carolyn's handwriting to the manuscript, she'd have proof, but Sarah wasn't sure how she could get a sample of Carolyn's handwriting.

Sarah moved on, recalling the reference to Debby's landlady, which she had been reminded of last night when she had been flipping through the book and had reread the passage *She was close to her co-worker and the woman she was staying with, and later with me.* "Did you know who Debby's landlady was?"

"Debby's landlady? You mean Olive?"

"Olive Cavanaugh? I thought she was Debby's co-worker."

"She was both. Debby used to live in one of those board-inghouses, but her house had a small fire. She moved out and lived in the basement of Olive's house for a while."

Sarah realized that she'd read the passage wrong—*her co-worker and the woman she was staying with.* Debby's co-worker and her landlady had been one and the same.

"They became very close after that," Carolyn said. "I'm pretty sure Olive knew about the trouble with the FBI even before I did."

And yet Olive hadn't wanted to talk about Debby to Sarah. What was she hiding?

"Olive and Debby would close up the shop at the end of the day," Carolyn said, "and they'd go to the village green. Debby would cut up pieces of fabric into tiny strips and leave them for the birds to build their nests with. Debby liked see-ing the scraps in the nests, she thought it was pretty. Olive would just laugh at her, but she'd sit while Debby cut the fabric up."

A vivid picture came into Sarah's mind, the sight of Olive cutting up pieces of fabric for the birds at Bradford Manor. Olive must have been doing that for years, even before she moved to the nursing home. Who would have thought that Debby's little habit would have been perpetuated in Olive?

"Thank you so much, Carolyn," Sarah said. "You've been such a help."

"No problem. If you find Debby, will you let me know?"

"Of course. And I hope you don't mind my saying this, but I'll be praying for you and your father."

"I don't mind at all. I just wish ...," she hesitated. "I don't think he's the same man he used to be. He's changed."

"Changed how?"

"Oh ... I don't know, maybe it's time I try to reach out to him again. I'll have to think about it." It sounded like she was talking to herself, but then her voice firmed as she said, "Have a good day, Sarah. Good-bye."

After hanging up, Sarah sat there for a moment.

Carolyn had mentioned that Olive had laughed at Debby for cutting up the fabric scraps for the birds, but she was the one doing it now. It was as if she was making up for the terrible thing that had happened to Debby, a way to assuage some type of guilt. She couldn't imagine what Olive would feel guilty about, but the answer to that might explain why she wouldn't talk to Sarah about Debby. The author of the book had been filled with remorse at not defending Debby. Could Olive be the author after all?

Sarah wasn't going to let Olive put her off again. She'd go see her tomorrow. There had to be a way to encourage her to tell Sarah about Debby.

arah entered Bradford Manor Nursing Home and immediately looked toward the birdcage. She was surprised not to find Olive there. Then she chided herself—she had come here plenty of times and Olive hadn't been cutting fabric for the birds.

She went to visit her father first. Dad had caught a mild cold, and because of his age, the nurses were watching him closely and forcing him to stay in bed awhile longer so he could heal. He chafed at the orders and grumbled the entire time Sarah sat beside him, except he would grumble about different things—the breakfast he'd eaten, Sarah's brother's baseball bat left out in the yard, the lawn mower not working, the checkers game he'd played with Mr. Blodgett yesterday.

"Here Dad." From her purse, Sarah pulled out an old, cracked leather batting glove and gave it to him. "I found it in one of Mom's old boxes."

"My glove." His eyes lit up. "Your mom bought this for me. I had a great batting average. It was. . . . "

Tiffany and a doctor then entered her father's room. "I'm sorry, Mrs. Hart, but could we borrow your dad for a bit? The doctor's just doing his rounds and wanted to check up on your dad's cold. If you want to come back in about ten minutes, we'll be done by then."

"Thanks, Tiffany. I'll be back, Dad." Sarah waved to him from the doorway of his room.

Sarah went out in search of Olive Cavanaugh. She found her in her wheelchair out on the back patio, chatting animatedly with Mr. Blodgett, her father's checkers partner. He was smiling and nodding at everything she said, although Sarah doubted he could hear a single word.

Olive apparently knew that as well, because her wicked sense of humor was coming out. Sarah overheard the end of the tale she was spinning for Mr. Blodgett.

"And then the cows broke through the fence and wandered into his neighbor's pasture and ate up all his alfalfa," Olive said. "He had to pay his neighbor back for all the damage. And the next week, his barn burned down. And then his electricity was accidentally shut off because of a mix-up at the electrical company. And so he lived up to his nickname of the Unluckiest Man on Earth. The End. Isn't that a charming story?"

Mr. Blodgett smiled and nodded.

"Olive Cavanaugh, you scoundrel," Sarah told her.

Olive turned in her wheelchair and grinned up at Sarah. "Oh Chuck is just happy to have somebody near him. He

really doesn't care if you're telling him juicy gossip or a re-
ceipe for patty cakes. Isn't that right?" she asked him, and
he nodded and smiled.

"Olive, I wanted to talk to you about Debby Neely again."
Sarah steeled herself for Olive's reluctance. Might as well just
get to the point.

Olive sighed. "Sarah, I don't know anything."

"Yes, you do," Mr. Blodgett said.

Sarah and Olive stared at him, mouths agape. He stared
back.

"What did you say?" Olive said.

"You tell her what you told me last week," he said. His
voice was pitched rather loud, and he spoke slowly.

"I thought...but...you can hear just fine!" Olive said.

"Not as well as I used to," he admitted, "but I'm not
stone-cold deaf. And my grandson was born deaf, so his parents taught me how to read lips a little too. That comes in
handy."

Sarah realized her mouth was still open, and she closed
it.

He nodded at her. "I heard you ask your dad about Debby
Neely. And then you talked to Olive about her. So I hung out
with both of them 'cause I was curious," he said. "By the way,
your father is a terrible checkers player."

Sarah smiled.

"Your dad only talks about old baseball players and your
mom's cooking, but Olive here likes to talk about what's
bothering her."

"I do not," she said. "I thought I wasn't being heard."

"Then you shouldn't tell dumb stories to a deaf man," he replied.

Olive huffed.

Mr. Blodgett stood up on legs that were a little shaky at first, but then he found his footing. "So you tell Sarah about Debby." He then leaned toward Sarah. "And I'd appreciate it if you would keep my secret from the other folks for a little while longer. Mrs. Russo tells me lots of interesting tidbits about her Russian mafia family." He winked at her and shuffled away.

"Of all the nerve," Olive said. But the edges of her mouth curved with her normal good humor. "I guess it serves me right. I shouldn't have teased him with that laundry list I read to him."

"Olive!"

Olive grinned at her. "I couldn't resist, especially when he laughed every time I said, 'purple socks.' Come to think of it, that should have clued me in."

Sarah sat in the chair Mr. Blodgett had vacated. "It might be possible to prove Debby is innocent."

"Really? How?"

"I'm wondering if she had some type of neurological disease. There's evidence she had trouble with her hands shaking. You can tell from her quilting stitches."

"If that's true, she wouldn't have been able to make the bomb."

"Exactly. I left a message with a neurologist at UMass Hospital."

Olive nodded. "You probably know by now that Debby lived with me and Jim? Jim loved Debby, she was just like a kid sister to him."

"You took her in after her boardinghouse fire?"

"We were good friends by then, and I hated the decrepit condition of her room. I had already asked her to move in with us, but she didn't want to impose. The fire gave me more reason to try to convince her, and she finally agreed."

"How long did she live with you?"

"About a year. She and I would sit together in the evenings after supper and just chat. She'd usually work on a dress she was making to sell, although...," Olive suddenly turned to Sarah. "Will you take me to my room? I have something to show you."

Sarah released the brakes on her wheelchair and wheeled her to her room.

"Park me anywhere, then go look in the back of that bottom drawer." She pointed to the bureau in the corner.

Sarah did as Olive told her and found a paper-wrapped parcel. It felt like another one of Debby's dresses. "This?"

"Yes, open it for me, will you?"

Sarah undid the string surrounding the brown paper and pulled apart the stiff, brittle folds. Inside lay nestled an unfinished quilt that glimmered like a nest of multicolored jewels.

"Debby said that this quilt was all she'd brought with her when she ran away," Olive said. "She worked on it sometimes when we sat together. I should have just given it to you before, knowing how you feel about quilts, but I didn't want to get Debby in any more trouble than I already had." Olive raised a shaky hand to cover her eyes.

"In trouble? How could you have gotten Debby in trouble?"

"It was my fault the FBI found her." Olive's voice trembled. "I'm the one who told her to confide in ... that police officer. What's-his-name."

"Dale Wexler?"

"That's him. And then a month later, the FBI came to take her away."

"But Olive, Dale didn't turn Debby in."

The older woman looked at her. "What?"

"I spoke to Tom Amsden, and he was very proud of the fact that he told the FBI about Debby."

"Who?" Olive asked.

"Tom Amsden. A lawyer in Maple Hill at the time."

"I don't remember him."

The author of the book had clearly mentioned the lawyer. Perhaps Olive wasn't the author after all.

"You thought Debby was arrested because you told her to talk to Dale?" Sarah asked.

"Oh, I didn't think he'd deliberately turned her in. I thought Dale had tried to find a way to help her, and it got the attention of the FBI. But if he didn't ...," Olive sighed. "All these years I thought she was arrested because of what he'd done."

Olive held her hands out for the quilt. When Sarah placed it in her hands, Olive stroked the material softly, eventually offering the quilt back to Sarah. "You take it. Debby never finished it, but maybe you'd want to?"

"Olive, I'd be honored to take the quilt." Not only was it a lovely quilt, but she hoped that by studying it, she might be able to find out more about Debby and her shaking hands, maybe something she didn't already know.

There was a knock at the door, and Mr. Blodgett came in.

"Hi, Mr. Blodgett."

"Sarah, I was just sitting with your father, and he said something I thought would be important to you." His voice was a little loud, but it seemed he was trying to hurry his words.

"What did he say?"

"Well, just now, your dad was talking about playing baseball and his teammates."

Probably because of the batting glove she'd given to him.

Mr. Blodgett said, "One of the people your dad played with was Dean Wexler. I know him. He's Dale Wexler's father."

"Sarah! I have something for you," Liam said as Sarah and Martha entered the café.

Sarah was surprised to feel a happy shiver at the sight of Liam at the counter. But she had time to process her feelings before she responded because a very insistent corgi waylaid her by sitting on her shoes and waiting for her to pet him. Naturally, she obliged. "Murphy, I have a feeling you're terribly spoiled, and you don't mind it at all."

Liam smiled but didn't say anything. Sarah fleetingly thought of the concern for his daughter he'd shown on their date, and she wondered if he'd feel comfortable enough with her to tell her about it. *Well, Lord, it's all in your time.*

Sarah and Martha sat at a table near the window, and in a few minutes, Liam had set a chai latte with extra whipped cream in front of Sarah. "Karen is making that triple sugar smoothie for you right now, Martha," Liam said.

"It's not *that* sweet," Martha said.

"Here you go." Liam set a piece of paper in front of Sarah that was covered with writing in long bold lines that was completely unintelligible.

"What's this?"

"*This* is Dale Wexler's handwriting," he said. "So you can check it against the handwriting on that manuscript."

"Liam, how in the world did you get this?"

"Easy. He came into the café yesterday, and I asked him if he knew a good mechanic. Then I had him write down the guy's name and number, and directions to the shop."

"Liam, you're a genius!" Sarah said. Liam opened his mouth to say something, but a customer waved from the bookstore area. He just gave the ladies a jaunty salute and wandered off to help the customer.

At a glance, the handwriting didn't look anything like the cramped, wavering writing on the manuscript. These were strong, bold strokes, much like Dale's personality. But the s's and lowercase g's—were those g's?—might be similar to the mystery handwriting. Sarah couldn't wait to double-check when she got home.

"This might not even be a good test," she said. "Handwriting could change drastically in fifty years."

"Not that much," Martha said. "At least, mine still looks pretty close to my handwriting on those high school papers my mom kept."

"I just don't want to jump to conclusions. If there's one thing I've seen while looking into this mystery, it's that there's always another side to the story."

"So you're certain Olive isn't the author of that book?"

Sarah nodded. "Aside from the fact that she didn't know about the lawyer, I convinced her to let me look at that laundry list she had read to Mr. Blodgett." Sarah couldn't help smiling at Olive's audacity. "Her handwriting is completely different from the handwriting on that manuscript—Olive's letters are loose and large, and the other handwriting was cramped and jagged."

"So what's next?"

Sarah gave a grin. "Looking at Debby's quilt, of course!"

Sarah laid Debby's quilt out on her quilting frame, revealing a riot of color across the surface of the quilt top. Debby had been making a starburst quilt, but she had altered the design to make it more complex, using dozens of different fabrics rather than the six or so that usually repeated throughout a starburst pattern.

Sarah remembered how she'd been able to find her Grandma Molly's hometown through the quilt Grandma Molly had made for Sarah's father. Sarah had found clues in the fabrics of the quilt that had helped her identify where Grandma Molly was originally from. Because Debby had used so many different fabrics in her quilt, Sarah had high hopes that she would be able to find something that would lead her to Debby's hometown. Once she figured that out, she might be able to discover where the bombing had occurred and, finally, where Debby had been imprisoned. Everything was connected.

Sarah's job was easier with this quilt because Debby had only completed the quilting in one section in the center. Since she hadn't yet sewn on the binding, it was easy to lift up the top layer around the edges of the quilt to look at the backs of the fabric pieces.

Sarah made notes in her notebook as she examined each piece. Debby had used a large variety of fabrics—from silk to satin to velvet to cotton lawn—but the backs showed no identifying marks.

The telephone rang, interrupting her about halfway through examining all the pieces. She answered the phone rather absently, her mind still focused on the quilt. "Hello?"

"Mrs. Hart? This is Dr. Emily Michaels from UMass Hospital. Ernie Maplethorpe's doctor passed your message on to me. I'm a specialist in neurological disorders that affect motor function."

Dr. Michaels immediately captured all of Sarah's attention. "I hope you can help me." She explained about the deterioration of Debby's work and her theory about her shaking hands, and asked if Debby could have had a neurological disorder.

"Most definitely," Dr. Michaels said, "but the only way to know for certain is to undergo genetic testing."

"You mean, a test could prove she has a specific disorder? Would that kind of testing hold up in a court of law?"

"You'd have to speak to a lawyer about that, but genetic testing doesn't lie. Some disorders that affect the hands can be extremely debilitating."

"Would a woman whose hands shook because of a neurological disorder be able to hide the shaking well enough that no one else would know?"

"Oh definitely. She could hide it by pressing her hands against something, like a tabletop or her leg. The shaking would disappear."

Sarah guessed that was probably how Debby controlled the shaking enough to quilt her dresses. By pressing her arm and part of her hand against her leg, she could still the shaking but be able to manipulate the sewing needle.

"Thank you so much for your time, Dr. Michaels."

"You're welcome. Give me a call me if you find Debby. I can administer the tests myself."

After hanging up, Sarah returned with renewed determination to the quilt. Now that she had a way to prove Debby's innocence, she had to find her.

Several hours later, Sarah sat back and stretched her aching back. Of all the fabric pieces she could easily see, none of them had any markings to give her a clue about where they were from. Sarah needed to look at the pieces in the center of the quilt. She would have to undo Debby's quilting stitches in their elaborate patterns before she could look at the backs of the pieces, but it seemed a terrible shame to undo those beautiful stitches.

Sarah's eye fell on the batting between the backing and the pieced top. It was cotton that had yellowed with age, and she could see tiny cotton seeds between the fibers. They made a playful pattern against the parchment-colored batting.

On second look, those weren't cotton seeds. Sarah grabbed her magnifying glass. She had restored other quilts with cotton seeds stuck in the batting, and these seeds didn't look the same. They were a variety of different shapes, sizes, and colors. They looked almost like birdseed. Sarah gently grasped a corner of the batting and lifted it up so she could look at the underside of the backing fabric.

"Zurakowski's Fine Birdseed" stretched across the material.

Debby had used thick, white cotton birdseed sacks for her quilt back, cutting the sacks into large squares and piecing them together. Sarah had no idea why Debby had used birdseed sacks, though the fact that she had used so many different fabrics to piece the top suggested she hadn't had money to buy new fabric and had made do with the scraps she had acquired. Perhaps she hadn't had the money or means to buy large enough pieces of fabric for the back, and so had improvised.

Regardless, Sarah now had her first clue about Debby's whereabouts. She wasn't really surprised that Debby's birds had once again shown her the way.

CHAPTER TWENTY-FOUR

I t took several days of Internet searching and her son Jason's help, but Sarah found the penitentiary where Debby Neely had been sent.

Zurakowski's Fine Birdseed had been in business in Ryeland, a small town outside of Albany, New York. A search for bombed courthouses in Ryeland turned up a newspaper article about a woman named Debby Lee Smith being charged with the bombing, which had occurred in 1959. Sarah had asked Jason to search legal databases she couldn't access, and he discovered that Debby had been sentenced to ninety-nine years in the Ingram Women's Penitentiary several miles outside Albany. She applied for visitation and received it sooner than she expected, perhaps due to a well-placed call Jason made.

He drove her to the penitentiary, talking to her the entire way about what she could expect from the facilities and from the inmates. She laughingly told him to stop. "I'm not naive, Jason. I know that I essentially don't know anything about Debby, and she's had a tough, tough life. I don't expect us to become bosom buddies."

The penitentiary was predominantly steel and concrete, punctuated by stone. It had a gloomy atmosphere, like a soaked rain slicker. Sarah followed everything they told her to do and stuck close to her son. Something about the concrete walls and floors seemed even harder than pavement, and colder than Maple Hill winters.

The visiting area was a large room with metal tables and benches bolted to the floor. The concrete floor here was smoother, slicker, and it ran all the way to the walls and up in a gentle slope like the sides of a bathtub. The stone walls were brightly whitewashed, but they smelled like old paint.

A tall female security guard seemed larger than life, perhaps an illusion of bulk caused by her gray uniform, and she told them which numbered bench to sit at. When all the visitors were seated, a loud buzzing sounded, and a metal gate at the far end slid open. Inmates walked in. There were a few joyful cries, but mostly casual hugs and kisses.

And last of all came Debby.

Sarah recognized her from the photo. She still had a beautiful heart-shaped face, and while there were lines in her olive skin and creases at her eyes, those eyes were still bright when they landed on Sarah and Jason.

She sat slowly, like a wary cat—or maybe like an older cat who has to be cautious with her brittle bones. Up close,

Sarah could see the shadows under her eyes that looked like they'd been tattooed there, the deep lines along the sides of her mouth.

"I'm Sarah. This is Jason."

"Debby."

Her voice reminded Sarah of chocolate milk, not too thick, not too sweet. But there was nothing sweet about her neutral gaze. Sarah reasoned that she should be glad Debby wasn't downright hostile about being forced to meet two complete strangers.

"I don't even know where to begin," Sarah said. "I guess I'll begin with this." She had laid the book on the table and pushed it toward Debby.

Debby lifted her hand from her lap to open the cover, and the shaking motion was larger and more obvious than Sarah had expected. She guessed the disease had worsened over the years.

Debby read the first page. "Where did you get this?"

"I found it in the Maple Hill library. Someone wrote it anonymously and then donated it to the collection."

"Who?"

"I don't know." Yet. "I've been talking to all kinds of people around Maple Hill who remember you, finding out more about you, and trying to figure out who wrote this."

Debby's eyes kept skimming the words, but now tears formed on her eyelashes. She wiped them away with a careless hand. "Olive," she whispered.

"Olive Cavanaugh?"

"It's her. She loved me like the sister I never had." Debby abruptly closed the book and slid it back over the table to Sarah. "So what? What do you want?"

"I know you were falsely convicted."

Debby closed her eyes in concentration, and her face relaxed, her shoulders dropped. After a while, she opened her eyes again. "I don't want to talk about it."

Sarah wasn't sure what to say. She didn't want to pain Debby but felt she needed to know everything Sarah had found. "I saw your dresses, and your quilt. They're gorgeous."

Debby forced a thin smile, and Sarah regretted saying anything. Debby couldn't sew anymore—it was obvious from the shaking in her hands. "I'm so sorry," Sarah said. "It must be hard for you. But I needed to tell you that they led me to the discovery about your hands. I called a neurologist from UMass Hospital."

Something appeared in Debby's dark eyes, like a gleam on the surface of a stone.

"Dr. Michaels says that with your permission, she can perform some genetic tests to determine what neurological disease or disorder you might have. Those genetic tests might prove you would never have been able to make the bomb with your hands the way they were."

To Sarah's surprise, Debby's face remained stoic. She didn't say a word.

"Debby?"

"Why are you telling me this?"

"I'm a lawyer," Jason said. "If your tests are conclusive, I can help you try to get your sentence revoked."

"And what about the past fifty years?" Debby asked.

Sarah didn't know what to say to her. No one could erase those years. She had tried to prepare herself for anger, despair, but Debby's hopelessness was more deep-seated, her anger sharper, and her despair darker than Sarah had expected.

Debby squeezed her eyes shut, and when she opened them again, they were calmer.

"I'm sorry," Sarah said.

Debby dropped her head. "I can't say it's been all bad," she admitted. "With my hands this way...what kind of job could I have gotten in the real world? I can't even use the computers in the prison computer lab."

"You didn't tell anyone about your hands?"

She shook her head. "My sewing was my livelihood. I dropped out of high school to help support my family. When Mama died, it was just my brother and me, and we moved a lot. A couple of places, people found out about my hands and they started looking for mistakes in my sewing, and not paying me the full amount, or taking their business somewhere else." Then Debby asked, "Who's still at the Congregational Church?"

Sarah talked about the people whom she had spoken to, and Debby asked about people she hadn't known about.

"There are people who want to write to you," Sarah said. "Will that be okay?"

Debby hesitated for a few breaths, then nodded, once.

"Since I found out you were here," Sarah said, "I've been praying for you."

Debby's mouth softened slightly. "Thanks. It's been hard to cling to Jesus here. It's hard to have faith some days."

Sarah could imagine.

"But God is faithful," Debby whispered.

Amen.

Jason spoke to her then, about what to expect in the coming weeks and months as they arranged for the genetic tests and court dates.

And then the visit was over.

The good-bye was awkward for a moment. Debby didn't seem like a person who liked being touched. But then Debby extended a hand, which was slowly quivering, and Sarah took it between both of hers. Her skin was dry and cool, and felt a little like soft cotton cloth.

"Thank you," Debby said. "Even if none of this works out, thank you."

As Sarah and Jason walked out of the penitentiary, he gave Sarah a one-armed hug. "You did great, Mom. I'm proud of you."

Outside, it seemed her lungs opened wider and her heartbeat slowed. She couldn't imagine living in such a place for fifty years.

Thank you, Lord! You helped us find her. Now I pray you'll help us free her.

QUILTING MAY FREE A WOMAN IMPRISONED FOR FIFTY YEARS
By Sarah Hart, *Country Cottage quilting columnist*

Deborah Lee Smith's exquisitely quilted dresses and vests are rich in detail and embroidery, but the stiches also provided clues pointing to a specific genetic neurological disorder. Modern technology can now do genetic testing for these disorders, and depending on the outcome, Debby may be able to have her ninety-nine-year prison sentence revoked.

Debby was known as Debby Neely when she lived in Maple Hill from 1960 to 1962. She attended the Congregational Church and sang in the choir, and she worked at Pleiter's Handmade Gifts, which later became The Galleria. The beautiful quilted dresses and vests she sold at Pleiter's were in very high demand. She had many friends and was especially good with children. But a false witness accused her of planting an explosive device in a federal courthouse, and the FBI eventually found her in our quiet little town.

A mysterious friend of Debby's wrote an account of her character and her time in Maple Hill, and when I found the book fifty years later, I became curious about who Debby Neely was and what stories her quilted garments would tell me.

Much gratitude is owed to C.J. Pleiter Wyatt, owner of The Galleria, for providing the resources needed to track down Debby's one-of-a-kind works of art. I was overwhelmed by the generosity and kindness of Maple Hill residents whom I contacted about seeing Debby's dresses. Everywhere I turned were openhearted people more than willing to let me study, photograph, and sometimes carefully borrow their heirloom garments. Thank you to everyone in Maple Hill who trusted me with your priceless treasures.

Debby's stitching led me to realize that she might have a neurological disorder that affected her hands, which would have made it impossible for her to make the bomb she was accused of creating. Debby is currently being tested by Dr. Emily Michaels, a neurologist at University of Massachusetts Hospital. Debby's lawyer is also working to have her released as soon as possible.

The sixties were a turbulent time of great change, and it saddens me that this woman was swept up in the machinations of that false witness, who happened to be the true criminal, a man with no regard for human life. Now we are hopeful that Debby can move forward—after being held back for so long—thanks to the generosity of Maple Hill residents.

Sarah reread the last line of her column. "My editor Mark made me put that last line in. I thought it was a little cheesy."

"No, it's perfect," Chloe said. "It forms a nice ending to the story."

"The only thing missing is the identity of the author of that book," Liam said. He'd left Karen in charge of the café this Saturday morning—much to her delight, despite the increased traffic—for a routine checkup at the eye doctor, and had surprised Sarah by dropping by her house on the way back.

Sarah went to refill her coffee cup from the coffee maker. "Debby thought it was Olive, but she emphatically denied it when I spoke to her before writing this column. And I truly don't think Olive would lie about something like that. So now I'm still clueless about who the author is. But the important thing is that Debby is going to be freed."

"I hope you sent a copy to Tom Amsden," Chloe said as she balanced on her crutches and washed her cereal bowl in the sink. "He deserves to know the truth."

"I sent a copy to Carolyn, who called to tell me how happy she is about how things turned out. She says she's going to visit Debby soon."

Chloe hobbled toward the kitchen door. "I better go upstairs to finish packing. You've been so wonderful, Sarah, but I'm looking forward to going home."

Sarah sat with Liam at the kitchen table. "It must be nice to be playing hooky today."

"I try to do it about once a month. Let Murphy think he's the one in charge of the café."

"You mean he's not King of the Universe? Could have fooled me."

"How are your kids?" Liam asked.

Sarah chatted about Jason helping Debby, and Maggie buying a hideous armoire that sold for three times what she paid for it, and the twins' toothpick project, due on Monday, which was being perfected today. "In fact, Jason is going to drop the girls off soon so they can work on the project here for a while. How's Caitlin?"

Liam stilled for a split second before he smiled and said, "Trying to con me into buying her a new car."

Sarah looked at her coffee cup. In the second before he answered, she knew that something was bothering him about his daughter, but apparently he didn't wanted to share it with her. That was okay—maybe someday...

"I'm sorry, Sarah," he said. "Whenever I ask you about your family, you answer with truth—whether it's funny or sad or happy or troubling. If you ask me about mine, you deserve an answer from me too. It's just hard sometimes for me to share what's really happening."

"Is Caitlin okay?"

"She's fine. It's her old man who's a wreck."

"What's wrong?"

"I just really don't like the guy she's dating, and it looks like it might get serious. I don't want my girl to get hurt."

Sarah touched his hand. "I understand. It's so hard to let them make their own decisions after how many years of picking out their clothes and packing their lunches." Sarah smiled. "But you'll always be her father and you'll always be there for her."

"You're right. And I promise, from now on, no more masks. I'll work harder to open up when you ask how I'm doing or about my family."

Liam's words caused an involuntary smile from Sarah.

She thought she heard voices in the front of the house and wondered if the twins had arrived, but it was Chloe who hobbled into the kitchen.

"Chloe, did you need—"

Her words cut off as Tom Amsden came into the kitchen, a revolver in his gnarled hand that swung from Chloe's back to point straight at them.

Sarah's heart rose into her throat and she couldn't breathe. Tom's face was bright red, his white hair wild around his face. His steps were slow but still steady as he approached them. Sarah nervously eyed his right hand, which shook slightly as it held the gun.

Lord Jesus, Sarah prayed frantically, *please don't let Amy or Audrey arrive now. Please keep them safe!*

"How could you let her go?" Tom yelled.

"Who? Debby?"

"Yes, that miscreant. How could you let that murderer out on the street?"

"But—" Chloe began, as Tom motioned with the gun.

"Move into the living room. All of you. Now!"

Sarah slowly made her way to the living room and heard a car door slam. Chloe and Liam followed at a slower pace, Liam keeping himself between Chloe and Tom.

Out of the corner of her eye Sarah saw movement through the window, then the darting figures of her granddaughters racing into the Dowlings' yard. Audrey had her cell phone glued to her ear as she ran, and their faces were both pale.

Thank you, Lord. They must have arrived and seen Tom somehow without him seeing them. It looked like Audrey was calling the police. Now Sarah just had to stall Tom until the police arrived.

Tom corralled them in front of the fireplace.

"Now you're going to call them off," he said.

"Call who off?" Sarah asked.

"The doctors. The lawyers. Everyone helping her."

"Why?"

"Because she can't be freed! I did everything I could to make sure she paid for the lives she ruined."

Sarah saw Chloe moving slowly, sliding a crutch out from under her arm and grabbing it with her hand. Sarah tried to keep Tom's gaze on her and not the young woman.

"You didn't do anything except turn a poor innocent woman in," Sarah said. "The FBI provided all the evidence that convicted her."

"Ha. I made sure she had an incompetent lawyer. I made sure the ex-boyfriend would look better than she did to the jury."

"Why go through the trouble?"

"Because *she's* trouble," he said. "Her and her revolution, with their 'free love' and counterculture. Anarchists is what they are. They thrive on chaos and madness."

Tom seemed to be thriving on chaos and madness himself.

"So now you're going to call them all off. She has to serve out her full sentence, all ninety-nine years. Then she can be forgiven."

He punctuated his speech with short jabs in the air with the revolver. Sarah could tell he was becoming more agitated with each wild accusation and statement. Tom's mind wasn't right.

"She can't be freed," Tom was saying. "She's guilty."

"Debby's not guilty," Chloe said.

"Yes she is!" Tom swung the gun toward Chloe.

But Chloe was ready. She took advantage of the momentum of his moving arm, and jabbed out hard with the top of the crutch she was holding. She hit him solidly in the wrist, making his arm swing wide. The gun went off as it flew out of his hand.

The sharp explosion pierced Sarah's ears, and acrid smoke burned her nose and made her eyes water.

Liam launched himself at Tom, knocking them both to the ground.

Sarah frantically blinked the tears away. She skirted around their struggling bodies while rubbing at her eyes. She reached for the gun, a dark shape against the Oriental carpet.

Her front door banged open. Police Chief Nate Webber and Officer Hopkins rushed into the house. "Police!"

Sarah sagged against a wall as Liam rolled to the side and the officers grabbed Tom, who was still struggling.

"No!" he shouted. "She's guilty!"

"Calm down," Officer Hopkins tried to tell him, but Tom only yelled louder.

"She can't be freed!"

As Officer Hopkins dragged Tom out of the house, Sarah rushed to Chloe and Liam. "Are you all right?"

Chloe sank to the couch. "A little sore. One of his legs clipped me, but I think the cast absorbed most of the blow."

"You shouldn't have risked your life that way," Sarah said.

"I had to get the gun away from him. Your granddaughters were outside." She leaned back against the cushions. Except for color high in her cheekbones, she looked fine.

"Are you all right?" Sarah asked Liam and laid a hand on his arm.

"I'm fine." He covered her hand with one of his own and squeezed before letting go.

"No injuries?" Chief Webber asked them.

"No," Chloe said.

"Where are Audrey and Amy?" Sarah asked.

"They're outside with Officer Pratt."

Sarah hurried out of the house, and as soon as she appeared in the open doorway, the twins hurled themselves into her arms. She gathered them tightly to herself, smelling the sunlight on their hair and feeling the softness of their skin against hers.

"It's fine now," Sarah said. "We're safe."

Abby McCormick, the reporter from the *Maple Hill Monitor*, lost no time in getting to the scene of all the action. No sooner had Sarah sat weakly down on one of the porch steps than Abby had come almost sprinting up to her. "Sarah, how are you doing?"

She couldn't speak for a moment, and her two granddaughters pressed closer to her on each side. "We're fine," she finally said.

Abby plied her with questions, which Sarah was okay answering as long as she didn't have to let go of Amy and Audrey. Liam helped Chloe out to the porch so she could be near Sarah and answer a few questions herself. But midway through, Imogene Dowling came across the yard toward Sarah's house, looking a bit like a blueberry in her cerulean muumuu with the ruffles around the square neckline.

"Sarah, I'm so glad you're okay," Imogene said. She managed to enfold Sarah, Audrey, and Amy in a gigantic hug. "And poor Chloe." She squeezed past Sarah to hug her, crutches and all, where she stood leaning against the porch railing. "And Liam." He gently patted her back as she hugged him. "Hi, Abby." Sarah was glad Abby didn't receive one of Imogene's firm squeezes; it looked like Imogene could squish Abby's tall, rawboned frame.

"Here, Sarah," Imogene handed her an envelope. "The postman accidentally delivered this to our house this morning instead of yours. What with everything that's happened, I didn't go through the mail until now. Look who it's from."

A firm hand had written: *Debby Lee Smith, Ingram Women's Penitentiary*.

Sarah ripped open the letter and scanned it while Liam, Chloe, Imogene, and Abby stood waiting in anticipation.

"Well?" Abby demanded.

Sarah started reading the letter to them all, but Liam interrupted her halfway through.

"Everybody who helped you with this should hear this letter."

"Liam, that's a wonderful idea."

"How about you pick a meeting place and time, and I'll print it when I print this piece about Tom Amsden," Abby said.

"Monday at The Spotted Dog, four o'clock." But before that meeting would take place, Sarah hoped to talk with Dale Wexler.

CHAPTER TWENTY-FIVE

ale's handwriting had changed dramatically in fifty years. It had gotten less cramped, the strokes stronger, longer, and more confident. That's why Sarah hadn't thought it was the same handwriting, at first. But he still made his lowercase g's with that odd slant to the tail, and his s's still looked like lightning bolts.

Now, and especially after seeing the photograph of the choir, she knew why the handwriting had changed so much. She looked at the two pages in her hands, one a page from the manuscript with several corrections made in the author's script, and the other the note with directions to Dale's mechanic.

"Sorry I'm late." Janet entered The Spotted Dog and sat down at the table Sarah and Martha had commandeered in the corner.

Since Janet and Dale had been friends for so long, she had been the one to arrange a time to meet with Dale. Sarah didn't know if Dale would willingly come to meet her, especially since he had been hiding so much about his relationship with Debby and the book he wrote. Janet would have to be the one to ask him to lunch, just to catch up. Then maybe they could introduce the topic of the book.

Liam approached the table and asked Janet, "Want anything?"

"No," she said, but then, "Oh, but those chai drinks you have are so tasty."

When Liam had gone to get Janet's chai latte, Sarah asked her, "He's coming?"

She nodded, a little sadly. "I told him to meet me here for lunch, but I'm not hungry now. I haven't had much appetite since you showed me the handwriting samples yesterday. It's all I can think of."

Martha's gaze landed on the door to the café. "There he is."

Dale walked a few paces into the café before he saw them. When he recognized Sarah, his step faltered for a moment. "Hi there," he said.

"Dale, this is my friend Martha Maplethorpe," Sarah said. "Have a seat."

"You're joining Janet and me for lunch? That's great."

"Actually, we'd like to talk to you about Debby Neely. We found the book you wrote about her," Sarah said.

His expression froze for several long seconds, then he gave a smile that didn't crease his eyes. "I kind of assumed you did. But I thought I might remain anonymous. How'd you figure it out?"

"There were lots of things." Sarah said. "But I didn't really put it all together until I saw your handwriting on the note Liam gave me. It matches the notes made on the original manuscript."

"I can't believe your mom kept that," Dale said.

"And when Janet told me about Debby's arrest, she said you were helping Mrs. Griggs to her car. The author mentioned how the FBI car almost ran Mrs. Griggs over."

"Huh."

"And then I realized your father played baseball with my dad, but when I first talked to you, I asked if you knew my mother, and you said no. But my mom went to every one of my dad's baseball games. She knew all his teammates. You were lying."

"Dale," Janet said. "Did you really write that book?"

He slowly nodded.

"I'm one of your oldest friends," she said. "I was your wife's best friend. We helped each other through our spouses' deaths. Why didn't you ever tell me about this?"

"It's one thing to publish your confession anonymously to get it off your chest. It's another to admit to being a coward. No one likes having someone else know about their sins."

"You weren't a coward," Sarah insisted.

"Yes, I was. I didn't do anything to step forward, to protect her, and then I couldn't even figure out where she'd gone. When the FBI arrested her, I was too far away to hear if they called her by her real name. I asked the people who had been near her, but they didn't remember. They had been shocked Debby was being arrested. After that happened, I promised myself I'd never be a coward again."

And he hadn't. This man standing here, who had become chief of police, was nothing like the timid-looking man in the choir photo, with the scared eyes and hesitant smile.

He shook his head. "I don't know why she ever told me about her past. She shouldn't have. I was a police officer."

"Olive suggested Debby talk to you," Sarah said. "She hoped you'd be able to help her."

"I admit, when she first told me about it all, I was torn. She was a fugitive from the law, and I had vowed to uphold that law. But she was also my friend, and I knew she couldn't have made a bomb. She just wasn't that type of person."

"You wrote that book out of remorse because you told Tom Amsden about Debby."

"I shouldn't have done it." His hand curled into a fist on the table. "Tom was a friend of my father's, and he was Carolyn's dad. I thought we could trust him, but he called the FBI on Debby. I didn't know he'd done that until after they'd taken her away. He said it was our civic duty and that Debby was guilty. He wouldn't listen no matter what I said." He stared at his clasped hands. "It was my fault the

FBI found Debby. It was my fault she went to jail for a crime she didn't commit."

Janet placed a hand gently on Dale's shoulder.

"I know how you knew my dad, but how did you know my mom?" Sarah asked.

"Ruth did some secretarial work for my dad. We had a tape recorder because my dad liked those kinds of gadgets, so I recorded the book and Ruth typed it out for me. William had it printed at his friend's magazine press because he knew he could trust his friend not to tell anyone about the book. He had it bound for me, and then I asked Ruth to donate it to the library."

"I wondered why you did that," Sarah said.

"I needed it to be out there, to keep me accountable, if only for my own peace of mind. I wanted it in a public place so that I wouldn't forget what I'd done."

"But Dale," Janet said gently, "even though what happened to Debby was terrible, it made you into a better man." Dale shook his head, but Janet kept going. "You became a better cop after that happened. I remember when you first joined the police department, and you wondered if you were only becoming a police officer because your grandpa had been one, and if you'd ever make a good cop. And then after Debby was gone, you knew that being a cop was what you were meant to do, and that you were going to be the best cop you could be."

"It wasn't worth the price," Dale said.

"You can't change the past. This is the man God made you into, and you're not half-bad."

She smiled, and he gave a half smile in return.

On Monday Sarah arrived at The Spotted Dog earlier than the announced four o'clock, but it was already filled with people who eagerly looked to her when she entered. Some she recognized from the Congregational Church, but some she didn't know at all. Yet they all smiled at her and had obviously come because of Debby's letter.

"Sarah!" Martha waved to her from where she sat at the counter.

With Chloe trudging behind her, Sarah made her way to the counter so the young woman could sit down. There were three drinks ready and waiting.

"There are so many people here," Sarah whispered to Martha.

"Yup, and it's still early. I think Liam will have a full house by four o'clock."

"They all want to hear Debby's letter?"

"Of course they do! Although...," Martha leaned close, "I heard Eloise DuBois listed her dress on eBay!"

Liam joined them at that moment and sat down. "I should give you a cut of my earnings this afternoon." He gave Sarah a wink.

Dale Wexler and Janet came into the café then, chatting with a few people they knew from church. They waved at Sarah, then sat down together.

"Well, it's four o'clock," Martha said. "I don't know about anybody else, but I'm eager to hear what Debby had to say."

Sarah stood up rather hesitatingly, but the room obliged her by quieting.

"Thank you for coming," she said. "And thank you all for helping me when I was investigating about Debby. I think you'll like what she has to say." She cleared her throat, and read the letter.

Dear Mrs. Hart,

I hope you don't mind, but because of my hands, I have asked my friend Becky to write this letter for me while I dictate to her.

Your visit surprised me but it also gave me hope, when I had been working so long to forget what hope felt like. I have been in Ingram for almost fifty years, and I had almost forgotten about Maple Hill, but the memories coming back to me are sweet and dear.

I am touched by how you have investigated my neurological disorder to secure my release. Thank you for your efforts for me, a woman you barely knew in your childhood.

When I first came here, I was bitter and angry at God. I thought he had abandoned me. But all this was in his plan. When I was finally able to let go of my anger and not let it control me, I could see that. I still struggle with the bitterness, but God is faithful.

I can also see that in the time I have spent here, God has used me to help many women know him better and grow in their faith. I don't know why he'd use someone like me, since I feel so weak, but he has. And it feels great when he does.

Thank you again for your visit and all you have done for me. I would love to hear more from Maple Hill and from the good folks who were so kind to me.

In Christ,

Debby Lee Smith

Sarah heard a few sniffles as she finished reading. She herself had cried when she first read the letter.

Finally Liam stood and raised a mug. "To Debby." Some people raised their own glasses and a smattering of applause broke out. Friends started chatting with each other about the letter.

Debby had touched other women's lives because she had been touched by the people here in this café, all gathered around her. And Sarah couldn't think of a better way for God to show his beauty than in the warm, friendly hearts of the people of her home, Maple Hill.

ABOUT THE AUTHOR

Camy Tang grew up in Hawaii and now lives in San Jose, California, with her engineer husband and rambunctious dog Snickers. She graduated from Stanford University and worked as a biologist researcher for nine years, but now she writes full time. She is a staff worker for her church youth group, and she leads one of the worship teams for Sunday service. She's also training for her very first marathon, which will be in December in Hawaii so her parents can cheer her on and her cousins can yell at her to go faster. On her blog, she ponders knitting, spinning wool, dogs, running, the Never-Ending Diet, and other tantalizing things.

HERE'S A SNEAK PEEK AT THE NEXT
PATCHWORK MYSTERIES BOOK!

YESTERDAY'S SECRETS

BY KELLY ANN RILEY

 CHAPTER ONE

May sunlight danced through the oak leaves and warmed Sarah Hart's back as she worked in the little garden behind her house. She relished the feel of the cool soil between her fingers as she yanked a weed encroaching on the perimeter of one of her heirloom tomato plants.

"Be gone, you dastardly villain!" she said with dramatic flair as she tossed the weed into a growing pile. The night before, she'd fallen asleep reading one of her favorite Agatha Christie mysteries, and this morning, melodrama peppered her speech.

She leaned back on her heels and surveyed her botanical kingdom. Green fruit dotted the leafy tomato plants. Several tomatoes had swelled to the size of golf balls, and she couldn't wait for the first tomato sandwich of the season. Lacy sprigs from her baby carrots waved in the breeze. Cucumber plants crept up the trellis, and her zucchini and pepper plants flourished on their mounds of soil.

Even though her back ached now, it had been worth coming out here and taking a break from her current quilting project. The birds singing in the trees and the soft spring air made it a perfect day to relax outdoors and enjoy the beginning of a new season. She sighed and stood, brushing the dirt off her knees. Even with obligations awaiting her, surely nothing could disturb the peace of such a glorious day.

She gathered up her tools and the basket of yanked weeds and strode to the backdoor of her cozy Queen Anne-style home. She kicked off her garden shoes and was reaching for the door handle when someone said, "Sarah?"

Sarah jumped and dropped her basket, the dirt and weeds scattering across the porch.

"Oh, I'm sorry. I didn't mean to startle you." A petite woman with bright red hair bent down to help clean up the mess. The sound of amusement in her voice triggered the right memory.

"Suzy Carmichael!" Sarah exclaimed. Except for occasional photos with the yearly Christmas card, she hadn't seen her college roommate since graduation. "I'd give you a hug, but I'm covered in dirt."

Suzy laughed. "You're a sight for sore eyes. I can't believe how many years have passed."

"I can't either, and here you are," Sarah shook her head in amazement. "We have a lot of catching up to do. Would you like to come in? I have some strawberry iced tea in the refrigerator."

"That sounds great," Suzy said as Sarah opened the door. "I love strawberry season. Phoenix is nice, but I miss seeing the green fields this time of year. Does Maple Hill still have the Strawberry Festival?"

Sarah set her basket and tools by the sink. "In two weeks on Memorial Day weekend. The weather has been perfect, so there are an abundance of strawberries this year. Then in July we're having a big fair to celebrate the quasquibicentennial."

"The quas— what?"

Sarah laughed. "The town's two-hundred-twenty-fifth anniversary. No doubt tourists will flock in. It's great for the town and my daughter-in-law's business. Have you been downtown yet? She owns Magpie's Antiques on the square."

"How fun! I read about your son moving back to Maple Hill in your Christmas letter. He's a lawyer, right? You must be so proud of him. How are they adjusting to life in a small town?"

Sarah set out the pitcher and tall ice-filled glasses on the kitchen table near Suzy. "Jason's doing well, but then of course he grew up here." She filled Suzy's glass with the pink-tinged tea. "It was a little rough in the beginning for their girls, since they left friends behind in California. The twins are turning thirteen this month, so you can imagine how important their social life is becoming to them. They seem to be settling in fine now. I'm so thrilled they're here."

Suzy tasted the tea and added sugar, her spoon clinking on the glass. "I know what you mean. Luckily two of my three have settled in Phoenix. My youngest is expecting her first baby any time now, which will be my third grandchild and the first girl."

"Congratulations!" Sarah beamed. "Babies are even more fun when you're the grandmother."

"Oh, I know! I'm a bit anxious to get back. I just wish ..." She sighed and gazed out the window. "You have such a lovely place. So homey. It suits you. I just wish I hadn't stayed away all these years. And I wish I could've come back for Gerry's funeral. You were in my thoughts and prayers."

Suzy reached across the table and grasped Sarah's hand. "I really, really liked him and thought you two were the perfect couple, even back in college."

"Please don't feel bad." Sarah squeezed Suzy's hand. "Your note was very touching, and I knew if you could've been here, you would've come."

"I just feel like I've let so many people down in the past. I'm going to try extra hard to make sure my Uncle Carroll is taken care of right," she said, determination in her voice.

Sarah studied Suzy while she lifted her glass and took several long swallows. Time had deepened the lines around green eyes that had sparkled with continuous mischief in their college days. The dusting of silver highlights throughout her bright short locks lent a distinguished air, and if Sarah wasn't mistaken, they'd been artfully enhanced. Her petite frame, dressed in a purple pantsuit, had broadened slightly but was still athletic looking. Overall, the years seemed to have been good to her old friend.

Suzy set her tea down, drawing circles in the condensation with her finger. "I only wish it wasn't a sad occasion that brought me back. I don't know if you've heard, but my cousin was killed in a car accident a couple of days ago."

"Oh Suzy, I'm so sorry. I read about the car accident in the paper. I didn't realize the woman was your cousin. I don't think I ever met her."

"I don't think you did either. Her mother was my mom's sister. Dawn and I weren't close. Too much of an age difference. When you and I were in college, she was only six. And then, of course, I moved away after. In fact, she was the only one of the cousins who stayed in Maple Hill. Wanted to be close to her parents. She was their only child.

"He's in his eighties now and he's been really dependent on Dawn. His health has been steadily failing, but with Dawn's help and her preparing meals for him, he's been able to stay in his home."

"This must be so hard for him."

"It is, and it's going to get worse. I'm afraid I need to get him into assisted living and arrange for his house to be sold. He hates the idea, but I don't see that we have a choice. Without Dawn, he has no assistance, and he says he doesn't have the funds to hire someone to come into his house."

"Change can be hard at any age," Sarah said, thinking of her own father living at Bradford Manor. "But he may like the social life and activities at a care facility. I know my father likes the company. There's always someone to talk to."

"I don't know," Suzy said. "He's a tough old guy. You'd understand if you met him. He served in World War II and then started his own car dealership. He did well, considering his snarly personality. I guess he knew how to hire the right people." She sighed. "This move is going to be a nightmare."

"Is there anything I can do to help?" Sarah asked.

"Just talking about it has helped, and I seem to have dominated the conversation with my troubles when I'd really like to talk about the good old days." She lifted her watch. "But, I need to stop by and check on Uncle Carroll and see what all needs to be done in that house. I got here yesterday just in time for the funeral today. I hope I can wrap up things in a couple of days."

"It sounds like you're going to be busy. How about I treat you both to dinner at The Old Mill tonight? That way you won't have to cook."

"I'd love to, but I don't know about Uncle Carroll. Other than going to church occasionally, he's pretty much homebound from what I understand. But," Suzy clapped her hands together, "even if he doesn't want to go, a girls' night out sounds wonderful. Would you like to ride over with me to Uncle Carroll's? It should only take me a minute to check on things, and we can see if he'd like to go to dinner."

"Great! It's a date then." Sarah refilled Suzy's glass, then excused herself to change out of her jeans and into a soft blue spring skirt and white peasant blouse. When she returned downstairs, she found Suzy in the living room examining a quilt Sarah had left on the back of the sofa, where she'd been doing some hand-stitching the night before.

"Pretty." Suzy lifted the delicate rose and lace Fan bed quilt.

"It belongs to a client and is over fifty years old. Some of the lace and stitching had torn loose here." Sarah ran her fingers over the corner where the damage had been done.

"I can't even tell where the old stitching stops and where you repaired it."

"I had to yellow the thread using tea. The lace was a bit harder to match. If you look closely, the pattern is slightly off."

"I'm still impressed. You were always artsy even in school. Do you get much business?"

"I stay busy enough. Some projects take longer than others. I do it mostly because I enjoy restoring someone else's handicraft. I hate to see beauty and history lost."

"I've never had a knack for sewing and doubt I'd have the time to learn if I tried." Suzy sighed and set down the quilt. "Well, are we ready?"

Sarah grabbed her new paisley purse. Suzy insisted on driving, so she and Sarah hopped in the white Taurus sedan.

Carroll Shepherd's house was located about twenty minutes across town.

Suzy parked in front of an old Victorian on Elm Street. "Funny how some things don't change. Although I was thinking when I dropped Carroll off after the funeral how the place looked smaller than I remembered, but maybe I'm just bigger." She laughed and set the parking brake.

They walked up the sidewalk to the spacious front porch that was bordered by a waist-high hedge. As they ascended the three wooden steps, Sarah caught a whiff of paint and sawdust before the breeze snatched it away.

"Is your uncle remodeling?" she asked as Suzy rang the doorbell.

"I have no idea. I don't keep in touch much with this side of the family," Suzy said, opening the screen door and trying the door handle. "Oh look, the door's cracked open." She pushed it open further.

"Uncle Carroll?" she called. "It's Suzy. Can we come in? I brought a friend."

When no answer came, Suzy glanced at Sarah, a wrinkle forming on her forehead. "He can't go far. He uses a walker and is confined to the first floor."

Suzy called his name again and entered the foyer. Her heels clicked on the hardwood floor as she walked down a hall and turned to the first opening on the right. She gasped.

"What is it?" Sarah rushed forward and skidded to a stop next to Suzy. She gazed into a large living room. A Tiffany lamp lay in the middle of the rug, glass shards from its broken shade fanned out across the room. An overturned end table rested beside it. Books lay tumbled on the floor beneath the shelves by the mantel, and the doors of a large china cabinet stood wide open.

"Uncle Carroll? Where are you?" Suzy called again, a panicked note in her voice. She darted down the hallway toward the back of the house. "The backdoor's open too," Suzy yelled from the depths of the house. "I think someone broke in!"

"Suzy, come back. Someone may still be here," Sarah called, her heart pounding. She dug through her purse for her cell phone.

A few moments later, Suzy reappeared with a broom in her hand. Her gaze turned to the wide staircase.

"Call the police! I'm checking upstairs," she said and charged up the staircase.

A Note from the Editors

Patchwork Mysteries was created by the Books and Inspirational Media Division of Guideposts, a nonprofit organization that touches millions of lives every day through products and services that inspire, encourage and uplift. Our magazines, books, prayer network (OurPrayer.org), and other outreach programs help people connect their faith-filled values to daily life.

Your purchase of Patchwork Mysteries makes a difference. When you buy Guideposts products, you're helping fund our work, which includes ministry to military personnel, prisons, hospitals, nursing homes and educational institutions. To learn more, visit GuidepostsFoundation.org.

To find out about our other publications and to enjoy free online resources such as inspirational newsletters, blogs, videos, Facebook and Twitter links, visit us at Guideposts.org.